Advance Praise for *The Silk Road*

"Jane Summer manages to capture that elusive, intricate mixture of hard-boiled sensitivity, utter loathing, and unconditional infatuation that precisely defines American adolescence. Like the best books written about those requisite roller-coaster years, *The Silk Road* is a novel for everyone—female, male, straight, gay, whatever—who was or plans to be young."

—Felice Picano

"Assisted by a veritable sex machine of a 440 Magnum V-8 Plymouth Barracuda, this narrative is an entirely original variation on the relentless theme of the seduction of the innocent old by the feral and Byronic young."

—Bertha Harris, author of *The Lover*

"A coming-of-age novel of rare charm and unique vision, *The Silk Road* is one well worth traveling."

—William J. Mann, author of *The Men From the Boys* and *The Biograph Girl*

"Jane Summer delivers an enchantingly meandering romp of a novel. Though she comes from a town called Hell, Paige, through her trust and curiosity, finds heaven in her fleeting and sometimes painful relationships."

—Maudy Benz, author of *Oh, Jackie*

"A truly impressive debut novel. Poetic and provocative, *The Silk Road* deftly explores both the anxiety and excitement of the teenage lesbian experience."

—Julia Watts, author of *Phases of the Moon* and *Wildwood Flowers*

The Silk Road

The Silk Road

A Novel

Jane Summer

alyson books
los angeles | new york

MANUFACTURED IN THE UNITED STATES OF AMERICA.

THIS TRADE PAPERBACK ORIGINAL IS PUBLISHED BY
ALYSON PUBLICATIONS,
P.O. BOX 4371, LOS ANGELES, CA 90078-4371.
DISTRIBUTION IN THE UNITED KINGDOM BY
TURNAROUND PUBLISHER SERVICES LTD.,
UNIT 3, OLYMPIA TRADING ESTATE, COBURG ROAD, WOOD GREEN,
LONDON N22 6TZ ENGLAND.

FIRST EDITION: MAY 2000

00 01 02 03 04 **a** 10 9 8 7 6 5 4 3 2 1

ISBN 1-55583-549-X

LIBRARY OF CONGRESS CATALOGING-IN-PUBLICATION DATA
  SUMMER, JANE.
    THE SILK ROAD : A NOVEL / JANE SUMMER.
    ISBN 1-55583-549-X
    1. LESBIANS—FICTION. I. TITLE.
  PS3569.U3815 S55 2000
  813'.6—DC21   00-027273

CREDITS
EXCERPT FROM "CECILIA" ©1969 BY PAUL SIMON. USED BY PERMISSION OF
  PAUL SIMON MUSIC.
EXCERPT FROM "CUT" FROM *ARIEL* BY SYLVIA PLATH. ©1963 BY TED HUGHES.
  COPYRIGHT RENEWED. REPRINTED BY PERMISSION OF HARPERCOLLINS
  PUBLISHERS INC.
EXCERPT FROM "FOR ARCHIE SMITH: 1917-1935" FROM *NOTEBOOK*: REVISED
  AND EXPANDED EDITION BY ROBERT LOWELL. ©1970 BY ROBERT LOWELL.
  COPYRIGHT RENEWED 1998 BY HARRIET LOWELL. REPRINTED BY PERMIS-
  SION OF FARRAR, STRAUS AND GIROUX, LLC.
EXCERPT FROM "A SEASON IN HELL" FROM *THE COMPLETE WORKS OF
  ARTHUR RIMBAUD*, TRANSLATED BY PAUL SCHMIDT. ENGLISH TRANSLA-
  TION ©1975 BY PAUL SCHMIDT. REPRINTED BY PERMISSION OF
  HARPERCOLLINS PUBLISHERS INC.
EXCERPT FROM "SONG FOR A LADY" FROM *LOVE POEMS*. ©1967 BY ANNE
  SEXTON. REPRINTED BY PERMISSION OF HOUGHTON MIFFLIN CO. ALL
  RIGHTS RESERVED.
COVER PHOTOGRAPHS BY PATRICK MORRISON.
COVER DESIGN BY B. ZINDA.

To Joanne Ahola

Although this book may seem authentic, especially to anyone who has ever been a teenager, it is a work of fiction. Dialogue is invention, characters creatures of the imagination, locales original conceptions.

But everything within is true.

①

People go through Hell just to make conversation. They tell you it was serendipity, that they had no choice, the thruway was at a standstill, they needed to find an alternate route. The truth is, they go through Hell for kicks. They see the thruway sign, HELL, EXIT 15, and have every intention of making the detour. Often they stop in town, gas up, dash into Vera's Luncheonette for a cigar or chewing gum, shifty eyes hoping to find and purchase amusing bumper stickers such as I'VE BEEN TO HELL AND BACK or THIS CAR HAS GONE THROUGH HELL. The bullheaded visitors make jokes about the town name. The residents' response humorless, they depart with no information about the etiology of Hell and no souvenir other than a cigar ring, a Bazooka comic, a cleaner windshield. What an unfriendly town.

Hell is one of New York State's many towns that were better off in the shiny-red 1950s. A personal injury law firm advertises on the billboard near the ramp off the highway, Hell's triumphal arch. The little local pride left in Hell's longtime residents is worn modestly, like the watch pinned to a nurse's mohair sweater, ticking on regardless of the children spraying sneezes into her face. There are no centennials anymore, and the parade tradition was abandoned a few years ago because the flag-waving spectators were staying home, doped up on television. Fourth of July picnics are still well attended—everyone likes a barbecued frankfurter—but this is Hell's concluding generation of fund-raising bakers. Someone should photograph the White Wonder Frosting and Banana Chiffon Cake (Mrs. Edward Clifford Tull), Rainbow Dessert Cake (Mrs. Lisbet Sundqvist), and Sugar Jumbles (Miss Mary Blear); nothing like that will ever be set out on a Sunday school table again.

Not situated near enough to the river piddling into the Atlantic (though in under ten minutes you can drive to the riverbank evenings, as teenagers do, roll a joint, kiss the neck of a girl in the passenger seat), the town never could offer homeowners majestic panoramas. Still, people move in year after year (the school system is good, they say) and transform the previous homeowner's property: Rooms are added, kitchens expanded, skylights installed, luxuriant hedges planted, motion-detecting lights wired in.

Unlike its affluent neighbor, Bubbling Brook, Hell flaunts no Mercedes-Benzes and Cadillacs snoozing in quarter-mile-long driveways. In Bubbling Brook five-bedroom estates command front lawns no one but the postman ever walks upon, though they're bouncy as a kitchen sponge, and the streets are quieter than butlers. Children in Hell, however, provide constant birdsong. They whoop it up no matter what season: tricycling in driveways, building twig forts on the lawn, roller-skating and sledding in the street, setting off firecrackers, and assembling teams for all sorts of ball games.

Hell houses show some variation, especially after new owners get their hammers on them, but they generally follow this plan: one bay window, one master bedroom, one children's bedroom, one playroom, one living room, one kitchen, one garage, one attic, and one crawl space. The garage is claimed by dads with rarely used power saws, the attic becomes an additional bedroom highly sought after by the house teen, and there are rumors that the crawl spaces are used for the punishment of children (true). Houses are oil-heated. There are few fireplaces. The similarity among the houses can be disorienting; when you walk into a neighbor's house it's both familiar and unfamiliar, like waking up in a hotel and not knowing where you are, in which direction to expect the window, the door.

Picture shrubs, the occasional daub of azalea radiance, the morning glory (considered a pestilence by people who know), and standard northeastern trees: oak, elm, maple, evergreen.

Hell isn't quite run-down. It has just lost its oomph. The 1950s were good to the town, and now it has no idea what to do.

Throughout Hell, at the mediocre hour between school recess and dinner, ninth grade girls acknowledge their homework. They sit at their desks or belly down on their beds, radios, volume low enough for parents not to hear, broadcasting songs that disturb everyone. Adults like to complain about the noise and that they can't understand any of the words. Headphoned boys lounging on beanbag chairs take the lyrics as seriously as the words of Christ. Girls doing homework to a background of radio rock are distracted by a growing stain of desire in their bodies; on their beds and in their hardback chairs, when the DJ plays a strung-out lead guitarist, some girls recoil and grow afraid, others rock and roll their hips in a way no extracurricular dance class ever demonstrated.

Paige Bergman listens—though no one "listens" to rock; you go downstream with it—to a song she knows by heart. The wonderful thing about adolescence is the ability to dally with conflict. Paige, though uneasy with the lyrics and convinced there's something wacko about the group's diehard fans (they torture cats, dive into quarry pools), loves this music, the vehemence of this music.

Hearing a favorite song on the radio gives everyone a rush. You jump to your feet and believe in your invincibility. You are positive you could get on stage and perform that song so perfectly nobody would even notice it was you singing and not a leather-clad Jim Morrison.

But for a girl it's not easy.

There are some girl singers on the radio. But there's no girl Jimi agonizing with a Fender, no female Keith Moon punching drums. Though no girls in Hell have a band, being a girl never stops Paige from abandoning her homework and pretending she's a member of a group performing on the bandstand of her bed. Standing on her chenille bedspread, Paige can see herself in full-body pose in the mirror. She takes her imaginary guitar in hand, and mouths all the words to the radio's "Eve of Destruction" while strumming uninventively. Why is that so satisfying?

Her mother very nearly ruined music. Now when Mozart ascends from her father's stereo system, Paige waltzes into it and just in time snaps herself right out of it, shuts her bedroom door, shakes herself off like a dog.

It's not that Paige doesn't like the music. Her father's music murmurs into her ear. This is how you feel when certain people— a favorite camp counselor, a new Spanish teacher—walk toward you: carnival lights, a synchronized universe, bruised with pleasure. It's almost intolerable.

But then the mother butts in....

In a plush burgundy seat in a concert hall in a whirlwind city, her mother had leaned across her father during the largo and whispered to Paige, "You're not supposed to tap your feet to classical music, dear."

A mother has no business being in her daughter's rapture, so from then on Paige would ignore the music of violins, the sonatas, symphonies, requiems. So there.

But rock and roll is hers, the name itself demanding toe-tapping, hand-clapping shimmy shimmy. And even when Paige stops to think about what she's doing up there on her chenille bedspread, she still can't stop herself. What else is she supposed to do? Not sing along? Sit in a hippie trance? Applaud politely?

She needs headphones for Christmas—it's the second time she has asked. Carefully she turns the radio up a notch. When she was in junior high, her parents had swung themselves into an ugly quarrel about decibels and popular music. Her mother made herself cartoonish at the dinner table by insisting, "That music is a bad influence on your daughter!" Her father rose to her defense and responded, "That's what they said about jazz." After the plates were cleared, they continued to argue, about nothing, the broken butter dish, the snow on the TV, putting in the storm windows. Paige knew what was up and crept away from the kitchen. It wasn't the music that caused her mother's anger. Paige prayed for the phone to ring, for a knock on the door, for her mother to calm down and not say anything to her father, especially in front of her.

Luckily, Mrs. Bergman had been too ashamed to tell her husband what she had seen that afternoon when she flung open Paige's door to tell her to turn the music down—or off, young lady, and do your homework!

Christine Jorgensen, big news in 1967. As far as parents were concerned, the nuclear bomb was nothing compared to a sex-change operation. Mrs. Bergman, who with her Jackie Kennedy sunglasses and slim figure thought herself more cosmopolitan than her neighbors, had been surprised to find herself riveted by Jorgensen's autobiography, although, of course, she was disgusted by the whole thing, as were all the women, the hens, of the neighborhood. Nevertheless, the women snapped up every magazine that ran a Jorgensen article, before and after pictures, though none of them talked about what it would be like to switch sex, to be a man, hair growing from your ears and that earthly thing between your legs cool as a mushroom.

Despite their own idle daydreaming as they lay in their lounge chairs, nursing iced coffees, no one ever ever ever imagined that one of their children, God forbid and knock on wood, would be compelled to mutilate himself that way. Some of the women believed that even thinking about it could make it so. The others dismissed the possibility with a wave of the hand. A few jokes followed (maybe that's my husband's problem, betcha Vera'd have the operation if the luncheonette made more money), and then they subdued themselves with pleasant thoughts of how ordinary their families were, how predictable, and what would they do about dinner.

Mrs. Bergman had stridden in, her bun tight and shiny, not even knocking a warning on Paige's door, hell-bent on pulling the plug on Paige's radio (it was a transistor). But what she saw when she opened the door booted her in the gut. She doubled over in horror, wrapping her arms around her patent leather waist. Mouth agape, she spun round and sped downstairs. She ran into her bathroom, took down her hair and put it up again. She caught her breath, then checked her lipstick in the mirror, checked her profile, as if to be sure it was still there. It was, as arrogant and stony as ever. She thought she resembled that lady in the Sargent painting, but that wouldn't mean anything to the hicks around here.

Until the day she dies, Eva Bergman will remain mortified about this incident, unable to speak to her husband, daughter, hairdresser, or lover about it.

Paige doesn't want to be a boy, at least she doesn't think she wants to be. The very notion of penis envy makes her and all her girlfriends laugh until they have side stitches. And though she may have been called a tomboy as a child, it was only because she wore pants, even in summer, detesting the exposure of skirts. But there was no way she would skin knees or climb trees: She feared she'd drop easy as a chestnut.

But maybe things aren't so funny. Should she worry that she had wanted to be Father when she and her childhood friends had played house? Did it mean she secretly did want to be a boy? Or had she just been accommodating, since everyone else insisted on being Mother and the youngest always had to be Baby? Whatever the reason, even as a small child she simply couldn't abide the idea of carrying a purse, staying home with the wah wah baby all day, and playing bridge with the gossips in curlers and hairnet. So, in the cast of playing house, what role did that leave her with?

It is precisely because she is a girl that what she had done had felt good.

The clean socks on her bed had been rolled up, each pair inside its other, by her visiting grandmother. The music was good, and Paige, at an age when she was half in the fantasy world of childhood and half in the experimental world of puberty, had stuffed a pair of socks in her pants and gyrated to the beat just like the stars on *American Bandstand*. And then, of course, her mother had charged in.

At the very same hour of the disaster, there was serenity elsewhere in Hell. Paige's classmates were at their homework: Hannah's mother had just brought up milk and cookies, Martine was petting the cat in her lap with her left hand and doing math with her right, Thomas was chewing the eraser end of his pencil while his older brother helped quiz him on his spelling.

Paige would never have thought it such a big deal if her mother hadn't reacted so strongly. Meeting her mother's gaze had been enough to shame her for years. The poison blood of humiliation ran from her heart, screeching throughout her body.

It is the end of the 1960s. Paige Bergman is one of Hell's mooning freshmen, pretty enough to not be singled out for teen torment. People her parents' age tell her she looks like Connie Stevens, if only she'd get that hair out of her face and put it up in a French twist. She's polite to adults, and while she has no special fondness for the police, she can't imagine calling them "pigs" as her friend Hannah does so casually. Once she went to a rally against the war (Vietnam) and, in her embarrassment when her father came early to pick her up, walked away without saying good-bye to her friends. She has never smoked marijuana or a Marlboro, never swallowed any pill other than penicillin and aspirin, nor has she inhaled any drug other than the Vicks VapoRub her grandmother smeared on her chest when she was eight. She dipped her tongue in her grandfather's beer once and found it vile. Kissing boys had been fun, but she didn't know what she was missing. Pretty normal, isn't it?

Paige lives in a two-story white house with black shutters, same as most of the teenagers who attend Lindbergh High, though shutter color can vary. Green's popular. Her bedroom, covered with psychedelia and oversize posters of rock stars and antiwar aphorisms in Day-Glo, is in the front of the house, facing the street. But what's to watch out the window? The Good Humor truck, a boy walking a basketball home, housewives ferrying groceries from sedan to kitchen, the cute mailman, a mutt pissing on her father's lawn, the streetlight winking on. She closes the curtains, lights a cone of incense, and, as her pinball attention rolls from her rock-and-roll fantasy to her homework to the Lava lamp, flomps on her bed with dramatic flair. She is Ophelia. Juliet. Marie Antoinette. She is Abe Lincoln. Che. Romeo. Paige Bergman is dead and gone.

Fooled you!

The old springs squeak, the metal frame quivers. Excluding her crib years, Paige has slept in this bed all her life, through the chicken pox, measles and German measles, flus, colds, and 24-hour bugs. The doctor has been to her bedside. Her father has sat on the twin mattress reading bedtime stories. Her mother has made its tight hospital corners. She and Hannah have pored over *Teen Beat* on its nubby bedspread. Paige has unlocked her Dear Diary sitting cross-legged here. On this bed, shoes still on, she has read three Nancy Drews and the ghoulish fairy tales in books her grandmother brought from another country.

Ever since she turned 11, Paige has rearranged the placement of the bed at least once a year. Mrs. Bergman, not at all pleased by that—she likes everything her way, it's efficient—wouldn't exactly yell at Paige. As a result, it was never clear whether Paige should complain to Hannah that her mother was angry or if her mother just thought Paige a dunce. But Mrs. Bergman made her scorn clear, mostly by intimating that something inauspicious would occur if she kept the bed in that position: "It's right under the overhead light, and you know the fixture's not very secure" or "The bed's too close to the radiator, you won't get any heat this winter" or "Why must you move it right under the window? The sun will yellow the bedspread."

Paige awaits the footsteps of parents. If her mother hears the bed creak, she'll come up to investigate Paige's progress with her homework. Her brother Jan has been gone for a couple of years, some fancy college, but Paige decided to stop missing him. When they were younger he kept stealing her diary and once tried to saw it open. Then he became interested in math and never seemed to pay her much attention, though he was looking out for her like guardian angels. Somehow Jan always managed to do just what his mother wanted. The high school pennants, the globe, the trophies, the books, and slide rules all remain in their place in his large bedroom.

Once Jan had been accepted by his first-choice college, the family seemed to wipe its hands, as if its work were done. The day Paige bounded into the living room to announce that she wanted to be a zookeeper, Eva made an exasperated sigh and told her that was ridiculous, her eyes never leaving whatever she was reading in her magazine. Paige dismissed any serious thoughts about her future.

Her guidance counselor, Miss Littler, who wears baby-doll clothes and has the pudgy cheeks and stiff hair to go with it, never recognized the A's and A+'s in French, as if language class were frivolous. Paige was insulted. For the midterm take-home exam, the students had to translate an excerpt of 250 words or two poems. Camus, Balzac, Hugo, and Dumas went unwillingly from

French into English. One brave soul took a stab at Baudelaire. Paige, however, worked from English to French. It was a way of working in code. Paige handed in her translation, liner notes from a popular musician's latest album. She received the highest mark in the class.

What's the French for "to groove"?

They don't teach you anything in school.

The 1970s approach. Fork in the road. Paige goes to Woodstock without her parents' knowledge. They shipped her off to Camp Melody, where she lives on cheese blintzes and ice cream, the kitchen being otherwise unprepared to accommodate a vegetarian. Between June 30 and the end of August, her father sends four care packages: cheese in a spray canister, potato chips, apricot leather, peanuts in the shell, Clark bars, salted pretzels, tins of smoked oysters, cheese ravioli in a can. Some say she eats better than the camp cook.

This is the summer of Paige's shadow. The cornfield, burnt by the sun. Someone steps on a snake basking in the dusty dirt path that leads from bunks to mess hall. The lake stinks of rot, ancient snapping turtles, and decaying reeds. The percussion instructor steps on a nail and receives a tetanus shot in the butt. Paige keeps waving her hand in front of her face as if clearing the air of a bee or gnats or a smell but can't shoo the shade cast over her. It seems she is wearing a hat with a wide brim, or sunglasses—when she laughs, tunes her guitar, writes home, she is in shadow, seeing but not seen.

A pair of legs in painter's pants walks past her bunk window, and the shadow lifts. Those are the legs of another camper, Nicola, who, to Paige's fascinated horror, will set a piano on fire during the performance of a piece by a 20th-century composer.

Paige and Nicola creep into the woods with the sack of peanuts her father sent, and when they have eaten their fill they snap open the rest and toss peanuts under the pines for squirrels. She feels like herself again when Nicola is around.

But after four weeks Nicola's parents show up in matching cof-fee-colored suits—he wears a tie in this heat, she wears her jump-suit tightly belted—and drive away with Nicola in a station wagon. And here is the shadow, returned, but Paige breaks through it with happiness twice more that summer, when she receives Nicola's postcard from Bayreuth (Paige never expected her handwriting to be so ordinary) and when Janis Joplin sings at Woodstock.

The head counselor (bassoonist) expects the music festival to be as quotidian an outing as the Newport festival was the year before. But in fact, the Woodstock Music and Art Fair will have so peculiar an effect on Paige that, in the newly waxed halls of Lindbergh High that September, she tells few people she has been there. She never will see the movie.

California hippies arrive in renovated hearses and VW buses. The unpredictability of the Hell's Angels urges Paige to scurry past them on her way to the Portosans in her garbage-bag raincoat. She feels welcome in the world, more so than in her nonmemory of being born and cradled in arms. The people who live along the highway line the roads to catch a glimpse of the spectacle, the closing of the New York State thruway due to a hajj of hippies. Paige hears a roar up ahead and suspects the locals are throwing rocks and brandishing shotguns. But as the Melody bus snails along, the locals are seen smiling, children in the rags of summer handing out free lemonade, and sienna farm families allow the purple-swathed counterculture to unroll sleeping bags on their property. Visitors will leave $10 of thanks, or a handshake, and muddy furrows in front yards. People are cheering.

The drugs, the mud, and the windstorm of motorcycles frighten so many of her fellow campers that they spend both nights and most of the days in the bus, which is parked in a potato field a mile from the stage. Paige, however, in her anonymity, feels profoundly important, excitable.

A brave few Camp Melody souls settle into the hillside, ready for music. The campers on either side of Paige boast about having already seen Joan Baez and Ritchie Havens in concert in New York City (chaperoned by their parents no doubt, smirks Paige). They arrived at Camp Melody with such optimism, eager to improve their folk-guitar riffs and self-inflated ballads so they could get back to school in the fall and hear their friends tell them they are as good as Dylan and should form a band, cut a record. Paige isn't serious about music; it is just something she has always done, like seesawing in the park or being the onion cutter at Thanksgiving. It placates her mother, who suggested Paige would be foolish if she didn't major in piano at camp. Paige wouldn't consider it. But neither did she get what she wanted. Because she wasn't allowed to sign up for electric guitar—boys only—she ended up being Camp Melody's sole flamenco student. The fervor, though mute, suited her, and she imagined a mania of heels circling her as she burned at the stake in the practice room.

Paige and the always game Joe (cornet) ditch the rest of the Melody troupe and inch down toward the stage. Despite such good seats, Paige is distracted. She keeps looking at Joe out of the corner of her eye. Is he trying to sidle closer to her? Or is it just the swelling multitudes pressing Joe's blue-jeaned thigh against her own? Will he get drunk on the beers being floated around the crowd and make a move on her, rest his head on her shoulder? Should she tell him she has a boyfriend at home? Paige wants to enjoy the scene but must instead remain vigilant.

What if he loves her? Paige tries to picture being his wife: They marry on the dunes at Cape Cod and share the same bed. She could do it—but she for sure wouldn't be washing his flannel shirts or making fondue or wearing Frederick's of Hollywood panties. She doesn't want him to expect these things of her, they frighten her, maybe because if she didn't do them well, he'd find a wife who was very pretty, a real woman, whatever that was. (One that adored the smell of men. One that was not afraid of beckoning with her cleavage. One that would never say no.) Or maybe because being a real woman, sitting in the passenger seat, being helped across the street, makes her feel like a child, debilitated.

Before Paige had left for camp that summer, John the Divine in his fringed suede jacket had taken her for a spin on his motorcycle. There was no guy who was more desirable. Yet Paige thinks she is the only girl in Hell who isn't pining away for him. And though the thought of deep touching with John the Divine is a thrill that brings her great happiness, she is disturbed that she doesn't want to be obligated to him. She will have a boyfriend on her terms, or maybe simply lose her virginity and be done with it.

A lot of the music is horrible, way off-key. And she had never liked many of the performers (Sly and the Family Stone, Santana, Grateful Dead). Who in the crowd suspects, this muddy night, that all of them in the vast audience would be exceptional forever?

And doesn't Paige belong to the family, the Woodstock club? She does, of course, and she does not. If only she could be relaxed and free with Joe, stand up and dance....

She hadn't made up her mind about Janis Joplin. Man-hungry. Recklessly drinking alcohol from a bottle. It's really pretty gross.

Yet something about Janis Joplin suddenly interests her. Paige nods off during The Grateful Dead's set, but when Janis Joplin appears, wasted as she is, the guys in the crowd going wild, ripping off their shirts, arms flailing in the air, war whoops sailing across the meadow, a new continent untethers itself inside Paige, or else her heart swims from left to right.

Something has happened. Maybe she is frenzied into fandom by the crowd, but for the first time Janis Joplin's singing gives Paige a strangled kind of feeling, and that is good.

She adamantly does not want Janis Joplin to leave the stage. She wants something, Janis Joplin's acknowledgment, whatever it is fans want. And she wants it so badly, she is afraid a small noise might come from her throat.

Paige, along with every guy in the crowd, envisions Janis Joplin's arms around her. But she is quick to tell herself it is more like the Matisse mother-baby print framed on her parents' wall than the grinding and slobbering embrace that is the fantasy of men.

It is confusing; they have nothing in common. Janis Joplin is the first woman Paige has ever seen with a tattoo, she drinks as if alcohol is ambrosia in a bottle, and she has been sexually extravagant. Paige, however, thinks piercing her ears extreme and certainly has not looked at her own naked crotch in ten years.

And yet when Janis Joplin sings, Paige feels at home with herself, truced.

On the far side of the damaged years, Paige will daydream: *Take me, Janis Joplin, in your lap and hum an unrecorded song.*

Tears hit her cheeks, disturbing reverie. Why is she crying?

Janis Joplin was supposed to cradle her until they ascended the world together, a comet waving bye-bye. Children who lose mothers feel this frustration and anger at being left behind, while simultaneously being at peace with remaining alive. Even though Janis Joplin was world-famous and Paige is nobody living nowhere, Janis Joplin's voice was big enough to hold her, and she had assumed that eventually she would crawl into it like a cat burrowing under the covers. This is what fans believe in, wonderful possibility.

Peers take Paige for a Joni Mitchell type, delicate like a soprano, meticulous the way thin-haired women can be. How little friends know about what goes on in friends' minds.

The relentless succession of deaths. Kennedy King Kennedy. Hendrix Joplin Morrison. All the kids feel adrift and spend a bunch of backyard nights looking up at the stars, but none are scared off dope. In fact, the deaths—both by assassination and overdose—romanticize mortality and drug use, and Paige imagines hitchhiking out to San Francisco to breathe deep and inhale Janis Joplin's ashes, flakes sticking to her lungs like a hickey or tick.

But that would be so unlike her. She doesn't tell anyone this is the story that leads her into sleep, and she stays loyal to her friend Hannah's sense of caution. Eventually Paige allows oblivion to consume Janis Joplin. You move on. You replace dream for dream.

For the duration of her time in Hell, Paige does passable school-work and experiments mildly with drugs, mostly for the exciting secrecy of it rather than any altered consciousness. That is also the reason Paige takes up French: Her parents don't speak it.

Heroin will increasingly fascinate her. The wreckage it causes. The paraphernalia. The physicality of it. She will try to be content with substitutes. Her own blood, the sight of it—she luxuriates in it; it is opium. The accidents (she slices her finger to the bone on a tin can) become calculated (her arm snags on rose thorns, etc.). But she will grow out of this behavior not because it bores her but because it humiliates.

As her life almost imperceptibly veers away from the path her classmates take—they will marry, get a mortgage or a trailer, have children, visit Disneyland—only one fear incubates: that the punch at the various parties she attends will be spiked with LSD and she'll spill the beans, rat, blab, snitch, let the cat out of the bag. Out of the same fear, she will absolutely refuse the once-friendly nitrous oxide at the dentist's.

But Paige keeps the secret. The secret becomes her wealth. The secret becomes her lover. After a while she's not even sure what the secret is and will spend many many years fishing it out of her brain waters. And then, with some regret, she will tell one person only, and then one more.

Other than her anxiety about squealing on herself, she is as fearless as the next 16-year-old. Chasing the thrill of physical euphoria lands some of those classmates in trouble with acid and amphetamines. Others contract venereal disease, ram cars into lampposts. Paige's personal teenage derangement centers around the secret, the pursuit of a phantom. She has the sometimes mistaken impression that love-ever-after will grow out of it. Paige is blindsided by her infatuation, and all that matters in the immediate future is that she win her learner's permit so the phantom takes her seriously. Try to imagine how seriously that will one day become.

After becoming old enough to vote, after losing her virginity, after familiarizing herself with clichés (which, having adapted to the idiom of someone else's language, makes her feel her life's a mockery, that she's in disguise) and shaving her legs, after figuring out Tampax and yielding to having her long hippie hair whacked off, Paige will have found the cesspool of true love.

In every graduating class there's a handful of kids who grow up different. Using an eight-inch knife, one of them in Paige's year will murder for money. Another will become a professional mud wrestler whose five kids will eat crackers in the dressing room while she's working and who'll send her a Mother's Day card every year for the rest of her life. And one student who brings only celery and diet soda for lunch will disappear overnight, her family leaving behind a house with a FOR SALE stake plunged into the insatiable heart of its kelly green lawn.

Unstable chemical bonds, highly reactive elements, free radicals. That's what these kids are, though others call them kids with a big question mark in their future. As the winter of her sophomore year descends, Paige becomes one of them. What in hell happened?

If you ask her yourself from the backseat of a Dodge Duster crossing Canada between Christmas and New Year's on a night the color of blood on a black-and-white TV, this is what she'd tell you somewhere in her 20s.

②

I should've worn my eyeglasses more often than I did. Real antique gold-wire frames, hand-tooled, excellent workmanship—or so the optician had commended.

The shop of Dr. Isadore Kraus, Optometrist, was one flight up creaky stairs in a three-story building whose street-level store sold prosthetic devices. Arranged in the display case were a pair of orthopedic shoes (one cross-sectioned), neck brace, corsets, walker, plastic legs, and three glass eyes: blue, green, and brown. A layer of dust covered everything. They did taxes on the third floor. As I squeaked into the shop, gray with meekness, a mouse, prescription in hand, a man in a white coat welcomed me with a gesture to enter. He put aside a bitten sauerkraut sandwich, hid it behind the countertop mirror. It made a bad smell, but I got used to it.

Dr. Kraus was a squat man, tufts of white hair sprouting from his skull and a mustache short and thick as the bristle brush my father uses to clean his suede shoes. When he rubbed his mustache with his index finger, which he did each time I tried out a new frame, it made a scratching noise, the sound of *maybe*. Once we both had agreed on a pair, he placed his ruler across my nose, measuring the distance from bridge to pupils. Maybe he touched a pressure point with his miniruler, I don't know, but I drifted into a state of complete relaxation. No fake smile, no squinting. He was looking into my eyes.

I hadn't wanted to choose eyeglasses alone, but Mother said, "You're a freshman now, you can do this on your own" (a perfect excuse when she had something better to do. Usually she said I was too young for everything). Hannah had band. Forget about my father; he's got no taste at all and says I look good in everything just to get out of having to make a judgment. He doesn't care about the way things look as long as they're functional. I'm sure that when he offered my used eyeglasses to the kids at his community center, it never occurred to him that they might care about how they look. Though he'd never say so, Papa thinks I am frivolous, just like my mother.

The first time I got glasses the optician, Dr. Nixon, cracked his gum in my face and leaned in so close I could see the blackheads on his nose. He insisted that only one pair of frames, retarded-looking ones, would fit me. He knew I looked ugly in them. I could see it in his face.

"I don't like these."

"They make you look like such a pretty little girl," the optician had said flatly then, turning to Mother, "Tell her to look in the mirror."

I folded my arms and turned away. I glared at the doorknob.

Mother picked up the mirror and shoved it in my face.

What I saw was the face of an eight-year-old behind glasses. I looked bushwhacked.

I wanted to snap the frame in two, to scratch the lenses with a safety pin. Mother said, "We'll take them."

That guy went bankrupt, hurrah.

The time I spend worrying. Just as I thought all milkmen were gentle with animals because ours kept a boxful of pet rabbits in his truck, so had I thought all opticians unscrupulous and contemptuous toward kids. Growing up is rarely more than learning such stuff, that milkmen eat rabbit.

Dr. Kraus, however, was one of the few real gentlemen I'd ever meet, right out of a novel: walking stick, ramrod posture, and a tendency toward making slight and deferential bows. Kindness affects me. That's why I have Blanche's line, "Whoever you are—I've always depended on the kindness of strangers," tacked over my desk. I've never known anyone who understands what I'm talking about.

Two weeks after my visit to the optometrist, I received a postcard saying my glasses were ready. This time I was adamant about going alone. It wasn't simply that I preferred few people to see me four-eyed. Isadore belonged to me. I didn't want my mother to ruin it by embarrassing me, didn't want to share him with Hannah. As he made adjustments to the fit, I realized I wouldn't see this man for another year, maybe longer if my prescription remained the same. How strange it is that you come so close to someone, you watch him chew a sandwich or scratch himself, you smell his breath, note the vein squiggling up his forehead, and then you both turn your backs, North-North magnets, and get on with it.

I filled in the exorbitant sum on my mother's blank check and tucked the receipt into the bib pocket of my overalls.

As I closed the glass DR. ISADORE KRAUS, OPTOMETRIST door behind me, bells tinkling, my head howled with emptiness. Even these golden glasses gave me that startled look. I had seen my reflection on the countertop mirror though I tried avoiding it. Eyeglasses. I hated the need. I wanted to hurl myself down the stairs, bound through a plate glass window. And Dr. Isadore Kraus thought I was "a nice girl." I might have cried if I had been the boo-hooing kind of girl, might have kicked something in the street, but the anxiety about getting on the right bus distracted me.

The bus was practically empty, and the driver wanted to talk...at least until a child ran into the street after a baseball. I slid five seats ahead when he slammed on the brakes, wondered during those horrible seconds whether I'd win a bruise or a cut that required stitches, but everyone was fine, the child never looked back, and the driver focused on the road, whistling "Windy." I scooted back to my original seat.

What a fraud I was, deceiving gullible Dr. Kraus. Nice girl, right! The last time I was nice without trying was in elementary school.

If you can peek at something with tiptoe eyes, as fathers in hospitals do when looking through the window to see their newborns in the nursery, so had I examined my new glasses, plaintive and compliant in their case. *I'm* not *wearing these*, I vowed to myself.

You break your own heart when you deny milk to a mewing kitten, when you ignore a lost child, when you hurl your favorite doll across the room. The glasses themselves were pretty cool, but like all eyeglasses they made me look like a dodo. Until John Lennon was photographed in his wire rims, wearing glasses where I lived was about as cool as wearing flood pants or caring about grades. So Dr. Kraus's antique frames spent more time in my shirt pocket, in my desk drawer, on the edge of the bathtub than on my nose. And as if they had life, I felt damned for my hissing neglect of them.

I did try getting on without my glasses, but it was no good. Even if I squinted at the television I only could distinguish people from couches because the people would move. Doing homework gave me a splitting headache. And once, after showering, I dusted myself with Grandmother's Fasteeth thinking it was talcum powder. I couldn't see the French teacher's whiskers or the parabolas on the blackboard, yet I tried to get passing grades despite schooldays spent in a myopic fog. But who needed a book or blackboard to learn "*Où est la piscine, Sylvie?*"

Nearsightedness made me a good listener, as I had loads of practice paying undivided attention to teachers' lessons, listening as hard as I could until I ran out of breath. That's one reason why I did well in French. But it also gave me the appearance of not having my head screwed on straight, a cocked ear setting my posture off balance. That's how I look in my yearbook photo. I seem to be asking "What's going on?" as if I'd come from another world, as if I were a big ignoramus.

By the end of high school my eyesight would worsen and I would have no choice but to wear my wire rims from the moment I woke until I lay down for sleep. My vision is so bad, it amazes me I don't need glasses for dreaming.

Everyone always wants to try on your glasses. "Whoa! These are strong!" they say, whipping them off their face, rubbing their eyes. My classmates' amazement at my ability to wear such strong lenses made me momentarily smug. But sooner or later someone would then call me Four Eyes or Professor, and I'd have to endure yet another recital, by neighbors or aunties, of Dorothy Parker's "Men don't make passes...." Glasses gave me the unwanted—and unwarranted—reputation of being studious. Teachers may favor students in glasses, but no one else takes you seriously. I never appreciated any of these ironies.

Someday someone will say to me, "It's so sexy when you wear glasses because I imagine taking them off." I'll never feel good about that either.

I am the spitting image of my mother at my age, or so Mother would tell me without failing to add that she, however, had perfect eyesight. "When you mature, boys are going to have the hots for you like they did for me."

The hots seemed an animal thing. I couldn't tell whether Mother was trying to flatter or frighten me. But all I could picture were the *National Geographic* females on television—the ones on savanna, steppe, vine and veldt, polar ice cap too—who, while a million people in TV land shovel dinner into their mouths, don't fight off the hairy beast, don't hyena for help. Boys did want to come over. Boys wanted to date me.

They weren't the boys who remind you of stainless steel. The boys who wanted to treat me to a strawberry float (or the latest James Bond movie or bowling and a Hershey bar) drooled and smelled of wet wool. I went out with them because I didn't know any good excuses. And because Mother insisted.

My belly iced up on all those dates. And it was the mothers I paid most attention to, those boys' mothers smiling in the background with mistaken assumptions of puppy love, those mothers getting ready to grow fond of little Paige Bergman, to make a place for me at their sticky Formica tables. Thanks to them, I was learning to live with being not what I seemed, the sweet and popular Paige Bergman up on Hickory Street who would never break Bruce's, Stuart's, Billy's, or Brian's heart.

I should have given a warning but instead would graduate Lindbergh High School with a host of housewives' long-standing hatred against me. Who did I think I was leading their sons on? Their open-fly, spitting-when-they-talk, cheddar-breathed sons who stared at my chest even in the dark of the movies? And I thought I was making sacrifices, doing the nerds a favor. It was my only consolation for being forced to spend time with these creeps.

Eventually, having realized I had to stop turning to my mother to help me out of the situation, a dentist's appointment became my standard excuse. My theory was that Mother made me go out with every boy who called because she was trying to assure herself of her own popularity. Because if she really wanted me to be popular she'd have let me get contacts.

"You're not old enough," she said.

I named the girls in my class who had them.

"Contact lenses need a lot of care. I don't think you're responsible enough yet."

"Please."

"No. End of discussion."

Did Grace Slick wear glasses, the Supremes, Joan Baez, Judy Collins? Name one female in movies wearing glasses who was supposed to be attractive. Not Greta Garbo, not Holly Golightly, not Pussy Galore.

Dorothy Parker was right. I was not a contender. I knew Mother wanted it that way. So I pocketed my glasses at every social opportunity—lunch period, study hall, recess—and perfected the art of spiteful behavior. (It really got to Mother when she told me my glasses were filthy, how could I see out of them, and I continued pouring Papa's minestrone down my throat.) Gym and all my classes were required wearing, as were any unfamiliar environments, though I did take chances here and there. Fading now is a scar across the bridge of my nose, somersaults while wearing my tortoiseshell frames.

I was certain people laughed at me when I swam in the ocean in glasses, but I couldn't have survived the monotonous beach without them. Once when I deliberately left them on my beach blanket and walked a straight line, a Hansel and Gretel line, down to the water, I still hadn't been able to find my way back. After stepping through the frigid Atlantic until it was up to my waist, I turned around, away from the great ships aimed for Portugal, unclamped the seaweed that had braceleted my ankles, and admitted it: I was lost, couldn't distinguish my family from the families of other seasiders.

Everyone was having such fun on their sandy claim, tanning, listening to Cousin Brucie, Dan Ingram, Harry Harrison on transistor radios, eating onion rings and franks, trying to pull off girls' bikini tops, lazily thumbing fashion magazines. I was trying to find which cluster I belonged to.

I pretended I could see where I was going. The sand was burning my feet. I felt pathetic.

At last I heard the bell of my mother's voice and followed it. Mother was laughing her head off.

"We watched you circle us three times!"

"I was looking for shells," I lied.

"You really don't need that," Mother said as I took a second slice of pizza. Why was she always being so mean? It's not that I had to worry about getting fat. I ignored her, took a bite. "Don't complain to me if you wake up tomorrow with pimples." Was that a warning or a hex? You couldn't tell with my mother. "OK, don't listen to me. But acne is in your genes." *Touché*, she sighed, zinging me and Papa at once.

My father did suffer adolescent acne, but what Mother doesn't know is that I like my father's complexion, its rugged history in scars (he has pitted skin and a blue shadow on his face from a thick beard; Mother was constantly tweezing the ingrown hairs from his face while his eyes watered as he sat on the lidded toilet seat).

Contact lenses wouldn't make me more attractive, and I really should do something about my hair—sleep in curlers, tie it back, blow-dry it at least. Who did she think she was talking to?

"I'm just trying to help." Eva's way of helping was to point out my pimples, especially if we had company. Just the previous week I had been watching television with Uncle Edbert with my chin in my hands, and she shouted, "Stop touching your face." Of course Uncle Edbert looked at me to see what she was talking about. "That'll give you more pimples. And you should stop eating those candy bars." It was chocolate that Grandmother had brought from Sweden.

Tons of kids were seeing dermatologists (in secret) who sent them home with special creams, soaps, and prescriptions for tetracycline. Eva, however, took me to some quack in a white coat who looked like Professor Rath in *The Blue Angel*. His nurse put black goggles on my face, scratching me as she did so. "Do not move," she ordered. Eva, the doc, and his scrawny nurse left the room. Someone threw a switch. I heard electrical crackling. They radiated my face.

For three days afterward the stench of burning flesh accompanied me everywhere, so I kept my distance from people. "You're red as a lobster!" Eva laughed. For three days my face would be on fire. All that for a week without pimples. It was such a success with Eva that she insisted I go back every few months.

I couldn't win. If I refused to go to the doctor, she'd make sure to point out my pimples. I think that was worse than having them at all.

One night it overwhelmed me, my lost cause with Eva. She'd watered me down. I'd look to my father for corroboration, but he'd just shrug. What could he do? "Just wait, darling. In a year or two your face will be peaches and cream," Papa said. I couldn't wait.

Anyway, it was too late. I had renounced beauty aids (pimple cream was the exception) as artificial and strode out of the house in bell-bottoms and sandals until October, Wallabees until April. I was a teenager.

Mother had had her chance to mother me in the go-go-boot years. She could have sent me to a beauty parlor instead of giving me a perm from a box, which fuzzed my hair and made it stink of burning rubber. She could have taken me to buy make-up. She could have discouraged Grandmother from making my clothes (that orange sweater nauseated me). She could have bought me a training bra so my back would look like all the other girls' backs when we sneaked into our gym suits showing each other as little flesh as possible. But it was OK. I would hate to be one of those girls wearing blue eye shadow and blow-drying a little flip in my hair.

The time I asked for money for a pocketbook, my parents' friends, Pride and Morton, had just arrived for dinner and Papa was taking their coats. Mother lifted a lid from a saucepan and in a cloud of steam said no and don't ask your father either.

All the girls had a pocketbook, even if it was just to hold gum and fountain pens. Mother said I'd have to wait until I was older, she didn't care what all the other girls were doing, and holding a wooden spoon stuck with grains of rice, rubbed cheeks hello with her guests.

Later in the evening I overheard a conversation about me. The men were in the kitchen clanking coffee cups and cutting up Papa's ice cream pie. The women were in the living room, mother humming a tune, Pride throwing me a kiss good night. I had just been sent up to my room with a big enough slice of pie. While settling on my bed with my plate and transistor, I heard Pride mention my name. Who can help eavesdropping on a conversation about themselves? Nobody.

I crept off the bed and tiptoed across the room, crouching right beside the door where the adults downstairs couldn't see me.

"You're behaving like all those men who never let their sons win a single game, not even checkers," Pride said. "Eva, buy Paige the pocketbook."

I got the pocketbook about a month later, a birthday gift from Pride. It doesn't matter now. You can never compete against a beautiful woman who's your mother.

If a chandelier could sing, it would sound like my mother's voice. I can hear her even when she's in a 25-member choir. My father says he fell in love with my mother's voice the minute he heard it.

My parents met at a rehearsal—Mother sang commercials, some movie music too—for chewing gum. Papa was the studio technician, until he went on disability. They honeymooned in Hawaii, and the photographs are still science fiction to me, my parents clowning in swimsuits, my parents living before I was born. I don't smile in pictures. I want to look serious. You never know what's going to happen. Look at my father.

When I was in elementary school, the neighbors next door told us our father had had a bad accident and was in the hospital and we could have dinner with them. All I remember is that they wouldn't let me eat the hot dog without the bun. Jan remembers there was no answer when he asked, "Is my father going to die?" He held a grudge against them for years, but not enough to egg them on Halloween. He just didn't say hello, and when we had new snow he made sure he was first to walk across their virgin lawn.

As far as I know, Jan and I were the only kids in school whose father had ever been electrocuted. People asked me if his hair stood on end. Or if he smelled of burning flesh. Papa has memory problems, though you can hardly tell, and when you can it's pretty funny. Once I asked him if I could have a brownie, and he said, "Just one." Five minutes later I asked again. He said, "Just one." I did it a third time and was full after that. When Papa couldn't remember meeting my friends and I'd have to introduce them all over again, they thought he was teasing them, so they laughed good-naturedly about it.

Papa was busier than ever after he stopped working a regular job. He built himself a study where he'd be reading three books at once. He hardly ever talked on the phone but had to have a radio or record player on, no matter what he was doing. On weekends, regardless of the weather, he walked in the woods carrying a basket for the collection of moss and mushrooms and twigs. He was supposed to work only part-time at the community center but often came home after I'd gone to sleep. His job was helping immigrants settle into Hell by tutoring them in English, taking them to the supermarket, and helping them fill out forms at the doctor's office.

To this day the people in Hell say immigrants bring down property values and the town is already running at full capacity. I know that's why folks weren't very friendly to us. I didn't care a dime. Papa came home with colorful food: pink jelly cakes, curried peas, potatoes and raisins, bread with herbs in it, whole fish with eyes, and pickled things my mother made him throw in the garbage before he even unscrewed the jars. He also knew how to say "I love you" in 17 languages.

The community center was simply two cinder-block rooms in a church basement. I sat in the corner on a folding chair whenever my father let me go with him. Though I brought books with me and Mother packed me a snack, I stayed still as a cat and listened to the accents, the ankle bracelets, sucked in the smells— pepper, menthol, sandalwood soap—which made me imagine I was traveling around the world. Some people's hair was so black it was blue. Everyone smiled at me from a distance, and I smiled back, not knowing their language.

Going to work with Mother was not nearly as pleasant. The bassist, Cracker, who had a son, a hyperactive kid in my grade named Litrell, gave me a bear hug that nearly broke my neck. How I'd grown, he'd say each time, and keep an eye out for Litrell who, if there's any sense in the boy's head, will be chasing after me soon enough. I could figure out why that frightened me, but I couldn't figure out why it was supposed to be a compliment. Anyway, if Litrell started bugging me, at least he wouldn't reek of pomade and cigars because, unlike his pop, Litrell didn't straighten his hair nor could he ever sit still long enough to light a stinking cigar.

The vending machines were usually out of root beer and M&Ms, and I habitually got myself locked into the women's bathroom. But that wasn't the worst of it.

The studio trombone player, an Elvis imitator, did something I wish my whole life was a dream. Mother and I had just walked into the reception area when a bunch of musicians came out on break. The trombonist tried to swing me off my feet. "Hey, you're getting to be a big kid, huh?" I'm sure my underwear showed. Then he sat me on his lap and started talking to me with his oily nose in my face and gray tongue sloshing around in his mouth. "Doncha remember me? It's nice to see you all grown up." He slobbered on my neck, and when I winced, he pinched me, he pinched my acorn-size breast and grinned, revealing a muck of food in his teeth.

Budding breasts are sore all the time, and though it hurt when he did that—I had tears in my eyes—I couldn't scream *ouch!* because it was worse than that.

The next thing I knew, I whopped him in the head with my elbow. He put me down and walked away.

I'm sure my mouth was still agape as I scanned the room to see who was my witness. Mother looked away and unpinned her hat. I've tried to forget the musician's name, but I know it's Jack Leever.

At home that evening, I told my mother I wasn't going back to the studio with her if Jack was there. She didn't ask why. She just took my Londonderry lipstick away and said, "You're too young for this," though I had already played spin the bottle dozens of times in the basements of Hell. Guess who started wearing frosted lipstick to work?

Head down, I walked the linoleum hallways and the road home from school, and though it may have looked otherwise I was not forlorn. I was watching my step. Hannah's mother said that wearing glasses only makes your eyes weaker. So I trained for 20/20 vision at every opportunity. Nothing happened, and I nearly fell down the stairs once. (It was just as embarrassing that I twisted my ankle and had to limp through my sixth-, seventh- and eighth-period classes.) If an object was farther than three feet away, I couldn't see it. Everybody was an overcoat to me. So what was the point in looking up?

No wonder being the object of someone's interest surprised me. Like a ton of bricks.

③

You had to be dead and buried to get any privacy. People weren't particularly meddlesome (excluding our neighbor Annette Goldstein), but Hell was a small town; you couldn't help being aware of comings and goings.

The automobile told the fullest story. Cars can't tiptoe, lie straight-faced, or sneak through backyards and thickets. More than one cheating husband has been caught not by the scent of a woman on his skin but by the butt of his car sticking out of a parking space at the Easyrest Motor Court. My brother, Jan, was grounded for a week after Mrs. Goldstein spotted our car outside the Village Tavern when Jan had told Mother he needed the car to go to the library. You don't have to be Sherlock Holmes to know who's up to what. Just follow the cars.

Hannah and I spent many hours car watching. Once, around 6 P.M., we settled onto a grassy spot on a rise overlooking the village green. With her mother's money, we had bought a Swiss cheese hero from Vera's Luncheonette. Vera sliced it in half on the diagonal, but we shared it by taking turns taking bites. Neither of us had germs, we agreed. This way we'd have a whole other sandwich after we'd finished the first.

The thruway traffic about 50 feet behind us whooshed by. We were blocked from the drivers' view by the billboard.

HAVE YOU BEEN SERIOUSLY INJURED?

ALL TYPES OF ACCIDENTS: AUTOMOBILE, CONSTRUCTION, SLIP & FALL, BRAIN INJURIES, BIRTH DEFECTS, MEDICAL MALPRACTICE, DEFECTIVE PRODUCTS, DOG BITES

DINO & MILLICENT, ATTORNEYS AT LAW
FREE CONSULTATION

We were minding our own business, debating the legalization of marijuana. Chief Duh's police car circled below us, looking like a toy. Then Hannah started in on her indignation about apartheid, and that's how I learned to pronounce the word before I had ever had to. Hell was apathetic to these issues, and Hannah considered that worse than if the people in town had been reactionary. I didn't care. I just thought neighbors should leave each other alone.

We were Gulliverish on that hill with all those small people below. I could hear Mrs. Davis's Thunderbird idling in Cluck-a-Doodle-Do's parking lot, poison clouds puffing out her muffler. She'd be serving cole slaw and a bucket of twice-fried chicken for dinner. Over by the hardware store the trunk of the Knechts' Tempest popped open to accommodate the lawn mower Herbert Knecht rented for his puny son to push. (I had a premonition he would mow the lawn in sandals and lose a toe doing it, but I never found out whether it came true.)

It was Hannah's turn to bite when I saw the car swerve into the gas station. I knew there was no way it was going to make it at that speed and angle, and indeed it crashed into the cement stanchion in front of the gas pump. I expected a much louder noise instead of that *pfft*. We saw drivers scrape by those cement pillars all the time. Most of the drivers were kids who had just gotten their license. It made me crack up. Hannah was scared by those crashes. But no one ever got hurt.

I recognized the driver of the latest crash as the same one who had been behind the wheel of the hit-and-run that killed Trudy, our neighbor's cat. I hadn't actually seen the car, but I'd heard it all right. Papa said hearing doesn't stand up as proof in a court of law, but how could you possibly have mistaken the gold LeSabre owned by that crabby lady down the street? Her axles squealed as the car pitched around our corner, and then she'd honk twice to let her husband know she was home, though he was stone deaf. She drove with her nose right up to the wheel and at one speed only, 50 miles per hour. Papa once yelled at her when we were little, said she drives like it's bumper cars. She hollered at him and nothing changed. We'd run from the street when she'd careen by, laughing at her though we knew she wanted to kill us. A person hates kids if they've never once been home for Halloween. We watched her from the bushes as she'd hose down the driveway to wash away the stench of our rotten eggs and shaving-cream curse words.

My car-motor acuity had been refined by my baby-sitters, inadvertent though it was. Baby-sitters filled me with dread. What would it be this time? Would they force me to take a puff of a cigarette? Wash my mouth out with soap for being disobedient? Eat all the cashews from the mixed nuts? Have slap fights in our living room with their boyfriends? As soon as our parents left, I'd wash up and go to bed just to get out of the baby-sitter's way. The one nice baby-sitter gave us Dentyne, but we only had her for a year before she graduated and went off to teacher's school.

We had Mitzi most of the time. She wasn't mean, but she was so stupid I felt uncomfortable being around her because she knew she was even dumber than us kids. If the TV didn't come on immediately she practically cried, and she spent most of the time at the kitchen table calculating how much money my mother owed her for four hours.

Mitzi, in her pink mohair sweater, and my brother, Jan, sat stupefied by TV while I lay upstairs in bed. It was hard to resist the edgy lullaby of criss-crossing cars on Hickory Street, but I had to remain awake until the heroic Peugeot turned the corner. Then and only then would I be relieved of my visions of kidnappers climbing up to my window, and car wrecks, shattered glass raining on my bloodied startled parents.

Once I heard my parents' Peugeot round the corner I was released into luxurious slumber.

When the Pontiac Firebird became the hottest car in Hell, two of our neighbors bought the same model in the same color: persimmon. I could tell without turning from my dinner plate which one of them was going over the speed limit on our block because the girl's motor rumbled like an old man hucking up his lungs.

Jan would try to stump me on the cars as they motored up and down our street: the high-pitched whir of the VW Bug, the Country Squire's reassuring hum, the GTO with the broken muffler that made your tonsils vibrate as it passed. I had perfect pitch when it came to cars. When Jan could no longer accuse me of cheating, having substituted his hands over my eyes for the dishrag blindfold, he began to lie to me, saying it was the neighbor's Comet station wagon when it could only have been the diaper delivery truck. I'd struggle to break free of his grip to see for myself I was right, and we'd fight until we were sweaty. If I dug my nails into Jan's arm he'd slap me in the head, and I'd cry. "Leave your brother alone!" Mother shouted from another room. What a joke.

While everyone's mother became more and more of an embarrassment as we grew up, my mother became repellent. She was more bossy and more prying than Hannah's or Amelia's mother, who mostly just worried about them dressing warmly enough, putting on weight, and getting good grades. Mine I couldn't stand to touch, even when our elbows knocked each other in our cramped little kitchen. When I found her reading my journal, I was unable to like her ever again.

People want me to say something nice about my mother. Frankly, to list Eva's good qualities makes me sick to a frenzy. I'll try: She's got a great voice, dinner guests tell her she's ravishing tonight, she won't use euphemisms for abortion and cancer. Period. I can't talk about it anymore, OK? Jan tried to shush me whenever I griped, though he never contradicted what I had to say about our mother. When I'd complain to Papa, he'd sigh and say, "She's your mother. She loves you," and eventually I learned he was no help. Hannah was repeatedly incredulous, as if each incident I'd recount was new, as if she couldn't contain in her head that my mother was impossible, Eva's always so nice to her on the phone. Grandmother considered the whole thing irrelevant.

My plump grandmother thought I was beautiful, and Hannah and Amelia envied my thick blond hair, but I knew my face was off, a bad forgery of the ravishing Eva Bergman. Hannah was getting fat on puddings and potato chips, Amelia was too tall for boyfriends, and I was growing ugly, squirrel-faced. To top it all, I had those damn glasses.

It was my freshman year, and I was wearing my glasses for all seven class periods, gym included, but it seemed safe enough to shuffle on home after school without them. By the end of the day the bridge of my nose was sore, a bright red footprint on each side, and I rubbed it using the gesture men on television use to convey weariness.

October in Hell is dismal, lots of mud and no fire in the leaves. Many of our neighbors went to Vermont to see the seasons change. Their kids returned bringing maple sugar candy to school that Monday. It tasted of the condensation of loveliness and was too sweet. Vermont must be idyllic, like the pictures of New England in our American history schoolbooks.

Hell is shades of gray: the pavement and the tires on it, the tree trunks and birds, even stratocumulus descendants of heaven. The walk home from school blisteringly dull, I considered running but didn't dare without glasses. The one day when my glasses broke, a teacher told me, "Now that I can see you out from hiding behind those glasses, you look morose," and I smiled though I didn't know whether that was good or bad. Even after I looked up the word in the dictionary I didn't know what he was picking up on, but I liked it. When you're a 14-year-old high school freshman, any aid to self-definition is useful.

I was morose!

Maybe there was a warning and I didn't understand, maybe I ignored it, but that autumn a meteor fell on Hickory Street. It took the form of a Buick Skylark, and it sat unpurring outside Dr. and Mrs. Goldstein's house, which was just up a block. Walking home from school that day, glasses in book bag, I approached the maroon haze. Squinting, I could tell it was a car. Hadn't ever seen this one before, maybe it belonged to their cousins or the Fuller Brush man.

The car reappeared in front of the Goldsteins' later that week, and then again and again, even once the snow fell. I never saw the Skylark drive up or drive off. I just saw it there.

A few weeks after first spotting the car, I sidled past it on a Friday, always a day for courage, the history homework in my book bag breaking my back. I peeked in.

She was the most beautiful woman I'd ever seen. I don't mean delicate or Miss America. I mean spellbinding, the way the Mona Lisa is, something to figure out. There in the driver's seat.

Through early winter she showed up in the Buick embraced by a fur collar and, when the thaw broke in January, turtleneck sweaters or silk scarves, those expensive ones with the stirrup motif. The neck makes the aristocrat, and, ministered by fur and silk like that, she was one.

There were 100 watts in her skull giving her the rosy, incandescent complexion of a fever. It seemed some force field made her skin searing to the touch, though I wouldn't know. Her butterscotch hair was pulled back in a bun at the nape of her neck, but you could tell it had a natural waviness. It was slightly darker underneath like dirt scratched in summer.

All I could see was her right profile, handsome the way Greek goddesses are in bas-relief. She waited unmoving behind the steering wheel, hands in her lap, composed as a department store nun, with a seriousness not unlike possession. The motor was always off, the windows rolled up. She did not honk. A white purse with tortoiseshell handle sat at attention on the seat next to her.

I think if she'd looked at me full on, I would have fallen under a spell.

The peckings of Hell's voracious crows and cardinals, the garbage collectors who set off the neighborhood dogs in a relay of barking, did not distract her. And rather than turning impatiently toward the Goldsteins' front door, she faced straight ahead and willed the sun to go down. Mother would have honked her head off, rapped at the front door harder than she should have.

I wanted to ask my parents about her. Except for once pointing out to my mother the car in front of the Goldsteins', I didn't mention her to either of my parents, didn't want them between us. Mother told me her kids were probably playing with the Goldstein kids, the house always a raffle of children, and she was waiting to pick them up. Papa, had I brought the car to his attention, would've suggested I tap on the window to see if the woman was OK. "Stop worrying about everything," Mother snapped at me.

Much as I tried to get the woman's attention over the months, she did not so much as scratch an itch. She did not yawn, sneeze, or check her bobby pins in the rearview mirror. Like one animal stalking another, she knew how to wait. I too was as patient as ruins. I would watch over her, be the good Samaritan, fairy godmother, guardian angel, knight in shining armor. So what if I was only a freshman? My feelings still counted.

The residents who passed the Buick on errands thought, like my mother, that there was nothing exceptional about a woman sitting in a car—what's so unusual about a parent waiting to pick up her children from a playmate's house, ferry them home for meat loaf and a bath? Yet within the span of a few weeks, I shuddered when I saw her car. I think I dreamt embarrassing dreams about her; she beckoned me from the other side of the water, whispered in my ear.

I wanted her to speak to me, to wash my neck, to steady me with her hands on my shoulders. But I could also hear my mother admonishing me, I was getting carried away. I was familiar with that, ever since Mother charged into my room when I was pretending to be a rock star. Ever since, I've been restrained around her, don't want her sniggering at me when I'm having pleasure.

On the days when the car wasn't there I was disappointed, cranky with Hannah and Amelia and insolent with my mother, who thwacked me with a spatula between my shoulder blades for refusing to vacuum the house (only because I knew Mother would stand there, fingering her lower lip, and watch me bend over and shove the appliance back and forth like her maid).

My friend Amelia wasn't what you'd call pretty, though I was the only one who thought so. She was very popular in school and by far the best artist in our grade, though she wasn't so good when it came to portraits: All her models, male and female, had her face. I think it was deliberate. And I always wondered how she knew what male anatomy looked like, but I didn't ask because it would have made me looked ignorant.

A showdown was simmering between Amelia and Hannah. I pretended not to notice. I didn't want to talk about it. Someday they'd both hate me, but in the meantime they were each a good friend to me. I was not a good friend back.

They wanted too much from me, to be best friends with big secrets. When I ran out of excuses for why I had to go home after having dinner at Amelia's, I'd just have to give in and sleep over. We had to share the same single bed, which I really didn't like. I thought if our skin touched I'd get a crossed eye and a hairy mole on my cheek too. I always ended up rolling onto her side because she was heavier than I was. She didn't mind, and we even giggled about it until her mother banged on the wall at 2 in the morning to tell us to shut up.

Still I worried about being swamped by Amelia. It was the same with Hannah, only she had bunk beds.

How could they understand I belonged to the woman in the Skylark?

I couldn't articulate what our point of convergence would be, or had been, though I don't really believe in reincarnation, but the lady in the Skylark and I would know each other. It was predestination, and I accepted that with utter conviction even though gurus are quacks.

Thus began the charade.

I washed my hair every day instead of four times a week in case I ran into her.

To impress her, I ostentatiously carried in my arms—instead of in my book bag—the existentialist novels we were reading in French.

On biting winter days I went underdressed, canvas sneakers and a ski sweater, to strut my independence, my contempt for the world, all the while knowing it offered the woman an opportunity to take me in from the cold. I got drenched in the rain; no self-respecting teenager carried an umbrella or scurried under awnings.

She was in my daydreams, always in the background, present the way an Almighty is. She seemed unreal real, like witches in fairy tales, but why would anyone hallucinate a Skylark? I wondered if she were an annunciation, and though I wasn't clear about the good word my messenger attempted to deliver, I listened to the night for hushed clues that never came.

Increasingly desperate for the sight of her, I discovered that agitation wasn't a half bad feeling. I could barely contain myself, wanting to talk about her and thus open the doors to any possible information. But I told no one about her. I didn't want anyone else jumping on board. At the same time I wanted Hannah and Amelia to get a look at her because if you were the only person who ever heard the Beatles, it wouldn't be much fun. Same with my lady in the car.

Surely Mother would know something. Their paths must have crossed, at the Meat-O-Mat? the dry cleaner? Women always know something about other women. Mother could at least find out her name from Mrs. Goldstein. But as I said, it was over between us.

I could've thrown a plate at her each time she made a snide remark or mocked me in front of my friends: Paige's small breasts, garbage breath, rat's nest hair, you're going out in *that*? you really should go back to the dermatologist, a little rouge would make you look less green....

I made it easy for my mother, my bombshell mother. I refused to compete. I wouldn't even consider wearing makeup and panty hose, preferred leather thong bracelets to pearls and my grand-mother's brooch. Mother thought it a disgrace for girls to go to school in jeans, patched jeans no less, my older brother wore a tie and button-down shirt when he was in high school. Grandmother bought me lacy white slips which I'd never wear, and silent Papa hid behind blue clouds of pipe smoke.

My ninth grade report card, all C's except for French. Straight A+'s. I was Madame Foiegras's pet, but there was no Advanced Placement class until junior year. I'd wait.

I sat in front of my parents at the dinner table while they undressed me as they perused my grades. "If you have such a talent for languages, you'd think you'd do more than grunt when you're at home," Mother said, signing on the line. She didn't mind my C's the way my father did because she hated to be out-smarted by her daughter.

Because I would not speak at dinner I was generally dismissed from the table as soon as I was done, unless Grandmother was visiting. I wouldn't talk to Jan when he phoned us long distance because I couldn't bear the notion of my mother listening in.

I wrote a poem for French class about "my mother's cold gray soul / the herring she is / slithering through dreams / stinking up the house" when we studied the Surrealists. Madame Foiegras wrote a whole page of comments and urged me to submit the poem to the French Club's *La Revue*. It was produced on the cheap, run off on a ditto machine, no chance of my mother seeing it and having Uncle Edbert translate it for her.

The longer the secrecy, the more worthwhile the secret. On days when the Buick showed up I was bursting out of my bones and unafraid of my mother. When the road in front of the Goldsteins' remained empty, it was a natural disaster, a whirlwind or freak thunderbolt that left a big, hurtful oil puddle behind just to rub it in. It was embarrassing for me when she didn't show.

I couldn't concentrate on homework and felt worse than crying when the car wasn't there (and sometimes when it was), but within a few days the car always came back. It was to be my meteor, the wonder that draws children running out of their houses in August, pointing to the sky murmuring only "Wow!" Falling star, particle of dust.

And then the Skylark vanished.

④

The shortcut to Hannah's ran through the school parking
lot. At night it wasn't safe: mean-looking dogs, rats hunching
over garbage, seniors drag racing without headlights, our police
chief and bullhorn, students puking beer, and even a murder (it
ended up being a knife wound to the head, waterfalls of blood).
Because of the perils, Hannah and I had an arrangement.

"The person walking home calls the other as soon as she
arrives," said Hannah, writing it in my notebook for emphasis.

"What's the point?" I wondered, watching her perfect left-
handed script. "If I get attacked by dogs on the way home or
popped by your neighbor's Dodge Coronet, by the time I call it'll
be too late."

"Mary, Mary, quite contrary," Hannah sang. "Oh, Paige, let's
just stick to the plan." I shrugged my shoulders and looked out the
window seeing nothing, birds, and how were those tweeters going
to help me with my frustration?

For years I'd taken the shortcut without incident. At night
the great open sky sheltering the parking lot made me want to
twirl around and around, but I never did in case someone was
watching. Instead, you just drank stars and loved the moon

moored behind the Poe-like scudders. If you were alone.

During the day it wasn't at all creepy. The worst that could happen would be that you'd have to trudge through your self-consciousness as you scurried past upperclassmen lounging on their cars corralled, rather than parked, in a wagon-train circle.

We were on the threshold of an early June sunset. Hannah and I had been studying together for the algebra regents. After we'd been at it almost two hours, her mother invited me to stay for dinner, but I didn't like the smell of it. I shoved my notes in my book bag and left for home through the shortcut. "Call you later, alligator!"

Massive sunsets, the smell of backyard barbecues, school finally, officially, unequivocally over—you bet I rejoiced! Freshman year was a real hump, and now that I was over it, I felt liberated. What a triumph it was to walk through school property this time of year. No more dress code, term papers, detention, rules against talking in the hallway, having to raise your hand, having to ask permission to go to the bathroom you were afraid to use anyway.

The school building wore the look of defeat. Upended chairs had been set atop desks. Halls deserted, you could actually see a pattern on the linoleum, which mournful custodians waxed with ponderous machines. Teachers' parking spaces were vacant. But the bell, like the alarm clock of someone who has died in his sleep, still rang throughout the building and across the grounds announcing the beginning and the end of phantom classes. Only the gymnasium remained open; for one week, smelling of erasers and old sneakers, it would accommodate the handful of us taking the state exams.

Summertime nudges in and high school kids loiter. You couldn't help it any more than you could avoid scratching your poison ivy. Kids wander the streets like goblins and settle in the parking lot. Someone has something cool to drink, passes around an ice cream sandwich, splits a juicy orange. You hear music in the streets, car radios rising and fading and rising again in the neighborhood.

Summer in Hell, we give out a collective sigh, loosen our belts, and slog on into the buggy season. Our statuesque housewives sunbathing in lawn chairs, reflectors positioned under their chins, let the phone ring, taste their own sweat mustache. "Hi, Mrs. Goldstein," I waved, and she wagged her reflector at me. Children eating peanut butter sandwiches under shady trees take an hour to finish lunch, the ant activity around them mesmerizing. "It's Paige!" One elbows the other one, the indifferent one who never had one of my peanut-butter pizza sandwiches. "Hey, Paige! Come and play with us!" said the child I knew holding up a magnifying glass. Cats snooze in under-bush burrows. Decapitated dads flat on their backs work ratchets under automobiles. Teenagers in parking lots burn out their car batteries playing the radio so loud because oh, how the sky has opened up to receive it.

Call the cops! That's how a lot of Hell residents reacted when a teenager with long hair appeared within shouting distance. Twice I personally saw Police Chief Norman Duh screech up in his squad car, Tabletalk Pie and Chuckles on the dash. With great effort he rose from the car and then threatened to arrest everyone, including me, though I was just cutting through. When he wagged his nightstick at us, silently I dared him to whomp me. I'd bleed, but I wouldn't whimper, and then I'd sue the bastard. But my body didn't understand what I was trying to tell it, and it started trembling and wouldn't stop until I got into bed that night. Dogs have that reaction too, going haywire over men in uniforms.

"You freakin' commies. Step away from your vehicles." Duh was an ass, always outsmarted by the hippies who refused to be goaded into fisticuffs and hid their marijuana quickly, successfully. Duh was too damn fat to bend down and beam his flashlight under the car seats. "Open da trunk!" he commanded, nightstick in hand, hippie boys giggling like girls. So while Duh stared at the spare tire and panted for breath, on the other side of the school the local greasers, including the chief's nephew Richie McFee, were hurling beer bottles at English classroom windows. Indeed, Chief Duh blamed their most recent vandalism on "the radical hippie element," though we all knew it was McFee, a senior two years in a row, who shattered the pane. The damage was exquisite, a giant snowflake.

As I cut through the parking lot, a bunch of guys were leaning on cars, smoking, fake boxing. A radio droned, but I couldn't make out the music. At first I assumed no one was looking at me—what a relief. It's weird when boys you don't want to look at you look at you, awful when they make sucking or coyote noises, and completely terrifying when they mention your breasts. (Mother once told me I should take being whistled at as a compliment. Sometimes I think she doesn't have enough brains to be afraid.)

I recognized the five guys, even if I didn't know all their names, and John Radnoti. Everyone knew John. John the Divine, we called him. Even in grammar school he was the most popular kid in the district. Boys wanted to be like him, girls wanted to date him, teachers wanted his respect, and parents told their children to stay away from the riffraff.

What was the physiognomy of cool? The sad truth of our public-school life was that to be cool you had to be reckless, indifferent, and not too smart. John was all that. Looking like Steve McQueen didn't hurt either.

None of my classmates knew much about John Radnoti other

than what we saw with our own eyes. We could plainly see he was gorgeous, that he hung out with the vocational-track kids, that he often cut class, that he smoked Marlboros in the parking lot. It was rumored that when John was nine, he had been bitten by a rat in his own home and had the teeth marks to prove it. It was rumored that during the spring floods, an alligator had slithered into his basement and John had tamed it. It was rumored that John had gotten a girl pregnant when he was in sixth grade. We were eager to believe any hearsay about him.

Radnoti father and son lived in one of Hell's two urban development apartments. The twin five-floor buildings were on the edge of Hell, next to the hardware store and across from the Easyrest Motor Court. Many of the apartment windows faced the sludgy river, which stank of sewage in the warmer months. Cheap paper decorations hung in the lobby doors as holidays approached: pumpkins with legs, a Puritan's hat atop a roasted turkey, cherry-cheeked Santa, cowlicked baby with the New Year on a banner across his diaper, Washington and Lincoln, an Easter egg and chick, a flag on a fireworks background. "How prosaic," Papa would snort while parking the car in front of the hardware store. I, however, found the decorations cheerful reminders of upcoming school holidays and festive puddings.

"How's it going?" John shouted, tucking his long, shiny hair behind an ear. Was he talking to me? "Hey, ahoy there! Bergman, come on over." He was.

I shifted my book bag with my brother Jan's college seal on it in an attempt to hide my scholarship behind my back and approached.

I smiled and wished I'd taken off my glasses before coming this close to him. Now it would be too obvious.

"You're Jan's sister, right?" John began picking seeds out of a baggie of marijuana. "Jan and I played varsity football together." I had been there when John, a fast and sneaky wide receiver, had been stretchered out of a game with a concussion. Later that afternoon, when Jan had dumped his bloody, snotty, muddy uniform right on top of my underwear in the washing machine, I'd had a fit, which was resolved by Mother ordering me to wash my socks, undershirts, and underwear in the sink. It wasn't fair of her, but envisioning Jan's spittle and nose blood in the rinse cycle made me never want to use the washing machine again anyway. And come to think of it, did I want my mother's avaricious hands fingering my personal lingerie?

"I saw you play a few times." (What a stupid game.) John flashed me a childishly happy smile, obviously enjoying having been recognized on the field.

I had never been this close to John Radnoti before. It was like when I saw Patty Duke at the jewelry store in the city or when our mayor waved to me in the Memorial Day parade before he resigned over tax evasion: You couldn't help smiling and feeling worthwhile.

John looked different close up, shorter, smaller, pretty actually. Long flirty eyelashes. A scar on the meaty part of his hand. I didn't know it at the time, but John's father had gone at him with a two-pronged barbecue fork while he was quietly watching TV. Clearly the rat-bite story was spread by that scar. Everyone had long ago noticed the slash across John's upper lip, the result of a fistfight with a math teacher who'd called him a nincompoop. The crucifix John had worn when we were in elementary school had been replaced with a silver star on a leather shoelace. It rested in the haystack of hair on his chest. "That's cool," I said, pointing to his heart.

"Some girl in hot pants gave it to me. She stole it from Busch's on Main Street." A red neckerchief was tied loosely around his neck. For a minute I imagined choking him with it. Ernie Busch was a classmate of mine, a real shrimp but a friendly kid, and I hated to see him made vulnerable by having teenagers steal from his father's store. I hadn't the words to object to stealing, but I had perfected the deadpan.

He hoisted himself onto the hood of the car and lay back against the windshield, basking, eyes shut, neck exposed, elite among animals. Had he growled or bared teeth I would not have been surprised. I guessed he was done with me. Probably my chest was too small.

Nose in the air, spine against the windshield, John was soothed by sun on the body, the wonderful ordinariness of the day, and the nearby shuffling of his pack's feet. Animal pleasure, idiocy of the highest order. There was nothing to be afraid of anymore. John's leather jacket was of thrift-shop provenance, his brain too simple for treachery.

I was seeing John Radnoti in his nakedness, and it felt strange, as if my skin were too big for me. Once a man walked up to me expecting me to know him, and I both recognized him and had never seen him before. Soon as he spoke, I realized it was my uncle, without his beard. His pink cheeks were an embarrassment to me, as if I had walked in on somebody undressing. I turned away from John just as I had turned away from my uncle. I couldn't witness any more.

John was kittenish. How wrong we had been about him. We thought John would knife you simply for passing him in the hallway. We thought he plowed through girls without knowing how to flirt, without needing to flirt. We thought he was Italian.

The truth was that he killed only mosquitoes, and he didn't feel so good about it. He was sweet to every girl, ugly or not. And he was born in the Bakony Forest of Hungarian parents. What did we know of that besides goulash and the Gabors?

The panther stretched, yawned, and leapt off the hood. Someone turned up the radio and played drums on the roof. John resumed picking out seeds. His cohorts were having the same conversation they'd been having when I was called over: "Hey, man, don't throw out those seeds!" "What are we going to do with them?" "C'mon, man, we gotta find a place to plant them." "How about a windowsill?" John's associates lived in adjoining apartment buildings just off Main Street, so the windowsill idea was quickly discarded, as the plants would be too visible. I was ready to leave and just waiting for a signal that I was dismissed when one of the guys suggested, "Down by the damn river?" I opened my big mouth, to my own surprise, and answered rather curtly, "Canadian geese ravage seedlings."

What they needed was someone's backyard. Mine.

John's eyes were every color, blue-brown-green, and I swear they were made for the sole purpose of supplication. One look into his sweetheart face, and I knew there was nothing sincere about him. That's what charm is.

"You have really beautiful hair," he said, reaching out to twirl a strand. "Is that auburn or dirty blond?" The guys held a spontaneous colloquy, a barbershop sextet with mud under their nails debating my hair color.

"Nah, that's ash blond. My sister has hair like that."

"Platinum blond?"

"Beach blond!" I looked at the one who said this like he was an idiot.

"It's 'bleach' blond, bozo," someone corrected.

"How many years did it take to grow this long? Three? Four?" John asked. Then, interrupting himself as if he had a lightbulb idea, "Hey," he sparkled, "want to help me out? Grow some seeds in your parents' backyard? Please?" He was sure, and the nodding heads were too, that Mr. and Mrs. Bergman, or any parents for that matter, wouldn't ever recognize the plants as cannabis.

Every girl wants to say yes to John the Divine, but what came out of my mouth was no. "You don't know my father," I answered, withholding the fact that Papa brews tea from the weeds out back and makes jam from weird berries collected on his Saturday walks. Parents' vagaries scrap every attempt at being hip.

"That's cool," he said. "It's cool. Let's go out sometime."

None of the boys who'd ever flirted with me had secondary-sex-characteristic hair, but now a young man—he had graduated, barely; I was just finishing ninth grade—stepped up to me and asked for the dance. Was that what it took to transform teenage girls into women, was it the attention of handsome critters? Even within that awkward parking lot conversation, I found myself wondering whether a push-up bra would be influential, theoretically speaking.

John jumped his motorcycle into ignition and, hollering through the tyrannical engine noise, said, "Hop on. I'll give you a ride." With my arms around his feminine waist, my book bag snug between us, my voice murmured to me with self-satisfaction, *So this is love.*

"Where have you been?" Hannah asked with exasperation. "I've been calling you for the past half hour."

Hannah annoyed me, my own personal gnat. But how could I get mad at her for worrying about me? When she had called the ASPCA after I told her about wild dogs in the parking lot, I cringed at her Samaritan spirit, and cringing made me feel guilty. After all, she was my best friend. But she was so uncool: She still kept a doll on her bed!

With all the nonchalance I could muster, I informed her, "John Radnoti gave me a ride on his motorcycle."

"Why?" Only Hannah would ask such a dumb question.

It was a good question.

And then I hardly thought about John the whole summer, that kind of love was no big deal. Shelling peanuts with my camp friends had been way more exciting. Anyway, I would be kidding myself if I thought John the Divine could be my boyfriend. He was being nice to me because he was my brother's teammate and he wanted me to plant his pot in our backyard. Simple as that.

But when I returned home from camp and for seven sophomore months afterward, John and I started hanging out together, and eventually he ran his fingers through my hair. John's smell was Ivory soap. I'd expected leather.

"Don't you like Valerie and Tina?" I asked one day after he'd kissed me in the school parking lot, where he'd been waiting by his bike to drive me home. It was appropriate, it was realistic, I'd believed, for Valerie Barbo and Tina Thomas to dream of going out with John. Rough girls, they smoked cigarettes out the school bus window, got drunk on beer, didn't study for tests and didn't care, played Truth on the floor in the girls' bathroom, were rude to substitute teachers, and tripped nerds like Hannah in the hallway. They were the bravest, though perhaps not most admirable, kind of girl. They were ready to go through red lights with a guy like John Radnoti.

In response, John just gave me a screwed-up face. He didn't seem to pay attention to them, other than to say Hey or offer a pat on the back when he bumped into them. Despite his reputation for being reckless and his school suspensions for "insubordination"—once he took his T-shirt off in the school cafeteria, once he walked out of algebra without permission—John had the sweetness. It was especially evident around his dad, who sat on the back steps of the hardware store watching the absence of boats on the river.

The whole town knew he was a stubble-bearded drunk, fingernails thick and yellow as horn. The folks who lived or worked in the center of Hell looked after him, the Gerhardts by sending along a stale-bread American cheese hero every now and then, the Meat-O-Mat handing over the nib of a mortadella roll, cups of hot coffee passed along by Vera at the luncheonette. The barber called him into the shop for a shave when business was slow, the fellas in the Village Tavern steered him homeward with a propelling pat on the back. Surely the newer people in town sneered at him, but I didn't think it such a bad life.

"Pop, this is Paige." He would not shake my hand when John introduced us in the darkness of their living room, which was disrupted by a single votive candle, eerily red, fortune-teller red. He simply made a grumble approximating the word *hah!* Radnoti was hollow as a clown, didn't care if it was mayonnaise or mustard on his sandwich, didn't disappoint himself because he'd made no plans or expectations. Sometimes I felt that way myself. He cleared his throat and, in deference to my feminine presence, left the room to spit down the sink.

There was never any mention of a Mrs. Radnoti, though John and I once visited his older sister who lived in the next county north of us. I didn't get to sit in her kitchen or see if she resembled her brother because she and her husband were having sex on the floor behind the couch when we walked in. John ushered me out the back door and called for his three nephews, who seemed to have come scrabbling out of the Earth itself, clutching cheese sandwiches and G.I. Joes. "Uncle John!" they shouted and cannonballed into his arms.

I'd watch John shovel his household's laundry into the washer at the Laundromat, iron his own shirts, order specific cuts of beef at the Meat-O-Mat. John came in two parts, and those contradictions gave him an immensity of freedom. He was on one hand a "good boy," and yet he always knew of a drug-plentiful Friday night party within a ten-mile radius of home.

John took me to those parties, the reason why I distrusted him. There was no good explanation for why he didn't take a tall girl, an experienced girl, Valerie or Tina.

The Triumph blasted us up the baronial driveways of rich kids from the Brook. At the last party we went to together I spent most of the time sitting on the kitchen counter with John, turning pages in the homeowner's newsmagazine to avoid the labor of maintaining a conversation with John as half-naked girls on acid draped themselves around him then wandered off. John paid them just enough attention so their feelings—and mine—weren't hurt, and continued petting my thigh as if he were subduing a four-legged thing.

"Long time, no see," pouted some older girl in a see-through purple sari, as she leaned her breasts up against John's knees and hugged his legs, which were dangling over the countertop.

"You look beautiful tonight, Cassandra," he said. Saying her name seemed such an obvious attempt at flattery, a gluttonous expression of his attraction to her. "Catch you later," he winked. (Oh, God, how embarrassing, who winks like that in real life?) And Cassandra walked off, giving me a scorching soap-opera look. Sometimes this boy-girl thing was just too ridiculous. "Don't pay any attention to her," John reassured me. "She's nothing. In fact, I almost forgot her name."

I was disturbed to hear him say she was "nothing" and wondered if he said that about me. If Hannah had been there, she would have taken John to task for being so dismissive, and I would have seeped myself into the rug like a spilled drink.

"I don't mind if you want to hang out with her. I know she's not 'nothing' to you."

His face a sudden blush of rage, John whipped around to me, grabbed my arms, and spluttered in my face, "Why do you have to give me this damn intellectual shit?"

It was hard when we stumbled. I smiled slimly, and it was fake, apologized though I wanted to say what an ignoramus he was if he thought *that* was intellectual, slid off the counter, and got a hitch with someone who was leaving the party to pick up beer and a pizza. Standing on the driveway, I tilted my head back to see the overhead moon. A light rain kissed my whole face. From the pizzeria I would walk the shiny black streets into Hell.

It was my virginity! Why else would John Radnoti want to go out with me? The year before we met, John was seen spending time with Clarissa Boylan, a twit even less interesting than her Fair Isle sweaters. No one had said it out loud, but we'd been thinking John liked her because the Boylans took him skiing in Colorado and to the Bahamas for Christmas. When she went off to college, John had seemed unmoved. He sashayed through the school hallways acknowledging every approaching girl with a tight kiss, and every kissed girl blushed or held her head a little higher. Tina and Valerie had wrapped their big chests in lamé just to get noticed by him. So what did I offer John Radnoti other than that ridiculous conquest? Why else would he have shown up at my house the week after that party where I walked out on him?

It was a relief for me to believe, though John never told me, that he frequently partied with girls like Cassandra and that he would eventually leave me. This way I didn't have to be pathetic with my heart broken, yet could reap all the benefits of having a boyfriend. One of the greatest of those advantages was that it had sprung me from my parents' house.

The stench of Mother and Papa filled almost every room. I didn't want to know exactly what the foulness was—armpit, piss, crotch sex, raw meat, hair spray, ant poison. No one ever complained about it as far as I knew—Jan had never said anything— and I certainly didn't want to draw my friends' attention to it by asking if they could smell it. But when I entered their bedroom, I was overcome. I'd get a sick headache and have to go to my bed. Unless I held my breath.

Sundays were the worst, as it was my chore to bring them the paper so they could read it leisurely in bed. Once Jan was gone I grew to hate the ritual. The one time I pretended to forget it was Sunday, Mother barreled into my room in her nightgown—oh, pardon me, her negligee—and demanded to know why the newspaper was still in the driveway, "Paige, answer me that!" Holy moley. I could see everything, her breasts shimmying, nipples big as saucers, pubic hair thick as pudding. If I ever found one of those hairs on my rug, I swear I'd throw up. "Look at me when I'm talking to you!"

After that incident I made every effort to ensure she remain in bed when in her negligee. I resumed my Sunday responsibility. Mother, still greasy with sleep, unkempt and tongue filmy, took the paper from me. Papa slept on, a benign beast or battleship in his hairy back rising and falling with breath. Mother made my skin shrivel. As she outstretched her arms, a wave of something steamy smelling enveloped me. It was swamp rot, where lizard things are born.

Having a boyfriend had thrown me a rope. The first day John came into my house and met my parents, he wore a white oxford shirt and black usher pants, nice and tight on him. He'd come straight from church. When Eva excused herself to change out of her bathrobe into house clothes, I heard a husky whisper in my ear, "Hungry?"

I shrugged and smiled. I'd eaten frozen waffles and strawberries for breakfast two hours earlier. I was voracious.

"You like Vera's Luncheonette? She has a Sunday breakfast special for $1.79."

"I'm going out!" I hollered.

"Eva, Justice...nice meeting you!" John shouted into my parents' bedroom. I flinched, as if a firecracker had gone off at my feet. I'd rather John act insolently than try to encourage familiarity with my parents. If he had gotten my father's name right, it would have been even more upsetting. I ran upstairs for a jacket.

"Where are you going, Paige?" Papa thundered.

"Vera's," I muttered to myself, not wanting to reveal anything to my parents. I felt bad for Papa when he didn't insist I answer him. I never knew a man of greater self-doubt than my father, but with his disability he could never be sure whether no one had answered him or whether he had forgotten they had.

"Tell that kid my name is Eustace! Eustace, dammit!"

"OK, Eustace Dammit," I said, and hearing the motorcycle's rumbling readiness, I flew down the stairs. I didn't immediately understand my enthusiasm. Was it the stupid pride of having a boyfriend? Or the eagerness to do away with my childhood encumbrances: the Sunday paper routine, all my baggy white underwear, my autograph book? Mother, too, was eager about something and bounced into the living room in her stretchy skirt and top, but when she realized John had left, her mouth drooped into a frown. She looked at me and stood back. Something had changed.

The kids at school also made a subtle adjustment to me. It's not that they treated me any differently, neither with admiration nor jealousy, when John held my hand. But they became somehow easier, as if they were trying to squeeze into the picture of my life. I felt magnanimous, Come on in! I knew it was the opposite of what you're supposed to do when you have a cute boyfriend, but I couldn't help it. Their company had made it all the more real for me.

Grown-ups—parents, nursery-school teachers, grandparents—had tucked me into bed, combed my hair, and buttoned up my winter jackets, but none of my peers ever hung a coat over my shivering shoulders or blew an eyelash off my cheek. With a boyfriend it was a whole new etiquette. I was about to receive entree, sexual experience, to see the world from the privileged perspective of being a couple, someone's girlfriend.

Despite the virgin and minor that I was, John treated me carefully, with self-restraint. I didn't know what he was waiting for. My 21st birthday? Someone sexy to come along? When we decided to spend a night together in the nation's capital, I hoped such circumspection would change.

The rain was inescapably cold the weekend we motorcycled down to D.C. for the antiwar march. I was shivering and wet the whole time, confused we hadn't planned better (why didn't John borrow his father's car?), astonished my mother allowed me go in the first place (wasn't John a virtual stranger?), ashamed the helmet flattened my hair against my head and the rain made my clothes stick to my body, showing my nipples. But I never worried we would skid off the road, get concussions, bloody knees. I never even thought about it until weeks later when Hannah refused John's offer of a spin around the block. She said I was the daredevil, not she.

The truth was I *knew* there would be no accident.

After arriving in D.C. close to midnight with nowhere to go in the rain, I found myself standing under a marquee advertising a martial arts double feature.

"Wanna?" John was counting dollars from his wallet, with which he gestured toward the ticket booth. "We can get some shut-eye." I was speechless, and began to be afraid. It took me time to understand the fear.

We bought the tickets, *Samurai II* and a Bruce Lee movie, slept the night in the seedy theater, and for breakfast shared a glob of Milk Duds that had melted in John's back pocket. The custodian handed John a cold orange soda and smiled kindly at me early that morning as we raised our feet so he could sweep under them.

"I would have thought you kids runaways, but I suspect you're here for the war," he whispered in a voice I loved like cellos, especially after that night of men grunting and swashbuckling. I smirked at the irony: We were there for the war. John engaged him in too long a conversation about jazz.

If I'd known John had no plans, no arrangements, I would have brought $40, but I assumed he was arranging the trip because I had seen him studying a road map. I knew John had no money for a hotel despite his occasional job laying carpet, but I'd been too delighted by his interest in something complicated like the Vietnam War and my own pending sexual encounter to bring up the mundane concerns of rain gear, food, hotel reservations. I hadn't cared where we stayed, but I'd imagined we'd meet a hippie who'd offer us a bed, cot, air mattress, or at least a blanket on the floor. I never pictured us in two greasy movie theater seats with my money in my shoe. I was a dunce not to have thought ahead, and God forbid Mother ever heard about it. She'd be sure to cluck. John wasn't as resourceful as I had initially thought, just a snake charmer and damn lucky. He even cajoled this toothless vet into swapping his decorated flak jacket for John's leather jacket, which was missing a button at the neck and had a huge wax stain on the right side, just by calling him "Brother" and putting his hand on the ex-soldier's arm. I guess he'd had enough war because he gave it up easily.

"Here, man, take it," the vet said, pulling the drab green jacket off his bloated body. "It saved my ass in Nam, but I can't tell whether that's good luck or crap. Keep the damn cigarettes," he said referring to the pack in the breast pocket. John accepted the jacket and embraced the vet. And almost every day, even in winter, John walked through Hell with SCHWARTZ on his chest, while Schwartz was probably back in Baltimore, where he's from, barely able to lift coffee cup to lips because John's jacket was tight as a peach around a pit.

And then I began having my first hallucinations. John was no longer any dreamboat. Rather, he had a Picasso head, ugly and distorted. And every time I looked over at him, my gaze went straight up his dark nostrils. My eyes had a will of their own; I couldn't train them away from that nasal forest. So forget about sex. We didn't even have one single solitary kiss that weekend. I had turned away. His hand around my shoulder made me want to slip out of my skin and walk off. Sometimes you just reach a limit with people.

During our long ride home, John pointing out the basics of nature—clouds, deer, a classic Maserati hardtop—all I could think about was how I would end it with him as soon as I got off that bike. What would I say?

But I became distracted.

We had just pulled up to the first traffic light you hit when you enter Hell from the highway, the big HAVE YOU BEEN SERIOUSLY INJURED? billboard straight ahead. We were stopped, red light. I was trying to keep my balance by holding on to the sides of my seat so I didn't have to put my arms around John. I felt the bike rumble under me and up my spine. I kept that pleasure a secret.

The light seemed to take hours. "Let's just go!" I shouted to John. He didn't hear. I was getting agitated, maybe it was because we were so close to home, not a pleasant prospect. Then, in the idling motors of the cars surrounding, something was familiar.

It was the Skylark. In front of us. I tugged on John's rice-paddy-green epaulets and told him, "Follow the Skylark!" The light changed. The Skylark's brake light went off. John turned toward me and lifted his helmet, smiling "Hhnnn?" The Skylark moved on through the green light.

We lost her. I could have cried. And if it wouldn't have started a whole discussion, I might have gotten off the bike and wandered home. But there were many ties tangling me to John. I swore I would cut out the knots with my teeth if necessary.

Peculiar as it was, I kept hoping the lady in the Skylark would see me with John. It would have given me legitimacy; everyone thought I was older than 15 when I'd hang out with John. Otherwise I was just a sophomore, too young to drive a car, too old to be chauffeured by parents. The age of invisibility.

Despite my resolve, John and I continued to see each other. I wanted to give having a boyfriend a try, to have that under my belt. "Paige! Eva! Justice!" John would shout from our foyer, having arrived uninvited, often when I'd come home from Hannah's thinking the day over, the whole cupcake of an evening mine. I never answered, pretending not to hear, feigning sleep. But John had enchanted Mother—"John, dear! What a surprise"—and she gave him the four-star treatment: smiles, the biggest piece of steak, the rest of the wine, even a damn shoulder massage. John's ugliness had dissipated, though I felt it was lying in wait just below the surface, like a headache, and I kept giving second chances to both John and myself. I went on the dates.

We'd had an ice storm later in the month. It came devilishly quick, making candy of our telephone lines, willow trees, and guy wires throughout town. John and I had been in the movies when the ice came to Hell, while he was laughing with his tongue hanging out of his mouth about something not at all funny. When we got out of the theater we saw the car was glazed with gravelly ice.

"This is out of sight, beautiful, man!" John shouted, buttoning up his pea coat. He looked positively weepy, then started skating on the pavement and whooping it up. People exiting the theater looked at him with great caution and interest. Everyone loves a public maniac.

"Yeah," I responded. It was a kind of high to agree on something with John. He took me in his arms like a ballroom dancer and waltzed me down the sidewalk. Tires were spinning and cars wove an intricate haphazard dance around us. I knew if we lost our footing—and we did—we might end up under the carriage of one of the cars slithering along the street. And though we'd both taken a hard fall, we were laughing, John at the pure joy of shenanigans and me at the irascible drivers honking.

With some effort and John's lighter we were able to open the frozen driver's-side door. There were, however, no windshield wipers on his father's car, nor did we have a scraper. So John drove, slowly, with his head out the window, sleet needling his face, his eyebrows frozen stiff and his lips blue, but John Radnoti would get us back. I nestled in his chivalry on the long ride home.

Or in his stupidity. Hannah, even my classmates the three Peters, would've called home for help. But that's the difference between sophomores, who back down, and grown men, who don't. To his credit, I confess he was a good driver—contemplation, instantaneous reflexes, courage. You wouldn't even have known a two-ton truck was cruising straight for you or cars were running red lights in your intersection if John were your driver. All you'd know was that John was looking straight ahead, one hand on the wheel, one lighting a cigarette, this was serious business, he could ask you to find a good radio station.

You might think John was the blessed driver and I his lucky passenger. Truth was, we were riding on *my* good fortune.

Buddhism came to Hell. Meetings at one more millionaire's house in the Brook, where people I didn't know sat on the floor chanting, took up most of John's social life. Instead of partying and handing out clumps of hash to those with the nerve to ask, which is what all the kids in school assumed he was doing, John was meditating on a Persian rug, accepting tea in bone china cups from a maid in a starched white uniform.

I think he got extra credit every time he brought a guest because he kept pressuring me to go. Finally I acquiesced.

The social buzz of the room settled like the shutting down of a motor, and then a low hum seemed to rise from the floor. Silently, mournfully, people wandered from one another, obedient children, and took positions on the carpet, keeping this deep hum in their throats. (I have since tried to make that noise. It feels as if I've swallowed too big a bite of potato or hamburger.) Everyone faced the same direction. I sat next to John, my knee touching his. He shifted so they didn't touch. He was taking this swami stuff seriously. Some fat greasy slob walked to the front of the room and began the chant.

My heaving giggles didn't pass unnoticed, though John said nothing, wrapped up in his own pleasure of finally having stretched his hamstrings so as to be comfortable in the lotus position. If I focused on the cherries in the crystal bowl on the millionaire's dining room table, I was able to keep quiet during the meditation, but I stopped at the chanting. I don't cheer, not with the cheerleaders, not at the rallies for Angela Davis, not at the trampling of the moon. I'm even too wary in groups, though most parents think it's shyness, to sing "Happy Birthday" with revelers.

Eventually he stopped asking me to go along with him every week. We were having trouble finding things we enjoyed doing together.

John took me to a comedy, and immediately I bought popcorn because who can wear a pretend smile of amusement and munch at the same time? I was never very hungry anymore. So when we dropped by Vera's Luncheonette, I mostly watched as John finished his meal—and my shake. "The usual?" Vera would ask John, and he'd nod and flash the smile women found irresistible, and they'd smile on him like Madonnas. John in his sainthood would chew in huge, slow burger bites, a bit of ketchup on his persistently kissable, but in the end unsatisfying, lips. He chewed with his mouth open. "Have change for the juke?" he'd manage, and I found it fascinating to look at the mix of meat and bread and relish in his wide mouth, forgetting the question on the other side of it. The smell of grilled meat on him was the smell of man, and that made me feel ladyish, but I also shuddered at what that meant. So much compliance, nylons, rouge, plucking, scouring, dustbins, and hospital corners.

He'd been carrying around a paperback book of guru sayings, his "prayer book," which sounded to me like a mess of fortune cookies. That ratty book became our conversations. John would read from it, "To live like a mosquito, one must berate the bowels" or some such nonsense, and I'd scoff. He'd try to change my mind by explaining what the wisdom meant, and when words failed him he ignored me, not in a mean way but like a psychotic who really doesn't recognize your presence.

He put coins in the jukebox, played "You Can't Always Get What You Want," as he did every time we came to Vera's. I thought the song meant something to him, reflecting how he never seemed to make much money or complete the coursework at the community college, but I was wrong. The song had an unsettling resonance for me.

Before I quit John I wanted him to show me about sex, to make the unimaginable commonplace. It seemed complicated, the timing, and immense, where to touch? It was the honor of having been initiated I really desired. Didn't want Eva to have one up on me with her knowledge of this overblown world. But I didn't know how long I could wait for John to take the initiative.

I had looked forward to him visiting me at my baby-sitting jobs, where we made out. Oh, what confusion, the first tongue! Was it a dead fish in my mouth or something enticing? I could have told Hannah I had French-kissed, but in the absence of love I had become merely an impersonator. John knocked on the door where I was baby-sitting, and I was indifferent about seeing him. And yet I was excited about the way he made us pant on the couch together.

Words were never spoken. We were shy. When he reached under my blouse I froze in fear that he'd find my breasts inconsequential. I have no idea why you can touch your own breast and it's about as exciting as scratching your head, but when someone you want to kiss does it you become hot-wired.

He pressed too hard; I didn't say anything, I wiggled into a different position. Still he came searching. But with enough of my squirmy repositioning, he finally got it and became gentle, which had the odd effect of making my body roar inside me.

I had faith in my body, and with the exception of the occasional pimple, my body delighted me, especially the way it fell into its syncopated rhythm when John pressed against me. I couldn't envision the mechanics of sexual intercourse, but from the instinctual way I responded to John's kisses I was positive bodies just knew what to do. So it was shocking when, my body all warmed up and ready to go, to do it on the neighbors' couch, they wouldn't be home for at least two hours, John stood up, announced, "Gotta go now," put on his cowboy hat and left.

I never asked where. I never told him he rubbed too hard. I assumed he was frightened. By my excitement, my being a minor.

Nothing was sexier than a guy in a rock and roll band. Tight pants, intense concentration, the ecstasy of music making. John was sexy like that, accomplished, "experienced," which made it more difficult to dredge up the sex issues—could he pinch less? could he not run away for once? could he give me a signal to unzip, unbutton, unhook, unlace, untie, *undress*, for God's sake? I would happily make the first move, but I didn't know what that could be.

Would I ever be able to talk about sex?

"Come to Winter Solstice Meditation?" he practically whined. You can imagine my reaction. But I went anyway and practically gagged on the dip, some yogurt concoction. Of course there were various quiches and bricks of cheese that stank of Jan's socks, as well as whole wheat pretzels that turned to sawdust in your mouth.

"Cool, huh?" said John. I smiled weakly, having no answer.

On New Year's Eve John brought cheap champagne and battered roses. I was drinking my father's homemade ginger ale and had a few sips of champagne from the glass John insisted on pouring for me. My parents were at their traditional celebration, hotel ballroom, big band music. We made out on the couch. I played with John's long sideburns and was ashamed of my tenderness.

John wanted to watch Guy Lombardo on television.

I walked outside and sat on the front stoop with my soda. It was a clear night, Big Dipper, North Star. Up the street the Goldsteins were throwing their own New Year's bash. The front door was open, a golden light beckoning from within. Cars lined the street as far as I could see.

Parked out front was the Skylark.

"Hey! You should see this guy! He's great!" John called to me. "Guy Lombardo!"

I didn't know what was going on with me. In a flash my body panicked even though I wasn't frightened, heart banging, face flushed, trembles. But just as quickly, maybe it was the champagne, gazing at the Skylark across the street put a crashing chord in my head, made me take John, our troubles, less seriously. It was like having a sprained ankle, then seeing concentration camp footage.

They've been singing that song for hundreds of years, and it doesn't make any difference. But with the rest of the ginger ale, too much of the ginger ale, which felt like the Big Bang theory in my mouth, I called it "a cup of kindness" and dedicated it to the driver at the Goldsteins' party.

The Skylark was mine. I knew from the way it gladdened me, maybe flirted with me, that something beyond a stupid New Year's song was out there for Paige Bergman.

In early February John said over the phone he had something to give me.

"I can't have anyone over. I have too much homework," I begged off.

"Fuck your homework," he said. It was unusual for him to lose his temper. "It won't take long. You'll never forget this, believe me. It's worth it."

While I waited for him to arrive in his father's unheated Chevy, I realized he was going to kill me. John Radnoti was going to strangle me with his red neckerchief. I'd given up on the idea that we would have sex, given up trying to understand why he wanted to be near me. But it was easy to see why he'd want to murder me: his reputation. I knew the truth about his virility: He was no Casanova.

John had found a way to drive to the edge of the river. We fish-tailed down a steep service road and crossed bumpety train tracks. The car skidded to a halt two feet from the river's edge.

Somewhere inside the sky was a winter sun. On the opposite shore a man in a hunting jacket was demolishing an abandoned shack. A small fire blazed in an oil drum. Nowhere did the river run. It was pure ice. We sat and stared in silence.

"See?" he said wide-eyed and agitated. "This is the essence of all things. This is the mind free of discord. This is nirvana." He elbowed me.

John was growing increasingly annoyed—because I wasn't impressed with the view? because his accomplishment of discovery was no big deal? because I believed in the glacier movement of the Ice Age?—and though it frightened me to have hurt him, I was resigned to his anger. What could I do? Walk out on John Radnoti? Put up a fight? Scream *help*?

He wrapped his scarf around my neck a little too tightly. "Let's walk on the river!" he grinned. He gave me an Eskimo kiss, shoved open his door, and stepped out.

I was looking at his face trying to figure everything out. I never could anticipate John's moods. And I didn't want to ask what he was thinking because that would show my ignorance, it would be prying, it might make him explode in anger. What about his enthusiasm? Childish. Many found such innocence appealing in a young man, but I was embarrassed by it, it reflected poor judgment, and people with poor judgment shouldn't operate a motor vehicle.

My whole life I'd been told never to walk on ice unless it's officially sanctioned. Grandmother had seen her sister vanish through the ice when they were girls skating in Sweden, her fur hat bobbing behind. More recently two boys were treated for hypothermia when they tried walking across this very same river 25 miles to the north.

John bent into the car and stretched out his arm to me.

"You go," I suggested (what a coward). "It's too cold out for me."

"You're scared, aren't you?" he ridiculed.

"Isn't it a little dangerous?" I was bursting to call him a stupid idiot, but school had always said that to him and that surely would put him over the homicidal edge. It made me crazy to have to be so thoughtful about what I said to him. It was like there was a chapter missing.

John was offended. "You don't trust me! How can you be a woman if you don't trust men? You'll never be able to love someone if you are afraid to open yourself to trusting him."

Finding the logic ridiculous, I took up his challenge.

I got out of the car. You could hear the groans of the ice as the current tore at the sheet, grinding berg against berg. I accepted his extended hand, walked on water.

Then I was sick of him.

We got back into the car. I thought John was expecting me to say this was romantic, but I now believe he was trying to share with me the forlorn feeling that had engulfed us both. We sat awhile in the jalopy and stared across the river without speaking, making breath smoke. John's nose, red with cold, made him look like he was about to cry.

The consciousness of all that touching. I was as empty of love as before I'd met John. I couldn't in a million years imagine letting him watch a baby being birthed from the mouth between my legs.

And by the end of March that was that, until a year later. He showed up at our front door wearing prayer beads and the same dopey grin. The smile charmed Mother, as always, into inviting him in for some iced tea though John, whom we were now to call Bubba or Babka or Babar, something like that, was more interested in the Jarlsberg my mother sliced for him. He ate every cheese-and-cracker she offered; she'd grown too bored to finish chewing the one she'd taken for herself.

John stayed for an unwelcome hour. From my bedroom I could hear him trying to persuade Mother to come to a *satsang* and meditate with his guru. "I don't know about that," she replied, "I do a bit too *much* thinking." Her "Would you like more iced tea?" was answered with "Swami takes iced tea with four sugars!" Mother sighed so hard I could hear her up the stairs, then she asked him what he was doing to avoid the draft. "The circle of light protects Swami's children," he responded. Mother tried changing the subject again, asking if he was seeing anyone. I could tell by the big silence downstairs that she was as shocked as I was when he answered that virginity was highly esteemed by Swami. "You mean celibacy?" she inquired.

"Purity of body," he smiled. Jeez!

Shortly after John left, I heard the medicine cabinet squeak open. Mother was reaching for her migraine medicine. The silver tray littered with cracker dust and sweating cheese rinds sat on the coffee table until Papa returned home and I was summoned to clean up and set the dinner table.

Before the week was out, John's bike barked into the driveway. Mother immediately turned down the radio, crouched behind her dresser and, pretending not to be home, wouldn't answer the door. Soon after that, we'd heard he'd headed for California. I'm sure there was a girl on the back of his Triumph. I was never jealous. I was emancipated.

Papa was confounded by my disinterest in his offer of Dutch crocuses for my birthday. "Paige doesn't want to be responsible for anything," Mother explained. "She doesn't want to have anyone or anything depend on her." I'd seen my father wilt during my parents' clenched-teeth arguments, and I resolved to never be in a position where I could inflict cruelty on a person, animal, or flower. So maybe, for once, my mother was right about something.

It was with remorse, though not regret, that I had broken up with John, especially since I did it in such a chicken-assed way, simple avoidance.

That secondhand motorcycle had released me from puberty, and I rejoiced in everything unfettered: motorcycles, drapey clothing, swishingly long hair, school holidays, smoking hashish, passing the written driver's license test, eating Rocky Road between meals in the backseat of a GTO convertible, "Suite: Judy Blue Eyes" erupting from the car radio, and we drove so very fast.

I had tottered on the balance beam in grammar school, and Mother never let me forget it. But once I'd grown into the sure equilibrium of adolescence as we, boyfriend and girlfriend, ate up hairpin corners on residential streets, I'd felt grand, as if I'd been singing opera or was Queen in a school production.

I had convulsions yearning for John's body or the way he'd learned to press my breasts in his hands. The convulsions didn't knock me to the ground or make me drool. Instead they felt like the horsepower was between my legs again. Although the shoebox my body reserved for pleasure would swell from here on to screaming exuberance, there would also be sadness in it, madness in it, and pain enough to bring the crack-ups of confessional poets and suburban housewives to heel at my feet.

So despite the opportunity, I didn't experience the astonishment of love with John Radnoti. But being his girlfriend had thrown a switch. I'd felt swift, a girl on horseback. It would take another white-water hormonal year, a year of comprehending sines and cosines, noble gases and the pluperfect, a year of memorizing hit songs, before true love would stop me, like a whiff of ammonia, in my tracks.

(5)

"Paige! Telephone!" my mother hollered up the stairs.

I had asked if we could put in another phone line when I was in junior high. We were two adolescents, a snoop, and an erstwhile businessman sharing just one line. "Not a chance in Hell," Eva spat out. "Why not?" I asked, and she answered the way she always answered when she didn't have a good answer. "Because I said so, and I'm the mother."

"What's she got against the phone company?" Amelia had asked when I told her my mother's reaction. It wasn't the phone company, and it wasn't the expense. What threatened Eva was that if I had my own phone she wouldn't be able to know who was calling, and she wouldn't be able to listen in. To take a call in the privacy of my room I had to put down the receiver on the kitchen phone, grab the phone in my father's study, run it upstairs and plug it into the jack in my bedroom, lift the receiver, go back downstairs to hang up the kitchen phone, then back up to my room. "Hello?"

I took the call in the kitchen where my mother did her best to eavesdrop. She quietly stirred her soup.

A Mrs. Gallagher on Chestnut Street was looking for a baby-sitter. She had a six-year-old boy. Regular baby-sitter cancelled last minute. I had been recommended by Annette Goldstein, who lived up the street (all three of her kids were so dull I nearly fell asleep before they did). Any possibility I could be available tonight? Dollar an hour. Dinner on the stove. They'd be home early. By 10 o'clock, 10:30 at the latest. Mr. Gallagher could pick me up in 15 minutes.

She was straightforward but not pushy. Had I said I was busy, Mrs. Gallagher would have thanked me anyway, and rather sweetly, I imagined.

"I'm going baby-sitting."

"Where?"

"Chestnut Street."

"Now?"

"Now."

"What about dinner?"

"I'm not hungry." As I walked out of the kitchen, I heard Eva thwomp the spoon on the stove.

He honked before I was ready. I tossed Hannah's Herman Hesse into my Greek shoulder bag and jumped down the stairs. Just as I was about to whirl out the front door, Papa appeared from his study, bifocals at the tip of his nose.

"Hey, I thought we were planning the garden tonight," said my dispirited father.

"Gotta baby-sit!"

"I want you to write down the number!" Mother insisted.

"Don't know it."

"What's their name?"

"I don't remember. Galahad or something."

"Don't slam…" Mother called after me.

I never keep people waiting. Sometimes I think being considerate is all I have going for me.

I walked across the frozen lawn toward a very large automobile. I saw myself do this, saw how low the pavilion of early starlight hung over my head. It was quickening, the astronomy in Hell, the constellations we all looked upon as if they were universal television. The winkles unleashed a mad dog of optimism inside me.

Mother was rapping on the bay window. I ignored her. She wanted to scold me for walking on the grass, my parents' latest restriction. Why the hell have grass if you can't walk on it?

Fumes from the muffler perfumed the evening. I bent to look through the car window. Mr. Gallagher sat in the driver's seat. He didn't smile hello when he saw me through the glass; he just leaned across the front seat and pulled the door handle open.

As I settled myself into the green leather seat, it seemed Gallagher's perfunctory "Hello" sounded more like questioning than a greeting. "Hi," I responded with the same doubtful inflection. "Tom Gallagher," he said offering his meaty hand for me to shake while he looked straight ahead. "Paige." And that was the extent of our conversation.

His voice was much higher than I'd expected from a man so large that he was all over the place, a giant squid. Arm flung across the seat. Belly proud and full. Left leg curled under him like a Buddha, an Ace support cuff at his thigh. He steered with two fingers. What a wacko. We would probably collide with something, run over a tricycle, or drive up on the curb. I was prepared but not scared.

Always the men picked me up, and the men drove me home, in the family car. The fathers were podiatrists, accountants, tax attorneys. They wore ill-fitting pants high on their waists, averted their eyes from mine like shy schoolboys, gave me my money folded once, cleared their throats before asking me my grade, kept their gaze on the road. They were, without exception, crappy drivers. Running over the curb leaving the driveway, tapping the accelerator, willfully blindered to all other cars, driving under the speed limit, crouching to the right side of the road. One guy even drove on the shoulder whenever possible.

Tom Gallagher had nothing in common with them: He drove an expensive automobile, and he drove it smack in the middle of the street, everybody look out. His tennis shorts revealed great knees knobby like hazelnuts. I don't recall ever seeing the bare legs of my other employers. And rather than being shy around me, he was just trying to figure out whether he was disinterested.

Drumming the headrest behind me to some imaginary frenzied tune, Gallagher must have thought himself a king. He stank of leisure and prosperity—bay rum aftershave. Even his clothes were arrogant: Lacoste polo shirt and tennis shorts in snow-blindness white.

I would end up knowing enough about this family to write a book. That Gallagher was nouveau riche—gas-fueled barbecue, tennis club membership—was immediately apparent. I would quickly learn he made his dough selling outdoor furniture though he preferred his tennis indoors. He didn't like bugs and bees or the sun on his jowls though he often hit golf balls at the driving range under the night lights. His wife, however, preferred outdoor tennis, the sun on her back, clouds clocking her game. It was on a tennis court, in fact, that she fell in love, a player on the adjoining court. But that took years for me to discover.

Until 14 months before, there had been no tennis courts in Hell, with the exception of the weed-cracked court at the high school. It had been in disrepair for as long as I could recall, out of commission even when my brother, Jan, was in school. It was used then and is used now as a storage area for wreckage from the Industrial Arts classroom. Jigsaws mossy with rust, desiccated fan belts, dislocated peens and bent nails, three-legged desks, plaster-of-Paris molds broken and heaped in a corner.

In Hell it was the newcomers who played tennis. At one time or another most boys in town played on a Little League team. Even those who hated the game, because they were called sissies when they struck out, played. In fact, the entire Hellcats team had a lineup of boys who were habitually taunted by neighborhood bullies on the walk home from a game, even when they traveled in groups. Instead of fighting back, they covered their ears, peed in their flannel baseball pants. Surprisingly, they didn't finish last in the league.

Bowling, too, was a popular pastime in Hell. Mr. Fry up on Pine Street owned the local bowling alley in Flounder. He told the county paper that 60% of the adult male population in Hell owned a bowling ball, and though he made up that figure, it was most likely true.

In gym we had played basketball, baseball, football, field hockey. But there was no tennis in Hell. It was a pastime solely for the country clubbers in the more affluent suburbs.

With the influx of young, well-off families, however, came the construction of an indoor tennis center just off the highway. A vast network of outdoor courts, supposedly open to the public, soon followed. The cost for a seasonal pass was sky-high, as was court time at the indoor place, but the courts were a source of many summer jobs, so few longtime residents complained.

When the contractors started killing trees to build more picture-window houses it was thought the construction would bring work to the townspeople and that a larger population would mean more customers for the local shops. What no one figured was that this was a supermobile generation that thought nothing of passing on the tuna melt and soggy potato chips at Vera's Luncheonette and driving 45 minutes across the state line for a lobster bib, butter dripping down the chin.

In fact, the newcomers would take almost all of their business elsewhere. They'd get their hair done in the city, have their fancy cars repaired at the dealership instead of at our service station. They'd dine in candlelit restaurants as often as they'd eat at home. They sneered at our Fung Lung, preferring China Moon in Bubbling Brook with its angle-sliced celery and trendy pu pu platter, which I personally thought you had to be a jerk to pronounce aloud. Even though China Moon didn't have chow mein, a fishtank, or bar and the owner didn't greet you at the door in a blue suit, it put Fung Lung out of business.

Baby-sitting was probably the one local pocket into which newcomers' money poured.

Gallagher plunged a cigar into his mouth. He was the boss, I got the message. Though it was winter, he wore only a leather jacket over his tennis whites. The heavy car cruised along our residential streets. Each time we gained speed, the g-forces nudged me into the plush seat. Luxury made total sense. Gallagher's other baby-sitters must have stiffened and clutched the armrest, but I liked the speed, the feeling of being the stone in the slingshot. Sometimes, especially when I was almost asleep, my body was kind enough to remind me of riding on John's motorcycle, and I checked out of wakefulness emancipated from worry, from caution, from gravity. The motorcycle memories gave me good dreams.

At Chestnut Street Gallagher swung the wheel to the right with his index finger, pulling into the driveway—power steering was so graceful. In our Peugeot, parking was a herky-jerky chore, which my mother accompanied with lots of elbow movement and curses. Eva hated the Peugeot. She wanted an Impala. With air conditioning.

He tapped the ember from the cigar and balanced the slimy thing in the ashtray.

The Gallaghers lived about a mile from us in a new neighborhood. Entire walls of the houses were often made of glass, very sophisticated. People in Hell resented the lot of them.

In a quest for status, the newcomers had walked away from their row houses and grabbed themselves a hunk of country only to turn their back on that too. Though they stayed in Hell, at least for a respectable period of time, few of them mowed their own lawns, and if they did it was with power mowers. You saw them bobbling across their acres clutching an iced tea and wearing the straw-hatted reminders of vacations where they did the limbo and got sunburnt. They joined country clubs instead of gouging gardens out of our alkaline soil. They installed automatic floodlights that ensured 24-hour brightness. They wired their houses with burglar alarms, which tended to scream during thunderstorms. They had central air-conditioning instead of old Westinghouse fans. They drove their children everywhere and hired entertainment for their birthday parties. Maids mopped the floors of their houses. Their telephones had two lines and a HOLD button.

Acting as if they owned Hell, the wives hollered to husbands putting in the yard. "It's Mort and Sylvia hurry up already they're calling from Florida." Women yakked in each other's driveway about clothing sales and household help. Mothers screamed their children's names and their children screamed right back, stomped their feet, and threw fits when they had to quit playing and wash for dinner. When I was growing up in Hell, the neighbors, surrogate moms and dads every one, were if not more respectful then simply more hushed, whistling for a dog or calling a child's name from the kitchen window. "Coming," we responded.

I had never seen so much jewelry in daylight, on women as well as men. An arm appears from a front door to take in the mail, charm bracelet tinkling. Chokers to pick up the baby-sitter. Pinky rings. Clip-on earrings. All gold and relatively hideous.

Then there was the lowdown on plastic surgeons, the face-lifts, the crow's feet, the silver hairs dyed black, the long and lacquered nails, the cases of diet sodas in garages. His car, her car. I didn't dislike the newcomers. But they were preposterous.

The Gallaghers' house was lit up like a stadium, outdoor fixtures aimed at the driveway, shrubbery, front lawn, crescent of pachysandra, and pathway. It was exhausting. Nailed above the mailbox a cast-iron nameplate proclaimed GALLAGHER. I would have liked to tell Gallagher the neighborhood was safe, he didn't need the lights or the name over the mailbox, but clearly the guy had a game plan. Unbeknownst to him, however, the fortress would fall of its own accord.

I followed Gallagher's waddle into the house. He pointed up the stairs, saying, "In the bedroom," without interrupting his bee-line into the kitchen. "Baby-sitter's here!" he yelled with a mouth full of something.

Most of the houses where I baby-sat were spick-and-span, each had an animal figure somewhere: a macraméd flamingo on the wall, salt and pepper shakers in the shape of kittens, a bronze frog paperweight. Head and Shoulders, the shampoo of choice. Every refrigerator had milk and the pickings of a casserole or chicken carcass. Luncheon meat. A bowl cradled bananas and apples on a breakfast table. The TVs always needed antenna adjustments (except for the Goldsteins', which was big as a stove and color), family photographs were on view either in the living room or den. These houses gave me the creeps; they smelled sour and were tight and anxious. Nothing seemed to move in them other than the hands on the kitchen clock: No curtain fluttered, no flower dropped petals, no cat tore at the rug. The Gallaghers' house was no different. Though they did have a cat, it had zero personality.

Despite the illumination outside, inside the house it was dark and haunted. There was absolutely no character to the place. But one good thing about the house was that it was immaculate. I personally prefer a bit of a mess, pets on sofas and no coasters ever.

In the living room and entranceway, scenes of impossibly bucolic courtship illustrated the Staffordshire plates neatly arranged on a shelf. I'd have my first French kiss facing these plates. A fifth of gin and scotch, a bottle of Kahlua, brandy snifters, and a silver cocktail set sparkled in a glass cabinet, but John and I would never break into it. We were both too respectful.

Two velveteen club chairs—were they brown? green?—sat knee to knee. A muted television set flickered in the den. There were no paintings in the living room or den, no potted plants either, and in the sole bookcase replicas of Model T–era cars took up more space than the books—abridged encyclopedia, AAA atlases, *The Peter Principle*, a big fat history of America, an art book. Some kind of award plaques were hung on the paneling in the den.

A wall-to-wall carpet ran up the stairs, spilled into the hallway and master bedroom. I took the stairs in search of the kid for whom I was being highly compensated to keep from bawling and swallowing poison.

The carpet, an overbearing red, was so plush it made footprints when you walked on it and had recently been shampooed (I could smell the chemical cleanser). Did going to Heaven feel as luxurious as ascending the Gallaghers' carpeted stairs? Halfway up, the carpet nearly tripped me it was so thick, and I had to clutch the banister to catch my balance. I could easily fall asleep and have dreams on this floor.

One day I would lie on it, though I had no idea at the time, flat on my back listening to Stravinsky.

The first room I glimpsed was the master bedroom. Paperbacks and an ashtray lay on one night table; a phone, lamp, business magazine, and three ball bearings in an ashtray on the other. A hideous oil painting of a wine jug and suede gloves hung over the bed, which was about as big as a swimming pool. What I couldn't see from the doorway was the almost life-size portrait of Mrs. Gallagher. When I finally would see it there'd be a slash in the canvas, but I would be able to say it wasn't a bad likeness, though the pea-colored satin drapery in the background and the bolts of cranberry taffeta wrapped around the sitter made Mrs. Gallagher look like a bonbon instead of beautiful.

A child's squeaky voice clattered from another room. I backed out of the master bedroom.

Sean, already in his pajamas, sat on the floor punching out perforated valentines with his mother, whose back was to the door. For a moment I watched from the doorway as mother and son spoke softly to each other, heads bent over their project, though Valentine's Day would be ending in a few hours. As I cleared my throat so as not to startle them, we heard a pots-and-pans crash from downstairs. Mrs. Gallagher whipped around, and Sean popped up like a jack-in-the-box.

Mrs. Gallagher, more weary than annoyed, as if she'd said it a hundred times before, sighed, "Oh, Tom," at the same time that she noticed me in the doorway. She smiled. At first it was the fake smile, the reflex smile. But I felt it shift to being real the way you feel a shadow come over you.

Smiling me the smile of saints and seductresses, eyes growing black and roomy, she made my heart spill its bucket of fresh blood. Crouched like a sinner at my feet was the woman in the Skylark.

"He's found Sean's Twinkies. I hid them in the stew pot," Mrs. Gallagher confided. I'm sure she completely misunderstood why I stood there dumbfounded. "Paige, right?"

What ethereal figure had I passed day after day in that Buick? Mrs. Gallagher was mundane as mundane could be—suburban housewife, mother of a preschooler, wife of a successful businessman. It never had occurred to me that the woman in the car could have been married, and married to such an overgrown man. Or that she would have lived surrounded by molded plastic bedroom furniture and decorative candles in the shape of dodo birds. Or that she'd play in a Valentine's Day mixed-doubles tennis tournament.

I had to be wrong, it was mistaken identity. Mrs. Gallagher wore the shag haircut of Keith Richards and Germaine Greer. The Skylark lady had a chignon. And where was the Buick? I hadn't seen it in the driveway.

But with my 15-year-old's trust in the untragedy of the world, I knew the woman on her knees before me was the Skylark woman, and as she got to her feet, I knew with a kind of sureness I've never had since then that Mrs. Gallagher would touch me in a way nobody ever had before.

"I'm Fiona." Mrs. Gallagher extended a hand, and I rapidly, clumsily took it, a life raft, her hand a life raft, large and dry and neither warm nor cold. Her gaze was severe, as if she were looking into my eyes to see if I was telling the truth. School principals can give you the same look. Seeing I was tongue-tied, she introduced me to Sean.

"Paige! Paige!" repeated Sean. "Paige!" And every time he said it he jumped in his cross-legged position.

Every other mother was Mrs. So and So. Mrs. Gallagher was Fiona.

Fiona gave Sean a noisy hug and smushed a kiss on his neck. "I have to get ready," she told us, and touching me on the shoulder, she walked out of the room. "Tom, have you seen my wristband?" I heard her holler to Gallagher.

"You sit here!" Sean said to me. He directed our valentine-making and within minutes was sitting in my lap, petting my long hair. "Why is your name Paige?" he asked, looking up my nostrils while I explained it was my mother's favorite name, so unwaveringly American.

Clearly Sean wasn't a child to cower before a new baby-sitter, to wail when his parents walked toward the door jingling car keys. Meek children were a baby-sitter's bane, and they always cried just as the parents walked toward the door and back in the door. Sean wasn't going to wail, and despite a snotty cold and grape-juice goatee, he was pretty huggable.

Sean and I walked to the hallway landing to say good-bye. Gallagher was helping his wife with her coat. There was something suddenly grotesque about her reaching back to find the left armhole, which eluded her even with Gallagher's help. It was a symbol of something, marriage, women married to men. It was an image utterly incompatible with my understanding of the woman in the Skylark. She'd put on her own coat.

"We'll be back by 10," Fiona bent down and whispered to Sean. And to me she said, "The fridge is yours, ice cream in the freezer. There's stuffed peppers on the stove, anything you want. Sean can show you where the cookies are." (Hannah is probably the only teenager in the world who would eat stuffed peppers, but I was amused by Fiona Gallagher's naïveté.) Sean swung my arm excitedly. His hand was small and sweaty.

"Bedtime is 8 o'clock on the dot, little fella," said Gallagher. He tickled Sean's belly. Sean squirmed.

"You said 8:30." The kid wasn't whimpering, just correcting his father.

"Eight-thirty," agreed Fiona. Sean did that half-giggling, half-panting thing kids do when they're happy. "Be good."

"If you give, what's your name again—?"

"Paige."

"—Paige any trouble I'll rip the skin right off your face," said Gallagher. I gasped.

"Daddy, don't say that!"

"Tom! That's a disgusting thing to say to anyone, let alone a child!" Fiona wasn't yelling, but there was venom in her voice, not what I'd expect from that spook angel in the Buick.

Gallagher, holding both their racquets, was embarrassed, his face got splotchy with blush. He'd meant to be funny. When he kissed his son's forehead it wrinkled in uncertainty.

While Fiona searched for her purse, Gallagher stood there, a sentry, legs wide apart, nervously humming. In another man it would be a threatening pose. In Gallagher it only accentuated his gut, the years spent off the college football field and the days spent in the patio furniture business. He couldn't regain his dignity. So he hummed to distract himself from himself.

Now I love watching people argue. I must hear the words they use at each other, watch how one refuses to be touched by the other, how the other beats down a door. But as a sophomore in high school I was extremely uncomfortable being in the vicinity of people fighting. In my parents' quarrels, Mother was snide, Papa skulked off, Mother said don't you walk away from me, Papa said God woman what do you want? and I crept up the stairs into my bedroom and closed the door as quietly as possible. My brother, Jan, used to turn up the TV when they argued until it caught their attention and they relented. Jan and I had had our own spats, but they were mostly confined to the yanking and tugging of something we both wanted, shoving each other out of the way, giving noogies in the arm, calling each other "moron." And unlike our parents, we grew out of the fights to the extent that Jan told me he was going to miss me when he left for college. I certainly missed him. I swapped the pillows on our beds after he left.

The Gallaghers' tense exchange created an immediate intimacy among the four of us, and I was sweating about it. I averted my eyes from poor, pathetic Gallagher as well as Fiona, who could've stung you just by looking at you. While I told myself I didn't have to baby-sit for them ever again, it felt like I'd just signed a contract.

Mothers left numbers. Pediatrician, Poison Control, the restaurant, the tennis club. See the notepad by the phone. They bent down to point out the first aid kit under the bathroom sink. They demonstrated the rope ladder in case of fire.

All an invitation to mishap.

But the Gallaghers didn't fret. And after all, if Annette Goldstein, who slobbers over her children at every opportunity and thinks they are more precious than their playmates, if she had recommended me, the Gallaghers had to be assured of my trustworthiness. I envied that about the Gallaghers, their confidence in the world. The more I got to know them, the more appreciative I became of their ability to walk into a restaurant, a party, a new neighborhood, and be completely at ease, impervious to curious onlookers. I'd never seen two people worry less about catastrophe than the Gallaghers. Everything could be fixed, they seemed to say, a thunderstruck home, a poisoned child, a fatal collision. At first I mistook that attitude for apathy. But I was to learn it was compensatory behavior. When you are petrified by everything within you, the world outside is irrelevant.

I heard Fiona's fury in the way she zipped her ski jacket.

Gallagher ushered her out, arm around her shoulders, and I didn't like it. Half out the door, he waved us good-bye.

Sean and I were already in the cookie jar when I heard Gallagher start the ignition. The headlights arched across the bedroom wall, then Gallagher burned rubber on Chestnut Street. I took up where Fiona had left off, sitting cross-legged on Sean's bedroom floor with a napkin piled with Fudgetown cookies between us. Sean took a sheet of valentines and punched one out: a red heart and a squirrel holding a BE MINE placard. "For you!" he said.

Fiona. What a ridiculous name. It both attracted and repelled me, like an old lady in a housedress sitting with her legs spread wide open on the city bus. Do you look or do you not? And yet what other name could possibly contain so much beauty? Fiona, amaryllis. Fiona, Polynesian island. Fiona, a libation.

（6）

When I started driving really fast, I began thinking, "Jesus, if I go off there…." I suppose that was natural, but it didn't slow me down…. Everything that day—everything in life, really—is a matter of fighting against your emotions, isn't it? Something tells you inside, "Don't go faster," but you do. —Mika Hakkinen, Formula One driver, interviewed in *Car* magazine, July 1998

Seniors take themselves too seriously. They think the rest of us are supposed to be awed as they strut down the school hallways, seniors on the verge of their magnificence, their lives more meaningful, more tormented than ours. Naturally, no self-respecting senior could possibly fritter away a Thursday evening reading Dr. Seuss to children.

Pansy had been the Gallaghers' first baby-sitter in Hell: They'd hired her even before all the boxes had been unpacked. She was the only teenager in all of Lindbergh High who still had the rosy cheeks of kindergarten and wore pink sweaters, but she had worked out for the Gallaghers OK because she was responsible, an honor student, and, living only two houses away, could walk herself home. I knew Pansy (her brother was one of Jan's nicer pals), but she didn't know me. Until Pansy entered 12th grade and got busy ministering to her own senior-class self-importance, she'd been an earnest student, the kind who hands in neat homework, hears everything the teacher says, and pouts when she gets a B. But now that she was a senior accepted by a hotshot college she had no time anymore for baby-sitting.

With Pansy unavailable and tennis still socially requisite, the Gallaghers needed a baby-sitter who could work on a regular basis. I should be kinder to Pansy. She started the whole story I'm telling you.

Gallagher put it to me: The offer was not just generous, it was extravagant. That was Gallagher. Ten bucks, Thursdays 7 to 10 P.M., a ride there and back. I accepted—for the cash, for the excuse to get out of my infernal house, for the chance to sit on Fiona Gallagher's furniture.

Thursday nights led to Friday nights, and sometimes I'd baby-sit three nights in a row into the weekend. Sean was a good boy. He never once cried except to whimper with his occasional "growing pains," which I resolved by sitting him on the toilet or massaging his legs, depending on where the pains struck. The psychological significance of Sean's discomfort didn't go unnoticed by me, and I envied him not wanting to grow up and lose his mother. Baby-sitting may have gotten me closer to Fiona, but I also enjoyed it because Sean was as much a comfort to me as I was to him. He liked to hold my hand while I read him bedtime stories, and I liked that too.

Fiona pulled a bit of talking out of me while she readied herself for her night out. We didn't have much time; she was not a fusspot like Mrs. Goldstein, who had to neaten the pillows on the couch, check that all doors were locked, point to the plate in the fridge and the vanilla fudge in the freezer for Fern's dinner, smooth out the gobs of foundation on her face and pick at her teased hair in the hall mirror, and make one last phone call, Dr. Goldstein all the while waiting silently at the front door, hat in his hand.

Fiona, on the other hand, gathers up her racquet and purse, tightens the kitchen faucet, gets in a jacket, and goes. All the mothers kiss their babies good-bye.

When the Gallaghers were going out fancy, Fiona applied makeup in the bathroom mirror and combed her hair, looking at herself with distrust, like an actor checking his makeup from every angle before going onstage. Mrs. Goldstein, however, smiled away any time she saw her mug in a mirror.

Whatever question she asked was the question I'd been wanting to answer: What are you reading? Would you like an aspirin for your headache? How's John? You look tired, are you all right?

Once they've asked your age and if you like school, adults then start in with the questions about your family. At that age, mere mention of my family acted as the freight holding me back from adulthood. Did anyone ever tell you you look like your mother? How late do your parents allow you to stay out? Does your father know you smoke? Shouldn't you call your parents and tell them where you are? No one meets grown-ups and asks what their parents do for a living, are you and your mother close?

Whenever Fiona mentioned my family I saw them differently, or, rather, I saw myself differently within the family. One time when I opened Fiona's freezer to read off the ice cream flavors to Sean, I realized I was smiling into the frosty shelves. Fiona saw my face and laughed, and I explained that Mother never brought ice cream home from the supermarket—she didn't like it—so opening Fiona's freezer was like being given the key to a soda fountain. Whining hadn't been my intention (I wasn't asking for sympathy), but what I'd said could have been taken that way. I practically held my breath until Fiona spoke.

"You don't have to *earn* kindness," Fiona responded. "Mothers are supposed to give kids ice cream money. That's what mothers do." She made it sound as if it's almost a child's responsibility to expect free Fudgsicles. And because she never criticized Eva, I had to work a bit to understand her comments, indirect and sub-tle. My posture improved when Fiona spoke to me, or that's how it felt. I was worthy! I was the girl promenading my boyfriend around town; I was the team captain, cool as dry ice.

I'd tried to hide Hannah from Fiona—she was so immature—but one Thursday I'd had a horrible headache and got Hannah to sub for me. I was afraid my reputation had been ruined. To try to restore my standing I introduced her to John, my grown-up boyfriend. If a man has a beard, he's an adult and his dating you makes you one too. That was my postulation. Fiona let me have John over when I baby-sat—no other parents did—because she knew we were "mature," a disgusting word.

If they hadn't exactly treated me like a peer, at least they didn't dismiss me for being a kid. Driving by me in Hell on weekend mornings, where I often wandered to meet up with Amelia for candy bar breakfasts, Gallagher honked and made me jump (it was his personality to honk when he could have waved). He'd stop that huge automobile and then come straight at me in reverse on Main Street. This was his way of inviting me to join his family for a Saturday cruise around town. I'd agree to meet up with him at his house, worrying all the while that Fiona might not want to go along, and it would be just me and Gallagher and Sean and my phenomenal boredom, which made it difficult to stay awake. (Luckily, that only happened twice, though it broke my heart both times.)

Gallagher did most of the talking, which wasn't much, and when we were quiet he hummed. Sometimes they solicited my opinion on current events. We agreed on nothing. But they were quiet about it. Fiona was actually amused by our differences, while I found them shocking. In a high school essay she had supported conscription, which would be the worst thing I'd ever learn about her. The My Lai disclosure passed right by her while it made me shudder until I gave myself a sick headache. And in May, when Hannah and I wandered the streets dazed after Kent State, Fiona asked me to baby-sit as if life were just using Comet, eating vanilla cones, and sleeping by your hairy husband. I never saw a newspaper in that house once, and next to ecology the hottest thing on the scene was battling apathy. The Gallaghers were the enemy.

During my early baby-sitting days, visits from my friends diminished the creepy-house factor that is part and parcel of working for a new baby-sitting client. True, I would be spooked when Hannah, John, or Amelia knocked, even though I'd been expecting them—after all, I didn't know the shadows of the house, and who isn't scared by a figure at the door?—but monsters from the deep lagoon of the crawl space and goblins in closets became, as Fiona would say, "Fig Newtons of the imagination" in the company of friends.

Once I grew familiar with the house, I preferred to baby-sit alone. But it was hard to turn John down. Part of me wanted John to be the first man I ever slept with, but most of me wanted something else, something beyond sexiness. The derangement of desire. It would make me feel at once as enormous as God and wee as a preemie. Grateful as I was for his kissing lessons, John would never be able to satisfy this rudimentary thing—I couldn't name it—this longing, this urgency to steal inside someone, receding like the nautilus into its pearly shell. John was not the person I wanted to visit inside out.

The more time I spent with the Gallaghers, the more reluctant I was to break up with John, afraid that their interest in me was based on my having a boyfriend who was old enough to do everything: drink, drive, shave, vote, enlist, go to jail. But our rapport also made it easier to leave John. I'd just wanted someone to take me places and wonder if I was cold. Friends don't do that when you're a sophomore. For one thing, no one can drive. And the only thing John knew about taking care of people who don't feel well was to give them a sandwich and a shot of whiskey.

The Gallaghers were a riptide, or at least Fiona was. I didn't know what in God's name was so interesting about seeing her, but whatever it was rushed right into the spot that would have been empty with missing John. I didn't tell Fiona we had broken up. I was afraid I'd be forfeiting my legitimacy.

Going out with John was supposed to be fun, but the whole thing had made me uncomfortable. I began to cut short our phone conversations and lied about baby-sitting so he wouldn't come visit. John grew angry, but I pretended nothing was wrong. I was ashamed, and a little scared, that I didn't know how to tell him I didn't want to be with him anymore.

Amelia and Hannah looked forward to hanging out with me in a house with a fully stocked fridge, color TV, and bar. It didn't take long before I understood the expression about wanting to pull your hair out: Amelia wouldn't stay away from the liquor cabinet, and in one night alone Hannah would eat substantial amounts of the Gallaghers' Chee-tos, leftover chicken, Poppycock (the name alone too much of an embarrassment for me to apologize to the Gallaghers or replace the caramel treat). Hannah was unstoppable. She sucked Popsicles and shoved

Twinkies down her gullet as if she couldn't breathe unless she was chewing something. She struck gold when she discovered half a dozen chocolate donuts in a pastry box in the oven. It hadn't occurred to her that she was being a glutton, and inconsiderate as well.

The hand towels in the bathroom were damp after they'd washed their hands, the afghan on the couch rumpled, cellophane Twinkie wrappings in the kitchen garbage. Amelia spun stations on the radio without having bothered to note the original dial setting, so I couldn't reset it before the Gallaghers returned.

Toddlers need to be distracted from desire; diverting their attention is an art. They want: to run headlong down the stairs, to play with knives, lollipops before dinner, to wear the dirty purple jumper. They cannot. As a good baby-sitter I had to perform feats of legerdemain, switch the talking teddy for the knife without the kid noticing. My friends were just like those children. Or maybe that's just how I treated them by trying to keep them happy without saying no or telling them what I was really up to, which was distracting them from the scotch, shutting cabinets filled with candy, hiding the knife behind my back.

Amelia was hyper, needed multiple stimuli. If I wouldn't allow her to drink the Gallaghers' rum and their Coke, then she wanted to snoop through the house. I'd let her do it before, when I baby-sat for the short people on Larch and the baloney eaters on Pine. She'd talk a mile a minute while poking her head into dark places like a dog on a scent. In those homes it was nosiness. Here it was a profanity.

In other homes she had found garter belts and satin underwear, checkbooks, personal letters, uppers and condoms in the medicine cabinet. But I warned her there was no spying here, and if she was going to get high she had to do it outside, on the back porch, and make sure no neighbors saw. On top of that, the Gallaghers apparently had no art books, which was the only thing that ever got Amelia to sit still and stop picking at her scalp. Wherever I was baby-sitting, after checking out the beds in every room, scrounging around the father's desk, and itemizing the medicine cabinet, she'd curl up, feet on the couch, and peruse the resident art book, in silence, for hours.

"Everyone has a coffee-table Da Vinci, at least an Impressionists!" Amelia said with exasperation. "I can't believe this house."

I'd hidden *The World of Dali* under the sink. I thought it was the creepiest kind of art anyway. I made sure visiting me was a total drag.

"The Gallaghers are my friends," I boasted, unsure whether it was a lie. "Don't go picking through their stuff." Amelia shrugged in indifference. Hannah, who always had to argue, said, "But you just met them. How could they be your friends? They're so bourgeois."

Hannah had insulted me, but I didn't show it. She was right, and it was to get worse, but in the meantime I was too confounded by my own tolerance for Fiona and by Fiona herself; how could a woman so gentle and considerate be indifferent to urban decay, pollution, napalm? She must have had some kind of fractured awareness, a chronic distraction, I thought.

Amelia had to leave, no question about it. Hannah would be manageable if I could get her to stop foraging. I had a trick.

I planted her in the bony Windsor chair under the harsh kitchen light and offered to do her French homework as long as she paid attention, no roving around while I wrote her essays and conjugated verbs. Hannah could study only so many irregular verbs in the discomfort of the kitchen before she'd leave the house of her own volition.

As I watched her split her split ends at the Gallaghers' breakfast table and waited for her to yawn, to depart, I thought she began to make involuntary piggy noises, and I saw there at the table that she had transformed into a greedy, snouty hog.

I could not breathe. These were my friends—I may not have told them secrets, but we'd sure laughed together and John I'd let put his tongue on mine—yet suddenly I was feeling suffocated by them. I began to see only what was grotesque in their faces, cringe when their skin grazed mine or I when smelled their breath during a momentary confidence. And now, my best friend asking personal questions, I pretended to speak no English. I needed air.

Sitting on the front stoop with the door open so I could hear Sean if he cried, I imagined my disgrace if the Gallaghers took the derriere indentation on the couch as mine, the bite marks in the pizza crust in the trash mine, the pee that used up the toilet paper mine. And what if they used my Twinkie wrapper as voodoo, putting a hex on me so I'd be splattered with pimples or lose control of my bowels or have moths zip into my ears on summer nights?

No traces, no trails, no evidence of me. "Leave the campsite cleaner than you found it," camp counselors drone. "Leave no traces behind, like you were never here." I should be one of Papa's epiphytes, need no drink or food or overcoat. Be an orchid, simply in need of a host, which is different from being a parasite. It would never be my Popsicle wrapper in the trash, never my hair in the sink. I'd be the baby-sitter who survived on air.

I returned to the house and to Hannah, who was pawing through kitchen drawers and the cookie jar. She was dense. She wanted to stay. I wanted her gone. And with that thought, sensing the squirreling of my own face—cool nose, cheeks growing furry, complexion graying—I avoided looking directly at her, Hannah the Hog.

"The Gallaghers really don't want me to have company when I'm baby-sitting," I said, washing our root beer glasses in the sink and feeling my whiskers twitch.

"They don't have to know. I'll leave before they get home."

"Hannah, what if Sean wakes up and sees you prowling around? And what if they come home early?"

"Funny, they didn't seem to mind *John* coming here!"

"Fine," I said, and decided to hate her.

I couldn't hate Hannah just because I had some ludicrous idea that Mrs. Gallagher would want to be my friend. I hated myself, my bushy tail, my white underbelly. How long, I wondered, would it be before others noticed?

"Have I done something wrong?" Hannah was passing me notes during French. "We never hang out anymore. What's going on? Why are we in a fight?"

A bold glare when I didn't send a message back but mouthed, *"Je ne sais pas."*

"Don't you want to be friends anymore?"

I was pretending to pay concentrated attention to Madame Foiegras at the blackboard. Hannah was acting like a sixth grader. Made me want to puke, her relentless prodding and probing. Picking at me like she was my mother, trying to psychoanalyze me.

She only let up because of the bee.

This bumblebee barreled into class, and everyone shrank back, even the boys.

"I'm allergic!" shrieked Philippe.

The bee landed on Hannah's head. I didn't know if I was about to crack up or cry.

"Bourdon," mumbled Madame. *"C'est un bourdon."* She explained calmly as she tried to shield the students, every single

one of whom hoped it would sting Hannah as it began haloing her head. *Let it sting Hannah, and then it will die and won't come after us,* my classmates were thinking. Hannah and I remained in our chairs, the others huddled in the corner behind the teacher.

I was distracted by Madame Foiegras. I'd never really noticed her kindness before. What other teacher would have acted so self-lessly for a bunch of thankless students?

Leisurely, my smile admiring Madame, I rose from my seat, watching the other kids dodge the buzzer, which was now enlarging its pool of potential victims. I followed its orbits, and when it returned to Hannah, who was squeezing her eyes shut, I shooed it out the window with my workbook. Madame slammed the window after the bee. "Voilà!" we said simultaneously, grinning at each other like people in cahoots. Class sighed. Everyone returned to their seats. What jerks.

No question about it, I sauntered back to my desk. Hannah's sweaty palm grabbed my arm as I passed. "*Merci*, Celestine," she said, calling me by the name I'd chosen for French class, because what's the French equivalent of Paige? "*Merci beaucoup.*" I shrugged and walked back to my desk.

As I sat myself down, Madame and I made eye contact. I'd had her for three years already but never before knew how to describe her face. I don't think anyone should ever be called homely, though that's how Hannah described her. She was blind. Madame had a trustworthy face, and when she smiled her eyelashes got moist with tears, making her eyes sparkly. In eighth grade I had found myself a little afraid of her, and yet I chose the name Celestine, which was Madame Foiegras's first name. She must have thought I liked her. Once you get out of grammar school, there's this comforting tension between student and teacher when they no longer take you down the hall by the hand or rearrange the barrettes that are slipping in your hair. The only teachers who touch you in high school are coaches, though there are the rare exceptions, such as in instances when a student, like John, takes a swing at a teacher or vice versa.

From the moment I first sat in Madame's classroom I was painfully aware of the tension, and I feared it might snap and she'd touch me, by accident, and I'd get cooties or something. I'd dreamt she smelled eggy and her face felt like peach fuzz when we rubbed noses, and I'd come to school in my nightgown, having forgotten to get dressed. I was horrified I'd let myself have such a dream, and even though it was just a dream I stayed away from Madame and regretted selecting my French name.

After the bumblebee incident, however, I was no longer afraid. Madame was on my side, and having one grown-up, Fiona, as an acquaintance, made me more comfortable with another sweet one, Madame. The same is true when you go to camp and make a friend, and from then on you're not shy of the other kids anymore.

Hannah got off my case for a while. She had to. I'd saved her from a teenager's worst nightmare: humiliation. Had she been stung, she would have yelped and cried, behavior unbecoming a sophomore, and no one would ever have let her forget it.

It was official, I was the Gallagher baby-sitter. I was up on Chestnut Street so often I could recognize the sound of the Gallaghers' neighbors' cars. Initially Gallagher picked me up and drove me home, and if Hannah had been visiting me on the job, he'd drive her home too. But after a few months Fiona would be the one to shuttle me home. You think I wanted to share that ride home with Hannah? Be dropped off first and let Hannah be alone with Fiona to learn something about her I didn't know? Or sit in the backseat where children go, talking to Tonka toys?

The more I knew about Fiona, the more I needed to know. It could have gone the other way—the more I learned, the more disinterested or disillusioned I became—but it didn't happen like that. Every stupid bit of information was valuable. The college she went to (University of Pennsylvania); the date of her birth (May 11, she was exactly twice my age that year); what size shoe she wore (7½); the story of her labor and Sean's delivery (when she pushed, she pushed and *everything* came out, but she wasn't embarrassed); the sandwiches her immigrant mother had made for her school lunches (herring on white bread with butter); she wasn't Irish at all (her maiden name Lando, Polish, probably from Landowski). None of it remarkable, yet all of it dear. This was the narration during my ride home in Mrs. Gallagher's car.

I had a suspicion she was more than a housewife. Maybe a witch, a spy with the CIA, a cat burglar. I didn't know, anything was possible. But there was something concealed, something close to the bone about Fiona, and I was 100% positive she would reveal it to me. It wasn't a case of hubris or confidence in my charisma; it was fact, as undeniable as hunger. Some things I just knew.

What the baby-sitter did: Thirty minutes after Sean was asleep, I'd tiptoe across the plush red carpet into the master bedroom. I picked out the cigarette butt with the lipstick on it, put it between my lips. Her warm Italian loafers adopted my feet. The cool silk sleeves of her shirts grazed my cheeks. I inhaled the perfume of sleep on her pillow. On my way out of the master bedroom I rubbed away my footprints.

That was a ritual of affection, though at the time I had no damn idea what I was doing.

The Buick Skylark had been junked. Who knows what possessed her, but Fiona was now driving a muscle car, a monstrous Plymouth Barracuda convertible with a 440 Magnum V-8 engine and a three-year lease. The color of the car was Plum Crazy, according to the dealer.

With its air filter vibrating through the aperture in the hood, that beast thundered like an outboard motor and could be heard coming from miles away. It terrorized young mothers in Hell the way polio and meningitis did. They froze in panic at the sound of the Barracuda grumbling up the block. *Where are my children?* the mothers squawked in their heads. *Are my babies playing in the street? sledding? chalking hopscotch games? riding bikes no hands? roller skating? chasing a baseball?*

But then they remember: On a beautiful day like this, the children are indoors watching television, eating graham crackers. (Actually the children are cutting their own bangs, stealing money from mother's pocketbook, lighting matches in the bathroom sink.)

I heard that Barracuda all over Hell no matter where I was. It was my Siren, it drove me crazy, and I trailed after Fiona, thrilled by the sound of that 400-plus horsepower every time. I once saw a blind man ski his way downhill by following the tinkle of a bell attached to his instructor's pole. That's how I followed Fiona's engine. Out of necessity.

But then the Barracuda seemed to be following *me*, showing up when I'd be eating pizza in town, passing by as I walked to Amelia's, grabbing a corner while I waited for the Good Humor man. Sometimes Fiona would notice me and offer a lift, and as long as I'd washed my hair that day and was relatively zit free, I'd accept the ride.

The only other vehicle that even came close to resembling Fiona's powerhouse motor was the rebuilt Mercury down the street, muffler still busted after all these years. And sometimes it threw me, made my heart go hard, but usually I could tell pretty quickly that it wasn't the Barracuda. The only car in Hell that could outperform Fiona's zero to 60 mph in six seconds was the Corvette owned by a classmate of Jan's who was now the owner of the gas station in town.

"Unseemly" for Fiona to be driving a car like that, I heard the mothers scoffing. These ladies, whose toddlers I'd baby-sat, were gossiping at the end of their driveways, leaning on broomsticks and rakes.

"What's a grown woman doing driving a hot rod!"

"Someday she's going to kill someone driving that fast!"

"And a mother no less!"

They didn't understand. Wasn't it obvious? Fiona drove fast because she was trying to get away. She was the bee caught in my classroom, battering its body against the same old window pane; the more lost it was, the wilder it grew. When she got to know me better she'd sing her theme song, "Don't Fence Me In," while shuttling me home at night.

She liked me OK. I knew because instead of dropping me off directly after baby-sitting, Fiona wanted to cruise through Hell and sometimes into the outskirts, always asking first if I was in a rush to get home. She could have dropped me off and then gone for her ride, but she didn't. And I could have walked home from the Gallaghers', but I preferred, I longed for, these after-baby-sitting drives. What a serenade, the swoop and ess of isolated back roads, the slow speed at which Fiona took me through darkness. How different was her driving at night, how lyrical. She didn't care that hot-doggers passed us, some even honking. Didn't rile her one bit.

I never knew which route Fiona would take or how long we'd be driving, it could be ten minutes or 40. Often we ended up chewing corners in the exclusive Debbie Court, a cul-de-sac punctuated with half a dozen new glass houses built on a promontory overlooking the village of Hell. Once when she stopped to take in the view, I told her that when I was a kid there was a horse farm up here and a dirt road named Skyline Path (now Debbie Court, a prissy name if you ask me). Jan and I would scramble up through the woods and gaze at the miniature Hell below. He would point out our own house to me, and I would imagine never going back again but sitting up here being God and watching over.

Fiona chuckled, "Being God."

Then we built ourselves a silence. We were confederates in this and many more unspoken nights. I had no idea how many drives there were ahead of us, never even thought about it, but I believed we'd be driving together until we died.

We had rain, lots of sad heavy rain. And then Hell froze over.

Driving me home one night during a freak spring storm, Fiona detoured into town for cigarettes. Never would the weather deter her from cruising in the Barracuda. Though she was the best driver I would ever know, she was oblivious to weather conditions an ordinary driver would certainly notice. It wasn't that she had special confidence in the Barracuda—I was sure she drove exactly the same way in the Skylark (once I learned to drive I was disappointed by the Barracuda, athletic as it was; maybe it was just too much car for me)—nor did she have an inflated sense of her own driving ability. With Fiona it was courage. If you had asked her, however, why she drove a car fast in the rain, she'd have said, "It's my dangerous blindness, my unwillingness to face reality, my immaturity." I bet some quack psychiatrist filled her head with that rot.

Hell was deserted. I could hear the whirring of a car stuck up on the hill. The tire chains on the town sand truck chimed. It was my favorite lullaby since it meant tomorrow would be a snow day, no school.

We parked smack in the center of the parking lot, ignoring the yellow lines, which weren't visible anyway. It felt like children ruling the world. It always does when it snows and all the borders are erased; you don't know where your lawn ends and the road begins.

"I'll keep the engine on so you stay warm," Fiona said, flicking off our headlights. I watched her skate toward the luncheonette. I rolled down the window, delighted by the carousel of snowflakes and my face a landing ground for them. It was the prettiest thing I had ever seen, and my head heard Tchaikovsky, though I hadn't been presumptuous enough to turn on the car radio.

Fiona crept up on me—I hadn't seen her return—and blew into the car. She combed her damp hair with her fingers, which were chokehold strong, probably from gripping her tennis racquet. Her face, wet with melted snow, looked unreal, as if she had the skin of diamonds.

"Locked up tight," she said. I thought Vera's would be, this hour on a Sunday. In fact, I was sure the luncheonette closed at 5 o'clock on Sundays, but I hadn't said anything because I didn't want Fiona to abort the drive. Being duplicitous left me with an iron taste in my mouth. It was not as unpleasant as I'd remembered.

We sat in the whirlwind of snow for a bit. I assumed Fiona was thinking where else to go for cigarettes, as she looked too preoccupied to be marveling at the snow on the windshield.

The friendly sight of headlights appeared from the rise ahead of the parking lot. A car crept toward us over the blanket of snow and pulled up beside us.

It was a Jaguar, a 1969 E-Type roadster, and in it was Fiona's friend Greta, hello, nice to meet you. She looked older than

Fiona and completely unremarkable except there was something extremely delicate about her, her skin a butterfly wing, be careful not to brush against her. It looked appallingly easy to be cruel to Greta, though most people experienced her as easy to indulge. Sickly babies are that way: no limit to the lollipops they're allowed. Greta wore tinted glasses though it was night. They made her appear nervous.

Fiona vanished into Greta's Jaguar—I wasn't sure of the color in the night, but it turned out to be pale yellow, barely yellow, lemon pith—and they had a quick chat. Then she returned; it took forever, if five minutes can be forever. Smoking a cigarette, two more in her hand, she opened the door to the Barracuda and a storm of snow blasted in. The air was cold, antiseptic.

The Jag drove off ponderously. I heard the snow crunch under its tires.

Fiona waited in the parking lot, smoking her cigarette and watching until the car disappeared from view. Something was off with Fiona, her face looked different. Slightly rearranged, puffy. It was a look I would see too often, a look that meant she was in another country but had left her ghost behind.

She put the car in gear. The tires whined. She tried reverse, but the tires still whined.

We were stuck on ice.

"You up for walking?" she asked gamely. I offered to try pushing the car, but she said she didn't want me getting hurt, and she said it all fuddy-duddy so that it made me feel very girlie.

Finding a phone to call Gallagher was unthinkable. Fiona was cultivating independence with a vengeance. Yet she was the most capable woman I knew. She strode into restaurants with no sign of self-consciousness. She drove an outrageous car in a sour little town. She had her child properly inoculated. Whatever she cooked made her home smell safe, rich as stew. She wore Bing-red lipstick.

She was playing tricks, all of it a hoax. Fiona thought of herself as a damaged woman.

Do I have X-ray vision? Her fear was obvious. There it was, right above her lip, the quiver in the nerve.

Fiona was playing housewife, and she played the role with excellence. Everyone was fooled: neighbors, nursery school teachers, butchers, hairstylists, plumbers, tennis pros, but not the teenage baby-sitter. I knew something was up when I first saw her in that Skylark.

Looking at two slippery miles ahead of us, we began the trudge home. The truth is, it never occurred to Fiona to call Gallagher. She'd been preoccupied ever since she'd gotten out of the Jaguar.

We walked in silence, and it felt like the night Jesus was born, all still and pristine and full of thunderous theatrical portent. I wanted something from Fiona—a piggyback, a searching question—and the next thing I knew she was holding my hand and apologizing. But that lasted about a split second; our fingers were freezing up when she let go of my hand, and I knew it. Yet I thought it was something about my hand that wasn't quite right. I sulked.

By the time we were halfway home, my hair was frozen and my fingertips numb, but I could have walked another two or even 20 miles with her. Saying good night to Fiona, like hearing the Barracuda buzz around the neighborhood, wounded me more than my fiercely red fingers.

When we arrived at Chestnut Street, Gallagher tossed us towels then scurried back into his den, illuminated by the flickering blue light of television. Fiona heated up a can of clam chowder, which we ate from those horrible brown bowls. There wasn't a chowder in New England that could beat the chowder of that night. And never in my life would I buy that brand of chowder, but instead I'd look at the red cans wistfully, my sadness trying to punch through my face in supermarkets all over the country, trying to make tears track down my cheeks. That soup became sacrosanct, as did every damn thing Fiona touched, said, purchased, read, drove, wrapped around her tongue.

It was Christmas for sure. I would never share that story with Hannah and Amelia. It would have left me with only a third the joy, though I couldn't have explained to them what was so interesting about eating soup with wet hair and a housewife.

Gallagher bounded into the kitchen all happy from watching *Seven Brides for Seven Brothers* and offered to drive me home during the commercial. I wanted to walk.

"You have a right to be contrary. You're a teenager!" said Gallagher. We grapple with whatever we can get our hands on, he continued, parents, politics, dress codes.

"Tom," Fiona said in my defense. But he was right. We found relief in enacting struggle. It's the best expression of emotional turmoil. It's like seizing the word that's at the tip of your tongue. We pursued the walk in the rain, strolling in blizzards, swimming out too far.

Sean croaked for his mommy, and Fiona went up to reassure him. The hair on his head would be damp from the short sleep he'd had; it would smell like buttermilk and strawberries, and Fiona would kiss him there again and again, trying to tell her son this is how she loved him.

From the kitchen I heard as he called out my name, "Paige! Paige!" and Gallagher shrugged, which meant he didn't know what his son wanted, but I should feel free to go up and see.

I stood in the doorway to Sean's room, and we waved to each

other. I stayed for a minute, watching Fiona comb Sean's dank curls with her fingers as the weight of sleep closed his eyes. Fiona kissed his forehead. Simultaneously we turned to leave.

I would walk home instead of accepting a ride from Gallagher to keep my wonderful evening contagion free. And perverse as it was, I wanted my mother to see what I'd been through, it might impress her. Before I left, Fiona promised she would call my parents to explain why I was late and that I was on my way home. And apparently she did, though it was one of those things Papa forgot as soon as he hung up the phone. As a result, there was a tense reunion when I walked through the door.

"Where have you been?" said Eva with her gritted teeth. I looked at Papa, but he was blank as a lampshade.

Rich people could be so refreshing, so calming. While Fiona's Plum Crazy Barracuda sat locked in an empty parking lot in the middle of Hell, she and Gallagher, by all appearances, were completely untroubled about it. Fiona would take a hot bath, Gallagher would roll her on top of him, and in the morning, he would call a tow truck, no harm done.

They were right, no harm done. Meanwhile, Eva was about to blow her top because I was home safe, soaked, late, and delighted.

That year my friends the three Peters played guitar and passed a lot of grass on to me; one of their older brothers was dealing, I won't rat. Even though the pot was usually free and they were my friends—I'd known them since kindergarten—I was afraid to get stoned with them. When I had been with John, I was afraid the punch would affect me like truth serum and I'd confess the lady in the car. Now who knew what I might say about Fiona? Maybe I'd blurt out what I did with her cigarette butts. Maybe I'd say how frightened I was of Amelia's mole. Who knew?

The crackle of a lit joint made me inexplicably lighthearted. Having my friends stoned and stupid gave me some breathing space. And it reminded me of campfires: humans in a meditative circle, counselors there to take care of the homesick and pass out marshmallows, the night air syrupy as melons.

After my friends got high we'd all smush into someone's car and set a course for the reservoir, where some of them took more drugs and sat in the mud while the rest of us tried to scale the dam wall.

Sometimes we'd drive the half-hour to the art-house theater. Even with subtitles I'd get nudged, *pssted,* and elbowed by my friends for whom I translated Truffaut and Renoir; and in the dark of the theater my body relaxed, calm as a guru. Sleep in a bed may subdue me, but sleep isn't as tranquil, sleep wasn't protected by an usher.

My group intimidated Hannah. Zeffirelli's *Romeo and Juliet,* which she'd seen eight times, was her favorite movie. She was so uncool, especially when she tried to speak French, her lips going out like a bird cheeping for worms. If she could only not talk about halitosis around them, if she could stop her habit of swinging her purse which always hit whomever was standing nearby, if she could stop scolding people who littered, if she didn't have to put lambswool in her ears when she showered. But what a successful psychiatrist she was going to be, wearing sensible long skirts, panty hose, and a pendant, not laughing when people talked about semen or toilet training.

Still, she was my friend.

Ever since school began in September, Hannah and I had spent two afternoons a week volunteering at Balloons & Bubbles, the day care center in Flounder, next town over.

B&B was in an area of Flounder recently demolished by steam

shovel and wrecking ball. Bricks and soda cans and tires and three-legged chairs filled the lots on either side of B&B. Sometimes a skinny kid would be sifting through the junk for treasure. I saw a fat rat slither under bricks one day in the rain.

The day care center was only 30 minutes from school on foot, straight along the highway, but Hannah preferred to take the bus. She said her feet were aching. One week it was fallen arches, then corns, plantar's warts, bunions. What a grandmother! Hannah was just lazy. Besides, I'd seen her feet in gym, and they looked fine.

The bus picked us up in Hell and dropped us off in front of Flounder's Ebenezer Baptist Church. The doors of the church were always wide open, and the sexton let us use the bathroom downstairs even though we were not members of the congregation. We avoided using the B&B bathroom because the stench of wet diapers singed the hairs in your nose and made your eyes spill water when you shut the door behind you.

Working at B&B made me feel real. Tagging along with Fiona Gallagher and an exhaustless heart and lying my head off to my best friends about it—no wonder I felt like a phony. But how could I possibly be a phony when a child would take me by the hand and drag me to the building blocks or when the children piled up on my lap all warm and holdable even if they smelled poopy or had a chicken pox scab.

In Flounder I was a complete stranger. Even the guy behind the counter in the newspaper store across from the center, his head in a halo of cigar smoke, never acknowledged recognizing me or Hannah from visit to visit, though I bought his homemade peanut brittle every single Thursday. For a year there was a piece of that brittle welded to the inside of my jacket pocket. It was my talisman, reminding me to be a stranger. If no one knows you, there can be no embarrassment. That's why when you pee in your pants in school you want to be sent to another school and never tell your story. But embarrassment vanishes. Shame is a tougher stain. You can move to every school in America, but it's still stuck to the skin on your face. Dwarf it in your secrets, mangle it so none of its appalling radiance can squeak through.

It was spring and the air smelled of mowed lawns and honeysuckle, smelled like a favorite aunt, the trees all in their apple blossom petticoats. I had been able to convince Hannah to walk home with me. She was kicking stones and swinging that damn purse, that renegade lasso, while I kept an eye on it to avoid getting beaned. I was daydreaming my Fiona Gallagher daydream, her finding me asleep on the couch when she arrives home from tennis, and at the moment of my reverie, I heard the Barracuda tumbling along the highway.

I turned, saw the car winding down the ramp. I'd had a hunk of peanut brittle melting in my mouth. I spat it out. My heart was going like I'd just seen a snake cross my path. Hannah just kept scuffing along.

Fiona hadn't noticed us.

From that day on, to increase my chances of seeing her, I insisted on walking home from B&B in the rain, in the sleet, in uncomfortable shoes, and in the darling blossoms of spring. And I heard her Barracuda nearly every time I worked in Flounder. I surmised that Fiona was on a schedule. I never said anything to Hannah, and so far she hadn't seen the car. Looking forward to the chance of glimpsing Fiona, I refused to use the church bathroom for fear that it might make me late for the Barracuda. And I refused to wait for Hannah and her galoshes or the purse she often forgot. I made her catch up or, my preference, take the bus home by herself.

I followed the engine as if it were the word of God.

"Hannah, let's jog." I knew she was too lazy to join me, so I rambled on.

Maybe I could beat Fiona to the crosswalk.

⑦

I wanted coincidence with Fiona. In addition to trying to run into her on my way home from B&B, I left for school 15 minutes earlier. For the first time since I can remember, I was in my underpants and shirt before Papa rapped "Wake-up time!" on my door. With the extra time I would take the long way, which wound past the Gallaghers' house, and without fail Fiona would be making coffee at the kitchen sink, Sean between her legs playing airplane or eating a breakfast banana. I was afraid she would turn and look out the window. What then? I wanted her to turn and look. What then?

If it was enough just to see her, if that made the day worthwhile, why did the word *abandonné*, "forlorn," resonate with me like a popular song?

When there was even just a one in a bazillion chance of bumping into Fiona, I made sure my hair was Breck clean, armpits thoroughly fumigated. Eventually I would begin dressing for her, dressing less ostentatiously, less like kids my age. No more bandana headbands, no suede-patched jeans, no sneakers with holes in them, no patchouli, no leather bracelets. Instead it would be halter tops, safari suits, and I'd shave my hairless legs.

A few weeks after Earth Day my homeroom class was assigned to clean up the riverbank behind Hell Hardware on Main Street. Amid the expressions of disgust and shouts from classmates who held up slimy things—a sludgy sock, a tire pumped full of muck, a headless doll slippery with ooze—I heard the purr of the Barracuda. Why did it break my heart?

The accelerating engine sounded as if Fiona were heading up to Debbie Court, the scenic part of Hell we had cruised during our drives home after my baby-sitting.

At the end of 1960s, surveyors with rezoning ordinances had announced that the crest overlooking the Village Green was no longer Bubbling Brook proper. The crest would be designated Hell. Property values sank, the Gallagher generation vultured in. Even if it was Hell, it was prime property, lofty, up on a hill, what rich people like.

When they changed the name of the dead-end street up there to the fatuous Debbie Court, after the contractor's wife, the long-time residents of Hell decided to hate the newcomers forever. Contractors hammered up a bunch of houses, one of which was spectacular, visible from most points in town, closer to rain than the church spire. If you had the patience—and Hannah and I had had the patience—eventually you'd see the shut eyes of the house open around 4 P.M., when the maid parted the curtains on the south side and that haughty house told those of us below we were boring it to death.

The house became part of the landscape of what I'll remember when I try to forget that I came from Hell. The riverbank filth. The Dino & Millicent billboard. The condescending, mysterious home on the hill. All will remind me of Fiona when I return to Hell to eat and run, bounce my nephew on my shoulders, give the parents a good-bye peck, cheek against cheek.

HAVE YOU BEEN SERIOUSLY INJURED?

I thrust my plastic garbage bag at Hannah and ran to catch a glimpse of Fiona. The car's butt essed up the hill.

The view of Hell is spectacular from up there. Fiona appreciated it, I'd thought, because it was so often included in our night-drive route. Debbie Court was a dead-end: She'd have to return momentarily. I'd wait at the bottom of the hill.

Twenty minutes later, no Fiona. Not even the most scenic view of Hell can be that entrancing. Maybe she ran out of gas, or a tire went *pfft*. If there had been an accident I'd have heard the ambulance, unless no one had been around to call for one. I headed after her. God, had she hit a child?

My thighs burned charging up that steep hill.

People write poetry about the wonderfulness of sunrise. I thought it was corny until I experienced it myself, except for me there was no sun involved. For me, the wonderfulness was seeing Fiona's car waiting up on the hill, shiny and whole.

The Barracuda was parked on the street in front of the grand house. The driveway was empty, the garage door closed. A jungle gym and a tent stood on the north side of the house, both empty of kids' laughter. A couple of small, hairy dogs bounced up and down in the large front window, yipping at me in the street. Otherwise the house seemed still, not lifeless, but like it was holding its breath, like there was someone in there hiding in the closet.

I laid my palms on the hood of Fiona's car: The engine was warm. Her purse sat in the passenger seat, a pack of Marlboros by the gearbox. The car was unlocked. Keys in the ignition. I thought of keeping guard over the car, but I didn't want Fiona to feel I was a leech. At my feet was an apple core. I was about to kick it away when I decided instead to stick it onto Fiona's antenna. Surely she would know it was me, her pixie, her puck. Her jinni.

Two Thursdays went by without a word from the Gallaghers, who usually called Wednesday night to confirm. I quaked when I dialed the Gallaghers, praying Fiona would pick up, but there was no answer. I assumed they weren't playing tennis and forgot about the baby-sitter. The following week I dropped a note to Sean in the mailbox, hoping it would remind Fiona about me. It didn't work, and I kept missing Fiona. She must have altered her schedule. She wasn't in the kitchen when I went to school, though the car was in the driveway. But without the Barracuda ribboning through Hell, Hell was wasteland and so was I.

When Fiona finally called it was a late Saturday morning. She kept clearing her throat and spoke in hoarse whispers. I could barely hear what she was saying, though I understood she wasn't asking me to baby-sit. She was under the impression that Gallagher had called me and explained everything. Then she said something about being out of the hospital and wanting to pay me for those lost Thursdays. She would be home all day if I wanted to stop by and pick up the money.

I wasn't going to accept the money but didn't protest too much about it. Perfect excuse to go over and see Fiona.

"Your friend Fiona Gallagher is crazy, you know," my mother said. She'd been hovering, just waiting for me to hang up the phone.

"Yeah?" I answered without emotion as I punched my arms into my Mexican sweater.

"Annette told me she had a nervous breakdown."

I despised her. For knowing something I didn't know about Fiona. For her cattiness toward the most considerate person, next to Madame Foiegras, that I knew. Dr. Goldstein had called Fiona a cobra. But Fiona was the lamb, deceived and cheerless, nuzzling her way toward imminent slaughter. The Goldsteins and Gallaghers had been playing Group Therapy, the board game ridiculously popular at the time. Dr. Goldstein had drawn a card: *Name the animal counterpart of each player.* The cobra the doctor saw was her high-wire anxiety triggered, the frenzied derangement of vertebrates squealing and scratching for their inviolate life. Dr. Goldstein distrusted Fiona, and I know why. She was no doll, no coquette, and the stethoscope did not impress her.

"She tried to kill herself. Annette found her. She was curled up in a fetal position. On her couch. Poor woman, what a shock." Mother was referring to poor woman Annette, not Fiona.

Although Mother hoped each dart of her information would sting, I didn't wince. The worst of what she said was the fetal position part because it meant that Fiona, so grown, so large a person, still wanted her mother. What could I possibly do for her? I was only 15, and all I knew about mothering was how to change diapers and administer a bottle.

For months Mother would savor repeating the thing about the fetal position, an obvious reference to the fact that I came out of her body, her fetid womb, and she would rub it in until I found her utterly revolting.

"Annette's a gossip." I walked out of the house.

I circled the Gallaghers' block three times after detouring through the cemetery, trying to prolong my anticipation and rehearsing how I would say hello. Was it true what Eva said? Would Fiona look like a madwoman? Be unkempt, hair like a robin's nest? Would she cackle? Would she recognize me? Try to choke me?

I was not afraid. It was Fiona, and I wanted to be her cure, especially if she did look like a nightmare.

It was a breeze picturing her in a madhouse. Somehow I had known this was coming. Fiona wasn't meant to live in Hell. Either she would continue cracking up or she would have to shed something and fly the heck out of town. In the meantime I could keep the secret even if the neighbors couldn't.

I'd pinched a batch of tulips from an old man's grave, b. 1883. Fiona would understand.

Gallagher had answered my *ding-dong*, held open the door as I entered, then quickly abandoned me. He appeared rushed, didn't offer water for the flowers, but wasn't in any way distressed. He seemed to have been expecting me to show up. Maybe he'd gone to get my money.

He was having a party, a Welcome Home from the Nuthouse party, though nobody was nursish. A radio played Sinatra. The lights were elegantly dim. There was cocktail laughter, and the sound of a high-heeled hostess accompanied a woman I'd never seen before, Gallagher's sister. No airplane noises came from Sean who, it turned out, was playing with Fern Goldstein at her house. It felt like the waiting room at a funeral home, people acting normal and peck-kissing each other hello while knowing something really weird is going on.

As I scouted among the tall people with that painful smile of being alone, not one person introduced himself or herself or smiled back at me. It's the same nonlook people give their waitress or someone behind a counter. I was too young to be consequential.

Fiona wasn't at the party, unless she looked so different I wasn't recognizing her. I could have turned and left. Someone might have felt a breeze when I opened the door, but no one would notice I'd gone.

Gallagher's was the only familiar face, but even he didn't look quite right. He seemed hollow as an Easter bunny, disemboweled.

Watching him mix a drink with ridiculous pinky flair, use filthy language with twinkling eyes, and flick dust off his leather shoes made his affectations painfully clear. Some small tenderness for him rose up in me like bile. I hoped I'd never grow up to be so insincere.

I decided I'd circle the room once. A woman in white tennis shoes I took for a caterer turned out to be Gallagher's Oregon aunt. The well-dressed couple mumbling to each other, holding drinks, grinding nuts between their teeth, were Fiona's college roommate and spouse. I thought the dumpy agitated woman on the couch who fiddled with her headband was distraught over Fiona, but she was just in a snit because her husband had shushed her.

I headed for the kitchen thinking I would leave the flowers on the table. Unfortunately it was covered with platters of cold cuts and pineapple rings and bakery boxes. I would put the bouquet in her car.

As I made my way toward the front door I heard a swish swish from the second-floor landing. Fiona had emerged from her bedroom in a shiny bathrobe. The late afternoon sunlight shone on her puffy face. That smile of hers did my whole body in, and I loved her. No one downstairs loved her as I did, I was sure. I mean, I would do all those things mothers are supposed to do for their kids, walk through fire, give her a kidney, insist that of the two of us she be pulled out of a burning car first. Overwhelmed with a sense of hopelessness, I even stopped wanting to be a person anymore and instead wanted to be silk so she could wrap me around her neck, or the telephone receiver she speaks into.

When she looked down at me I knew she understood the mess in my heart. I reached up to her, extending the unwrapped flowers. It looked as if she started to cry because her nose got fat and her upper lip pleated itself, but no tears showed up. I think that was the saddest face that ever would look down at me.

She accepted the flowers and in a hoarse voice told me to get the money from Tom, he had already put it aside, under the cookie jar. I shook my head no and stepped back.

Everyone in the room glanced up at Fiona's appearance. I could have sneered at the puzzlement on their faces when she smiled good-bye at me, but instead I strode out the door happy as marigolds.

Fiona's car was in the Meat-O-Mat parking lot. It was as conspicuous as a house on fire. I'd just left my friends in the pizzeria when I saw Fiona walk out of the butcher's clutching a paper bag with blood on it. She saw me and offered a lift. Flattered, I got in.

"Are you in a rush to get home?" she asked. But I wasn't going home. I just said, "Nope."

She tossed the meat into the backseat. I could feel the ignition rattle my tonsils. Being driven around in that car made me as close to being overjoyed as I'd been when I was a kid jumping out my bedroom window into the snowdrifts. Motorcycles and big-engined convertibles still drug me. I'm up for bold adventure.

"How about if we put the top down?" As Fiona leaned over me to unlatch the roof on my side, I smelled her. Girls in gym had the sour smell of distress and mildew. Housewives smelled of baloney and hair spray. Grandmas smelled of too much perfume, and it choked me the way inhaling talcum powder can. Fiona didn't smell at all like any of them. She smelled slightly mentholated, like Grandmother's ginger cookies, and slightly potatoey, as if she'd been born from the earth. It was the way her pillow had smelled when I shoved my face into it that baby-sitting night. Even her clothes in the hamper enchanted me. And then there was her perfume.

What did I know about perfume? At camp we'd crushed pine needles and smeared the resin on our necks. And when I was six, Uncle Edbert gave me Winnie-the-Pooh toilet water, which I, of course, emptied into the toilet. A woman's perfume is malicious, a scar, a reminder that haunts you all over the world wherever there are women and duty-free shops. One day I'll be waiting in the coat-check line at the Guggenheim and Fiona will ghost herself off the silk scarf of the Italian tourist ahead of me and I'll be a teenager again climbing the stairs to her bedroom with the innocent pleasure of pie.

The top was down, sun warning it was about to set. We drove very fast, Fiona serene but focused on the dialogue between the Barracuda and the road. A good driver is well-acquainted with disappointment, expecting the worst of people as they change lanes without signaling, pull out without looking, merge into your passenger door. Fiona was too preoccupied to expect the worst, but there was no cause to worry about crashing with Fiona, who had speed-of-light reflexes. Anyway, had she sent me through the windshield I'd have gone smiling because when you die with someone, you're connected forever.

I wanted to stand up and feel the anchor of my clothes and my hair pulling me from behind. All we needed was loud radio music, but I was sure Fiona wouldn't have known what to make of "The End" or "Hey Joe," The Doors and Hendrix.

We made dust as we swung into a slender parking space. Fiona got the parking right the first try. I followed her into the Bubbling Brook Nursery, trailing as she meandered through the stuffy hothouse.

"Uhh, I love this heat," she said. "This humid, *sultry*, VOLUPTUOUS heat." Fiona spoke like that, stringing together a chain of adjectives of increasing amplitude until they brought her to the mightiest one. "It's voluptuous," she repeated, then sniffed the air like a predator. The ropes in her neck stood out, and her eyes narrowed when she became vehement about something. No wonder they took her to the nuthouse. Passion is unbecoming in Hell.

Who says passion is an older woman's emotion? I slipped into it the moment I'd seen Fiona in that Skylark.

Fiona's blood, I was thinking, must be sweet as condensed milk. She wasn't a flatterer, a schemer, suspicious of teenagers. I couldn't imagine her being a very good liar. She wasn't nervous like the rest of the ladies I'd baby-sat for. Everything with her was emotional vehemence. Such intensity did away with all the superficialities that make me ill at ease. It made my age matter less. Fiona couldn't chuckle, but she could give you a real ha-ha-ha, solar-plexus laugh. She couldn't eat her dinner if it was OK; it had to be this side of delicious. Fiona was thick with emotion. If she wanted something, she seemed desperate for it, she demanded it. If she smoked a cigarette, it was deliberately and with great pleasure. When she was in the Barracuda, she wasn't just driving from here to there, she was *flying* that car. I loved it. I would have been her navigator in an instant. I pictured us doing the Grand Prix. The whole damn town was just jealous of the way Fiona could enjoy her pleasure.

And some people, Annette Goldstein for example, thought Fiona had no self-control—by which they meant wacko.

What's strangling me? Suddenly I was in octopus arms, my enthusiasm collapsed. I was choking on air.

It was Fiona's awful tennis dress—it resembled our gym suits, and when she bent over to smell the potting soil, not the plant, you could see practically everything.

Should I tell her? Do you tell a man his fly is open? Jan whacked me in the head for telling him that, but I was just faking him out. Would Fiona smack me? Turn red? Fiona would have shrugged her shoulders and laughed.

"Isn't it sensual...*organic*...PRIMEVAL?" She held a wad of dark damp dirt under my nose, squeezing it with such force I could see the tendon struggling at her wrist. "Just smell this."

Primeval? Quick, dictionary, vocabulary list—does that mean supernatural? Totem? Choice meat? It's dicey spending time with people older than you, all the words they know: *licentious, staples, neurasthenia, profiterole.* I evaded the question.

"It's swampy." Wrinkled my nose. Humidity feels like reptiles stalking me, crocodiles, geckos, horned toads, rattlers. "Makes my hair fuzzy."

Fiona laughed at that, though it wasn't intended to amuse. How wonderful to make someone laugh. My heart just beat itself out of my chest and swung maniacally like a hanging planter in hurricane country.

"Thanks for coming with me," she said, brushing the dirt off her hands. "It was nice." So what about the tennis outfit.

Before we left, Fiona bought mulch, two 20-pound bags. I don't know what possessed me, but I said let's not wait for the guy who's supposed to be right up to help us with it, and I took both bags into my arms. My legs solidified to iron as I stumbled through the parking lot and good thing Fiona walked in front of me so she couldn't see my apoplectic face. She popped the trunk, and I dumped the mulch into it.

The insides of my arms were red, and I felt a cool puddle of sweat in the center of my chest. Fiona looked me in the eye before starting the car. I couldn't read her expression. She could have been thinking of hiring me.

The nursery cashier came running out to give Fiona her change. "You should have let Mack carry those bags for you. Your shirt is all dirty now."

"It'll wash out," answered Fiona lackadaisically. I was embarrassed. Sawdust and dirt clung to my breasts in my white T-shirt. The cashier shrugged her shoulders and walked off. "I didn't realize you were so strong." Oh, God, I could have been a boy trying to impress a girl on a first date. "You're small, but I bet you have an iron interior."

We backed out. The body-hugging bucket seats were so low, I could barely see over the dash. Abruptly Fiona shoved the car into park and turned to me again. She dare-stared me, and I met her gaze for maybe five seconds; it seemed a long time. Oh, God, she was furious, what had I done? Was she sick of me already?

"Why don't you have dinner with us?" Fiona watched my face with such expectation that it defied any excuses I might have come up with. "Come on!" She nudged my knee and was smiling. I guessed she really was over her nervous breakdown.

"Tonight?"

"Why not? Have you ever had veal piccatta?"

"No." I was a vegetarian.

She knew how inexperienced I was; otherwise she would have asked me if I *liked* veal piccatta. But how thoughtful, as my grandmother would have said. How thoughtful.

"How old are you, Paige?" she asked me when we'd returned. Sure, I'd told her a few times already—I was a little insulted she hadn't remembered—but why should I expect my age to be important to Fiona Gallagher? And then I realized it wasn't that she'd forgotten because she didn't care but that she'd forgotten because she didn't want to believe I was so young—how could she be friends with a puny teenager?

I was sitting in Fiona's kitchen holding in two hands the chocolate soda she'd concocted for me. And it was because of that soda, despite her problem with my age, which would only get worse, that I loved Fiona Gallagher. When she'd learned that, though chocolate was the only sweet for me, I had never had a chocolate soda, she set about to change things. She poured U-Bet chocolate syrup into a tall glass, added a splash of milk, then with the precision of a pharmacist added the right amount of seltzer (which I also had not tasted before) and stirred.

"Here, taste this." Fiona knew it was good. And she wanted me to have it. That made me fall in love because in my house the girl never gets the best ear of corn or the last bite.

Fiona was one of the few people who looked right at me when talking to me. My grandmother always seemed to be talking to me from the kitchen sink while she filled the teapot, scoured the casserole dish, or peeled potatoes. Teachers talked to us with their noses practically grazing the blackboard. Parents hollered at us through rooms and up and down stairs. And when I'd be walking down the street with friends, everyone looked where they were going, rarely at each other.

But Fiona looked me straight in the eye as if she wanted to pick a fight, except it wasn't hostile. I think a lot of people were delighted by this. It meant she was paying undivided attention to a fool like you. And neither Hannah, John, nor Amelia were going to get in on it.

Lemon, garlic, thinly sliced mushrooms sizzled in the pan.

I said I was 16, but I didn't say barely.

"You're very quiet. Are you unhappy about something?" Fiona

turned from the stove to look at me full on. A dish towel was draped over her shoulder. I had a vision of her burping a baby; I guess it was Sean.

She heard me sigh.

"Paige, any time you want to talk to me about anything, anything at all, I'm here." I was hoping it was *she* who wanted to talk to *me* about something.

I spent the meal trying not to hyperventilate and deflecting Sean's embarrassing questions ("Why do you have that beauty mark on your neck?" "Can I try on your glasses?"), which made me feel exposed, naked. I couldn't see anyone's expression, and my glasses were dirty.

Profoundly nauseous to the point of sweating from my forehead, I made my veal square dance across my plate. The meatloaf-brown Gallagher dinnerware was making me woozy. Sean with greasy fingers tried to unbraid my hair.

Fiona asked if I'd like to take the rest of my dinner home. I did.

I scooted the paper plate up to my bedroom and with my fingers shoved Fiona's French beans and carrot salad into my mouth. The veal I had cut to bits during dinner I flushed down the toilet, saving only the biggest piece, putting it on my dresser under an upended highball glass I took from the kitchen. My fingers tasted delicious. I should have drenched the beans in the lemony sauce.

A month later my mother discovered it. "I've been looking for that glass for weeks—potatoes please, Eustace—it's Orrefors! Your grandmother brought those glasses over from Sweden. What were you doing with it? And what the hell was in there? It was covered with mold."

"Where did you put it?"

"In the garbage, of course!"

"You have no right to go into my room and take my stuff."

My mother sat up straight as she could. "I'd like you to clear the table."

Fiona wanted to know if I was unhappy? I could've thrown a plate at my mother's unblemished back.

"Breasts are all alike. Seen one pair, you've seen them all."
Gallagher made his pronouncement from a padded chaise lounge
in his backyard. Puffing a cigar in the late May sun, he let his
magazine spill onto the patio. Someone with his back to me
picked it up and began leafing through.

"Oh, please! Why do you even bother to say such ridiculous,
asinine things, Tom?" Fiona was in the vegetable patch, where
she was trying to encourage some tomatoes. Sean was inside
napping.

"Just ignore him. He says it just to get a rise out of us."
Gallagher's sister looked exactly like him, only fairer and shorter, two pudgy peas in a pod. The guests were Fiona's in-laws. I'd
seen them at the house when Fiona had come home from the
hospital.

After perusing the *Playboy*, Fiona's brother-in-law agreed
with her, while her sister-in-law had no opinion and went back
to her celebrity magazine and mixed drink. If asked for my opinion, I would have taken Fiona's side, though at the time I could-
n't understand the big deal about breasts.

"Well, if anyone should know, it would be you," Gallagher

mumbled in his wife's direction. Fiona gave him the firm grip of a
stare he couldn't shake.

If I hadn't already been noticed, I would have turned and crept
away, but Fiona blurted out, "Paige!" and everyone snapped their
heads around to look at me.

"I'm so glad you stopped by," she smiled warmly. Her arm
around my shoulder, I was introduced to the guests.

When people act surprised that you're going to shake their
hand, it's too late to pull back, and generally they're flattered, as
was the brother-in-law who looked exactly like F. Scott
Fitzgerald's photograph on the back of the Scribner paperbacks.
His wife, however, found shaking hands an inconvenience, as it
meant she'd either have to put down her drink or lose her place
in the magazine. Choosing the magazine, she practically harrumphed when I clasped her hand. I got a kick out of that. So did
Fiona; I caught the sympathy for me in her eye.

Sean awoke from his nap; we could hear him whimpering
upstairs. Fiona and I went to fetch him. "Come," she said, "I'm
sure he'd love to see you." Gallagher hollered something up to us;
we couldn't make it out. Often I'd heard Fiona implore Gallagher
to speak more civilly to his employees. Embarrassed to show her
face in the office because of his shouting, she made no attempt to
find out what her husband was howling up to her.

It was family Saturday. While Gallagher dropped off the in-
laws at the train station, Fiona opened a can of Hawaiian Punch
for Sean, and I was content just to be around Fiona, learning more
about her. When I saw, for example, that she rinsed the top of the
juice can under the tap before she put the can opener to it, I knew
incontrovertibly that she loved her son. I'd never seen anyone
take that kind of care before.

"Would you like to come with us to Vito's?" Fiona asked me,

and I told her sure, completely disregarding my homework and the fact that Hannah was expecting me. We waited for Gallagher to return, then piled into his car for the 40-minute drive to Vito's, a roadside stand on Route 22. Sausage-and-pepper heroes were Vito's specialty. I wouldn't ever bite into one of those, no way. Fiona ordered something even sloppier and more hazardous-sounding to me—cheese steak with onions and peppers—and when she offered it I took a bite, surreptitiously gnawing off only the bread and sauce and trying to make my lips touch the part of the bread that had her lipstick marks on it. Sean teased me with a French fry in front of my nose. I was quick and bit it. That's all I had an appetite for.

We had just left Route 22 when we had to slow for the toll-booth. Gallagher put his hero in his lap, Fiona turned around to supply us with more napkins in the back, and I wiped off Sean's ketchup beard. Suddenly Gallagher began tailgating the Camaro in front of us. The driver seemed unaware. "I'm not stopping," announced Gallagher, and before we could figure out what he was referring to, he had run through the tollgate on the heels of the car ahead of us.

"What the hell are you doing?" Fiona asked, wide-eyed. She swallowed hard because she'd had a big bite of steak in her mouth. "What could you possibly be thinking, Tom?"

He explained that he had only $100 bills on him, and he'd had no intention of stopping just to have them broken for the 25 cents.

"Don't you ever pull a stunt like that when you're in the car with me. Or with Sean. Or Paige."

Or Paige? Initially I interpreted that as Fiona being protective of me. Then I realized I had been invited along for a purpose: I kept the Gallaghers apart. I kept them apart so they could stay together. The un-go-between. I kept things cordial.

But soon I was invited along for another reason.

"Paige!" exclaimed Fiona in pleasant—I hoped—surprise at seeing me in the backseat. "You're eating with us?" she asked hopefully.

Gallagher had seen me walking past his house on my way home from Hannah's. I blushed, assuming he figured out why I took the route that led me to his house, but that was absurd; no one in the world had any notion of my schemes. He offered to take me out for dinner, and I said yes, praying Fiona would be coming too.

We picked up Sean from the Goldsteins' and drove 75 miles an hour to the Clam Box. In our plastic bibs, the four of us sucked lobster from the claw, Sean played dolls with the claws, Fiona asked the waiter for more lemon, and Gallagher belched out loud.

"Oh, Tom!" Fiona reprimanded, though she sounded more disappointed than annoyed.

"Paige, are you going to eat your coleslaw?" begged Sean with big, wanting eyes. Fiona, looking at me with the same eyes, stopped chewing in anticipation of my reply. I couldn't figure out whether she had wanted my coleslaw for herself or was trying to tell whether I really didn't want to give it away but was doing it out of courtesy. My enthusiastic, "No way!" set her jaw going again, and Sean reached for the soggy mess of it with both hands, knocking over Fiona's ice water. She laughed and said it was *freezing* cold dripping on her legs.

There had been no spaces in the restaurant parking lot, so Gallagher, audacious as ever, had parked smack in front of the restaurant, blocking everyone's way. Fiona had been exasperated throughout the meal. I may as well have been home in Hell for all the attention she paid me. By the time the timid maître d' approached our table to ask if it was our Lincoln parked out front blocking the exit, we were about to order coffee and dessert.

Gallagher left to repark the car, bib still around his neck. I leaned over the table and wiped butter from Sean's chin. When I sat down, Fiona placed her hand on my thigh. And this was the dilemma about everything between Fiona and me: Was that a friendly touch, a kindly "thank you," or was she trying to tell me something?

Of course it was just friendly, I told myself. But why then had she waited to touch me until Gallagher had left the table? Was it just coincidence? If not, why would such a beautiful wife be so suggestive with *me*? I even had a chin pimple that day.

I told myself I'd seen too many movies, was too familiar with the gesture under the table as an icon of sexual mischief. Fiona was above such ordinary behavior, wasn't she?

Being with Fiona was always momentous, full of implicit expectation. My "future" may have been one deflated hope, but the real time—the actual minutes and seconds—I spent in Fiona's presence, was nothing but providence. My optimism was unbounded. We would be together. I just didn't know *when* and therefore anticipated it every single time she came near me.

⑩

What a thrill----
my thumb instead of an onion.
—Sylvia Plath, "Cut"

That summer I was waitressing at a diner outside
Flounder. I asked to be a busboy—you didn't have to wear a hair
net or speak to the cretin customers—but the manager refused
and almost wouldn't hire me at all because I'd asked such a ludicrous question.

My mother acted like my getting the job was the greatest
accomplishment of my life. I heard her boasting to her brother,
my Uncle Edbert. It's not that she was proud of me. She was proud
of herself for telling me to lie about having a driver's license and
then vouching for it. Since I had only recently turned 16 and had-
n't yet gotten my license, I would have been considered an unre-
liable employee.

Uncle Edbert was Eva's confidant. He tried to convince me
that he and I were close, and though he never asked prying questions, he kept trying to buddy up to me. For example, after my first

week on the job he came over with a trophy. My name had been etched on it, but it didn't say Best Anything. There was no baseball player on top, no crossed hockey sticks, just a loving cup that was so small it didn't even hold a dollar's worth of dimes. Damn plastic trophy made me feel worse, not better, by rubbing my penny-ante job in my face.

The job was humiliating—requiring orthopedic shoes, stockings thick as support hose, a damn hair net, serving without complaint—and Mother knew it. She was gloating because I had been tamed, broken in.

Since my shift began at 5 in the morning, I had to take the bus, which stopped half a mile from my house; my parents would pick me up when my shift ended, at noon, if Eva was free and if Papa didn't forget. I was told not to rely on them, to make sure I had money for the bus. I hated walking through Hell in that polyester uniform, prayed no one I knew would see me. My manager said I wouldn't get a better shift until I'd been there through the summer. He knew perfectly well I'd be back in school by September. I was lowest on the totem pole.

I typed Fiona a letter at the end of July, then held my nose, plunged in, and sent it. The Gallaghers were in the Irish Alps, a part of the Catskills unclaimed by the big Jewish resorts. For two weeks I looked after their house: taking in the mail, watering the plants, feeding the cat. I never slept there, but on weekends I took a nap in Sean's room, and when I woke, having no idea where I was, thought for a moment that now was my chance to be a completely different person, to thrive on my amnesia.

But I had the cat responsibilities.

For months I had wanted something that would just be mine and Fiona's, something tangible: a ticket stub from a movie we might go to or a picture taken together. I was too embarrassed to speak of desire. What would I have said?

I missed her enormously, even though she was less than two hours away, and missing her was one of those good and bad feelings. If I wrote her a letter it would be a connection, a way of creating a link between us.

I didn't want to ask for anything: I knew how unhappy she was. But I was unhappy too, and Fiona would take me more seriously if she knew of my despair. She would see we were alike. She was the older one, she was the one who could help me, not any freaking guidance counselor or school psychologist's inkblots. I wrote:

Sean's Mr. Cat is fine, but I am lost. All my friends know what to be when they get out of school. They see pathways and doors and diplomas and kiddies. I see London fog and me in it bumping into strangers, conjugating verbs in my head or, worse, aloud like a derelict. What's the point? Maybe I should just get married and mop the floor.

My heart swelled when Fiona wrote back, and thank God Eva hadn't been home when the mail came. I still have one of the two pages of her reply.

Dear Paige,

Tom and Sean send their regards.

I'm not happy about the tone of your letter. Where's your enthusiasm? I would have written back sooner, but I wanted to think about what to say to you. So here it is—right between the eyes—and it's strictly between you and me.

The most important thing in your life is YOU and what you feel about YOURSELF, and you can only get a clear picture of yourself by expressing your own creativity. Whether that's by translating Proust or making Jell-O. And—there's one more thing for you to remember: You cannot find yourself in other people. Don't try to emulate me. Believe me—I have my own very great weaknesses.

I want you to know—I am your good friend and I know you like me and I like you too. I'm here if you want to talk about ANYTHING.

I hope I didn't offend you....

She offended me. How dare she think I was trying to "emulate" her (I had to look up the word). Was I taking up smoking cigarettes? Was I planning to live in Hell for the rest of my life? She missed the whole point.

And my bit about mopping the floor? That was a decoy. She was supposed to tell me not to get married, to take another path.

I was so embarrassed, scolded like a child. So I made sure that before the Gallaghers returned I was out of there. I would make Fiona want to see me, and I'd wait for her to call for baby-sitting.

Just after 6 o'clock one morning, after rinsing the parsley (every plate got a parsley garnish) and portioning a tray of tapioca into 36 parfait glasses, I walked out of the kitchen as usual to check my station. I was excited, at first, to see I had customers because not only had I been given the slow booths—no one wanted to sit back by the rest rooms—but also my shift was generally dead anyway, a few truckers off the interstate and an early-morning manager or two who ate enough Canadian bacon that their complexion turned as pink and meaty.

The people at my station turned out to be Fiona and a very sleepy Sean. She didn't notice me at first, and that's when I should have scrammed. But then a huge grin spilled over her once she spotted me, or my surprise? I started to cry, not in any weepy way, but out of shock, as if I'd been punched in the gut. I didn't let it show.

Everything enslaved me. The dopey uniform. Eva. My age. If only I could have driven off, the top down and my hair snapping in the wind. The frilly white collar on my uniform made me want to die.

My supervisor gave me a rude little shove. "There's customers at your station."

The Gallaghers had been back for almost a week, but I hadn't heard from them. I wasn't even sure Fiona remembered I worked at the diner when she decided to take Sean out for breakfast. Sometimes it seemed as if Fiona forgot all about me unless we were face-to-face, and even then I had my suspicions. Maybe one reason she never drove me straight home after baby-sitting was because she'd forgotten about me though I was sitting right there in that Barracuda passenger seat, keeping my lips together in case I had bad breath.

Fiona ordered tons of food. Fried eggs, French toast, cereal, bacon, fruit cup, blueberry pie. "How's the coffee?" she asked just like everyone else.

Each time I had to approach the table with a dish, I got goose bumps from embarrassment. She wanted to talk, but my supervisor was watching me. Anyway, I didn't want to speak to her when I was in my uniform; I might just as well have had food caught in my teeth or a bloodstain on my rear end.

As if wearing glasses hadn't been enough of an embarrassment. I would have gotten over my mortification in a flash if I had been assured Fiona wouldn't ever imagine me in my idiotic uniform. Or if I had known Fiona would one day say that I "enchant" her in my glasses. But then I would never have believed that anyone, especially not Fiona Gallagher, would say something like that to me.

Finally Fiona left. I heard her car rumble out of the parking lot. She left me a huge tip, $20. It was more than I made in a whole week of tips. It would be my lucky $20. When I got home I stashed it in a record album; everything personal or important had to be hidden from Eva. I had known enough to hide the second page of Fiona's note, which said *See you soon. Love, Fiona.* Love, Fiona. But how could I have known page 43 of *The Bell Jar* was not the best hiding spot?

In September, after I'd started my junior year, I'd go to take a look at that note. Often that summer I'd done that, just read it over and over, pressed it under my shirt where my heart was.

That page would be gone and has long since disappeared. Eva snatched it. I know because my copy of *The Bell Jar* had been sitting there, plain as day, on Eva's night table. I saw it from the doorway. I panicked. I had underscored passages in red pen, I had scribbled marginalia (in French, thank God), and I'd slipped Fiona's signature between its pages.

Eva came up behind me, and I heard myself say, "Mother, isn't that my book?"

"I don't know."

"Did you take it from my room?"

"I thought you were done with it."

"I asked you not to go into my room!"

"Yes, but I wanted to have a look at it. It's a best-seller. Everyone's reading it. Don't be so fussy."

Stalemate. I wasn't going to ask about the letter, and she was begging me to.

"You went into my room without asking."

"And why shouldn't I? Are you hiding something?"

I had wanted to decimate the book, to pick it up with a pair of Playtex gloves so I wouldn't have to touch Eva's greasy fingerprints, and burn it in the barbecue. I loved that book.

So I walked away showing no emotion, having perfected the

expression of ennui. I went to my bedroom and, despite my trembling, calmly raised the ceramic candlestick I made in art class, and I brought it down on my desk, thwam! Thwam! Thwam! After three smashes it finally broke, and without pause I dragged the jagged end piece along my left forearm from elbow to wrist, digging all the way. My blood bubbled up, what a pleasant surprise. It was the color of miracles and maraschino cherries, and it relieved me, like taking off panty hose or aspirin to a headache.

I slipped into a long-sleeved shirt and during dinner felt my blood tugging at my sleeve as it dried to crust.

No one in school had said anything, even though I wore three-quarter sleeves and had gym class, until Madame Foiegras, pacing the rows while we worked on a pop quiz, asked me if I had a cat, indicating my scratches with a nod of the head. When I said no, "Moi? Non, Madame. Je suis allergique!"—and I had said it jauntily—she looked saddened. I was trying to shrug her off and she knew it. The idea of her peeling back my shirt froze me up, though I'd rather have had her do it than the school nurses because she'd be gentle, afraid of hurting me. But it gave me the willies. What if she couldn't control herself? What if she tried to kiss my scratches and whispered mon petit chou-fleur?

I could have come up with an excuse for staying after class, giving Madame an opportunity to say she was worried about me. But if I had received sympathy from her, I'd have used up my quota, and it was Fiona I wanted to take notice.

⑪

For the last gasp of summer, my friends the three Peters invited me for a Nantucket weekend. Their friendship unbound me. It was so much easier to have fun with them than with Hannah or Amelia. Everything was just living, not worrying, emptying the sand from your shoes.

Maybe that's what being rich does to you, eliminates the bedrock of anxiety that defines animal life. All of us worry, warthog and whelk and midge and wild horse, about dinner, tuition, our daughter's wedding. But the rich wear white and repose while the domesticated animals linger, hoping for a scrap.

Two cars, both luxury models, to each Peter's family. Steak and lobster dinners, king crab luncheons with dusty wine bottles, something unusual to pass under their guests' noses—quiche, goat cheese, snow peas, crepes, tahini—to certify their sophistication. Among them were one yacht, two sunfish, a motorboat, and water skis. A senator for tea and cigars on the deck. Rose trellis clinging on the leeward side of a house.

Here I go with the mothers again. All the Peters' mothers knew how to shuck oysters, mix gin and tonics, and make me self-conscious, an uninvited guest. They snubbed me when I offered to help fry the morning bacon, hang the beach towels on the clothesline, pick up the snapper at the fishmonger's. While they accepted my help with chores, they never turned to face me unless they were looking me up and down like a sapling for sale. They were thinking no girl from Hell is going to weasel her way into their son's heart and bank account.

If they only knew the truth about me, that when Peter took me canoeing at night and pointed out the phosphorescence in the water, the burden of Fiona arose again in the face of the sea.

But I couldn't blame the mothers. What else were they to think about our spending our days on the nude beach? The boys weren't peeking at me any more than I was peeking at them, but it still felt weird being the only girl, like I had double-crossed my own self. And on top of it all, my breasts got sunburned the color of raspberry sherbet.

On Sunday I was taken two hours early to the commuter plane that went straight to Hell. Peter's mother didn't say good-bye or have a safe flight. She just gave me a tight, smile then drove off.

Something good will come my way. Patience.

That autumn Hannah had sent off five requests for college catalogs, arranged three campus visits, and attended two sessions with alumni representatives in the guidance office. She pressured me to do the same. "I'm not saying you have to apply early admissions, but Paige, have you looked at a single college catalog?" So I sat in on a meeting with one SUNY alum just to get Hannah off my back (and to get out of trig), but I hated the idea of going to an ordinary college.

"What is the percentage of students who go on to graduate school?" "Is the school involved in any community service programs?" "Does the science department support study abroad?" I was impressed with Hannah's questions, but I acted as if we'd devised them together and sat there looking well-informed. The other kids wanted to know how many coed dorms there were, whether you had to be on the meal plan, if you were allowed to drink beer on campus, how many papers you had to write per course, and stuff about sports, football mostly.

I'd cobbled together a question in case I got called on—"What's the student-teacher ratio?"—but when Seth asked my question the alum's nostrils flared. According to our class of '64 alum, that was the first issue addressed in the college catalog. He was either very proud of his green leisure suit (he kept yanking on the lapels as if to make us notice it) or he was too fat for it; it was cutting him under the armpits. He cracked open the catalog, tapped a finger on the appropriate paragraph, passed it around. Man, his fingers were fat, blood sausages every one and a class ring strangling the pinky.

The photos in the catalog showed students in groups laughing their hyena heads off, fortified by deep snows, playful in Frisbee springtimes. Look how earnest in their chem-lab safety glasses, how inimitably healthy in their snowflake sweaters. Where in the world do these people come from? Why would I want to go to school in the middle of nowhere? That's where I come from, and at least in Hell the winters are mild.

Not one of Hannah's choices was more than a morning's drive from Hell. What was the point of applying to colleges if you weren't planning to get way on out of here?

The Sorbonne was my idea of continuing education.

But my guidance counselor, Miss Littler (we called her Miss Hitler), had vocational school in mind for me. During our mandatory college counseling session, where each counselor was supposed to list five schools for the student to consider, Hitler said every soft-pencil aptitude test since kindergarten showed I had an ability with spacial relations—Will more cars fit on a block where there's parallel parking or on a block of nose-to-curb parking? She slid a piece of paper to me across the gray metal desk. On it in her curled-up wormy handwriting were the names of two vocational technology schools. Hitler didn't even have the consideration to give me my other three names.

"The supervisor of Hell's public works department is a graduate," she said, pointing to the first school with a pencil. The words were piped out of her red mouth. I felt like she was a movie with the sound track out of sync. "And if I'm not mistaken, Elma Irish, over in the Municipal Building, the police secretary, and Ralph Raugh, the receiver of taxes, are Ratsass alumni." I think that's what I heard. I wasn't really paying attention, too busy trying to see if it was really me, the French honors student, she was talking to.

Hitler's face didn't move at all when she spoke, only the dummy mouth, and I squinched my eyes looking for the ventriloquist. If her breath hadn't been so mildewy, I would have been insulted. Instead, I sat as far back from her as I could, my chair jammed up against the wall, and got mad. With guidance counselors like Hitler, it's no wonder seniors had nervous breakdowns and sailed off the radio tower still wearing the dress from the dance.

Being angry at such a lonelyheart made me feel guilty, until I realized Eva was behind this. "A college education is astronomical!" she had said at the dinner table. "We can't possibly afford to send the *two* of you to college." Jan was already in school when she went on with her diatribe, so guess who would be the one to lose out? Who cares? I could hitch to San Francisco.

"Paige'll get a loan," Papa had responded, supping soup. He then rolled his eyes at me, his chin over the soup plate. I had pretended not to notice. So did Eva. He could keep his wimpy brotherhood. If he was really on my side he'd have said, like fathers are supposed to, that I was a smart girl and would get a damn scholarship anywhere I pleased, that if the family had to scrimp a little, so be it for our only daughter.

I'd cleared the table clenching their steak knives in my hand, by the blade end. They left serrated marks across the meaty part of my palm.

Once I'd ripped down the pictures from my wall and packed my radio, books, and jeans, that would be it. I wasn't going to come back for her holidays or hysterectomy, not for semester breaks or summer vacations. Papa could call me on the phone if he wanted to talk, and Eva could go to hell.

After telling Hitler I'd consider her recommendations (though what I was thinking was *fuck you*), I was blindsided by a smack-in-the-head headache the moment I stepped out of her office. Brain heavy as lead, feeling poison gassed, I was going to vomit.

And then I figured it all out.

Spite is such an entertainment. And out of spite I would study my ass off, I would live French, translations of everything chattering in my mind: my trig homework, the cafeteria menu, the Vonnegut and Salinger and Hesse we read, Mother's disappointments, even Papa's silences, they are different in French. I would win the language department's Prix d'Or for outstanding work in French, be accepted at the Sorbonne, or receive full scholarship at Bennington, Vassar, Stony Brook, to study French. Show them all.

French came easy. Eva said I had inherited her ear. The ear had nothing to do with it—would she like me to Van Gogh mine and send it to her in a manila envelope? The talent was from my father, Lieutenant Eustace Bergman, who had worked in intelligence during World War II. I inherited my interest in cracking codes from him, and from Eva I learned of necessity to speak in a coded language. Voilà!

In winter's flinty early evenings, after Gallagher had treated me to a restaurant dinner with his family, all I could hope for as I lived off his largesse, the chill of his leather seats coming through my jeans as we returned home, was that Fiona would ask me to stay awhile, for instant cocoa. Most of the time she did, and when I would baby-sit in the afternoons, once she'd returned she always invited me for dinner.

"You can stay here as long as you like," she'd said. "Tom can call your parents and let them know you're with us."

I sat through those dinners on Chestnut Street, rarely eating much more than a dish of mashed potatoes, and stuck around to put Sean to bed while Fiona made phone calls and a pot of coffee. Gallagher was amused to find me doing homework in his den. (I had written my so-so college application essays on the couch in the Gallaghers' den, anticipating his any-minute-now bounding through the front door, tossing his suit jacket on the nearest club chair, and rubbing his hands together to indicate hunger. He could be so prosaic.) But he was affectionate in his weird way and was the only one outside of high school to call me Celestine.

While I found it pleasantly surprising that he offered me a haven from my parents, I hoped he would shower, swallow the meat loaf, button up a clean shirt, and go out with his guys to the driving range (which closed only when snow exceeded four inches and on the holidays) for the evening. It was mean of me, but it felt good when Sean, Fiona, and I were alone in the house.

So when she phoned me, "Sean has something to tell you: 'Can you come pick up your Christmas present, but can you walk because I'm in my pajamas and Daddy's not home to drive you and Mommy has to stay here with me?' " I was delighted.

Carrying a *bûche de Noël* I'd made with Hannah for a French project, knowing all the while I would give it to Fiona, I trudged through the light snow silencing Hell. By the time I got to the Gallaghers', the snow had soaked through my canvas sneakers and Mexican sweater, and my fingers were red and numb. I loved the discomfort. Fiona towel-dried my hair and insisted I wear her fuzzy pink slippers until my sneakers dried under the radiator. I preferred to be barefoot, as you can imagine. Sticking his head out the kitchen doorway, Sean watched while finishing his dinner.

"Where would you like this?" I asked, pointing to the cake I'd set on the shelf by the door. Fiona whisked it into the kitchen, peeled back the wax paper covering it. "Ooh la la!" she said, impressed. "Let's have some right now. Would you like a piece?" I nodded no thanks, Sean squealed "a *big* piece," and we sat at the kitchen table, Sean and Fiona enjoying the cake in huge mouthfuls and laughing with each other, me enjoying watching them.

"Save some for Daddy!"

Gallagher was visiting his sister's family for the weekend and would be home in time for Christmas. There would be cake left for him.

While Fiona bathed, I watched Sean take a few more bites of marinated flank steak and boiled potatoes, and encouraged him to chew so he wouldn't choke on the chunks he was feeding himself. We could hear Fiona singing "Hello, Dolly" in the tub and we both thought it funny.

"Your mom is very special," I whispered to Sean.

"Why?"

"Because she let you have dessert before you finished dinner."

"Oh, she always does!" Sean answered. Then he toddled

upstairs and handed me my Christmas present, which was a drawing of a pink whale.

"I love it!" I said and hugged him off his feet.

"Sean, get ready for bed now," Fiona called from her soak. "Paige will help you."

Sean burnished his face with a washcloth until it was shiny and apple-cheeked while I parted his hair, golden like Fiona's, with a wet comb. He looked too much a little man, it was creepy, so I mussed up his hair. He preferred it that way anyway. Respectfully, I waited in the hall as he entered his mother's bathroom for his night-night kiss. "Tuck me in, Paige," he said. I pulled his taxicab sheets up to his armpits. A fairy tale I invented about the talking toast with jam made him laugh until he got the hiccups. I offered him water, kissed him good night. Twice. I love a child's forehead.

It was awkward. I didn't know whether I should wait until Fiona got out of her tub to say good-bye, whether I should holler through the door, or whether I could simply leave without being rude.

I decided to leave, didn't want to be presumptuous—why would a woman twice my age be interested in having me hang around? I got my sweater from the kitchen.

Fiona stood in the hall. Clutching her bathrobe at the neck and belly button, she had a confused expression on her face, as if I'd hurt her with an inexplicable slap. Shook a cold tremor through me.

"You don't have to go...unless you want to." The ends of her hair were damp. "Tom and I got you a present too." I followed her into the den where a small white box, red ribboned, sat on Tom's desk.

I took my sweater off and sat at one end of the couch, Fiona in her bathrobe at the other end.

And then Fiona talked to me.

She named the names of her siblings and parents, all names of

kings and queens—William, Elizabeth, Sophia, Gus (Gustave)—
an intimate gesture, I thought.

She told me about Gallagher's persistent pursuit for her hand
in marriage, and I smiled grudgingly.

She admitted murdering her childhood pet goldfish by stab-
bing it with a pen in a pretend game of war. I did not absolve her
with platitudes, but rather felt heartbroken for the Fiona-child's
sorrowing.

She said that during her hospitalization another patient had
crawled into her bed the first night and slobbered kisses all over
her before the nurse dragged the unfortunate off. I rejoiced with
the news, though I wasn't quite sure what exactly the news was.
All I knew was that she was kissed by a girl and it didn't make her
violent or remarkably nauseated. I made no comment, remained
ravenous but poker-faced. We had begun speaking to each other
in code.

From my end of the couch, I could smell her. I inhaled her as
if she were oxygen. I barely said a word for fear of making a fool
of myself, every word I could say a heavy metal, drenched with
import. But everything she told me went into the mental file I
kept on her. For someone as legitimate as a housewife, she was
fascinating.

That night Fiona Gallagher had paid attention to me. Didn't
ask the usual—school, boyfriends, favorite activities—but instead
told me secrets. Over the course of the school year, Fiona would
want to know how I felt—about her breakdown, about my mean
parents, about André Breton, whom she'd read in college, in
French! And I'd tell her as best as I could.

Two minuscule hours had passed. "Well…" I said, intending to
leave. We walked into the hallway, and I got into my Mexican
sweater.

"You'll freeze in that sweater of yours," Fiona said. "Try this on." As Fiona helped me into her ski jacket, which had that scent that made me just want to fall down broken apart in tears, she took hold of me by the lapels and said, "Paige, you have to learn to let go," and before my eyes could drop out of my head with dejection, she remembered, "Your present!"

It was after 11 o'clock. Eva would be getting pissed. But I stayed, and in that ski jacket opened my present.

It had to be a joke.

What a hideous piece of jewelry! Maybe it would have looked good on one of Fiona's friends, but people like me just don't wear ostentatious metal, a chunky silver bracelet with a timepiece sunk into it. I'd wanted to love the gift, and here it turned out to be preposterous.

Maybe the watch was a message. Saying...*eternity*? Saying...*time to go*? *Time is running out*? And the bracelet? Was she chaining me up? Locking me out? Maybe the whole thing was an evil eye, an amulet, telling me to keep away from Fiona Gallagher.

Fiona helped me latch the silver chain around my wrist.

"Thank you," I managed to say. "You didn't have to—"

"Would you mind staying with me until these sleeping pills start working?"

The gassy smile slid right off my face. My guts caught a chill. Her request was odd—was she afraid of the dark? Most people would say so, and yet wasn't I waiting to hear it? Fiona had been sent to me, now I was sure. She made sentences out of my inchoate desires. "Please, don't do it if it makes you uncomfortable," she said seeing me hesitate. "These sleeping pills make me anxious, like I'm slipping, sinking, plummeting into a void.... Do you have any idea what I'm talking about?"

I nodded with innocent teenage audacity. Actually, I didn't care why she wanted me to stay. Whatever she asked of me I would give her.

Fiona pulled back the covers, and I turned away out of propriety so as not to see her underwear—if she even wore any to bed. She dumped her two pillows onto Gallagher's side of the bed, pulled up the blanket. Lying flat, she patted the bedside for me, come, sit. I sat. I wished I'd washed my hair that morning.

She took my hand and sat up on an elbow to get a closer look.

"You have a child's hands!" she said, surprised. "Your skin is so smooth. It's marble, alabaster." It was getting steamy in her jacket.

She placed her hand next to mine for comparison. There was that wedding band, good gold too, and her strong fingers, unpainted but neatly trimmed nails.

"Oh, Paige, you're so young." She sighed. I didn't want her to feel bad about not being young. I told her I liked her hands better than mine, they had character, and it was true. She laughed and told me to just wait until I was her age. I didn't think I would ever be her age and prayed for hands like hers with ropy veins the way I used to pray for a broken arm in a plaster cast.

Fiona enjoyed having a young friend far more than I enjoyed being her young friend. I never valued my age, never even recognized that my skin was soft and my joints always ready, my hair lustrous and my breasts firm, two halved lemons.

I held Fiona's hand until it twitched, though initially I thought she was clutching me out of affection, and her breathing became snorty. A cramp bit me in the calf from keeping still so long so as not to disturb her.

Once she was certainly asleep, I placed her hand—how heavy it was—by her side and limped out, switching off the light and squeaking the heavy front door behind me.

I was privileged to share such private time with Fiona Gallagher. Then why did I grow to resent being left brilliantly awake, alone?

I'd have to come back for the cake platter, and how delighted I was about that.

Billy McFee's laughter resonated throughout the neighborhood. The moon does howl. The December chill burned the air—it smelled crystal cold—that night in Hell, a smell of arctic isolation.

What could I do with my big Fiona love? If I were an artist, I'd paint her. If I were a chef, I'd make crepes suzette for her. If I were a man, I'd marry her.

The impossible laughter, ho et cetera, came bogeyman close as the fire truck drove up a parallel street, then faded heading north toward the high school. Here was mirth, broadcast from a megaphone. In September, October, potential assemblymen cruise the same streets blaring their slogans and platforms and thrusting pamphlets from Country Squire windows. But this was a pageant, searchlight on top of the red fire truck trained on a team of plastic reindeer.

The fire department Santa would be a bygone tradition within a few years' time. Or so held my father, a man with a penchant for predicting disaster. Catastrophe is a reliable source of self-satisfaction for him. Maybe that's why he's still married to my mother. Papa's greatest moment came in an aerogram from Lulea, when his father-in-law, Grandfather Gustavus with the mutton-chop sideburns, lamented the lack of fish in Sweden's lakes, the worst season in his long and declining memory. "Acid rain!" clapped my father. "I told him it would happen years ago!"

I would never know whether Papa's prediction came true.

Meanwhile, in the early 1970s, the Hell fire department show-cased a long-johned Marshall McFee every night the week before Christmas. Sweet propaganda for the children who believed his cotton beard couldn't be tugged off.

Grandmother Anna-Maj wanted to do it the traditional way, and she practically stamped her delicate, slippered foot. She said we should be celebrating Advent, we should use candles on the Christmas tree, we should open presents Christmas Eve day. I think she missed home, people calling her Swedish diminutives.

Sweden's cultural eminence in Hell rested firmly on massage and meatball, the darling of the suburban cocktail circuit. Oh, and, of course, clogs and promiscuity—nude beaches, legal pros-titution, extramarital sex. I know I was a disappointment to Grandmother because all being Swedish meant to me was lin-gonberry jam. My brother, Jan, was better than I at patronizing Grandmother, but she was on to him. She knew he was proud of having Swedish blood because he thought it meant he had a right to think he'd marry one of those busty blond women wading in the Baltic in bikini bottoms. Why that was attractive I'll never know. Jan and his wanky friend Clifford even entered the SAS Strindberg Contest. You had to write an essay or a play. The prize was a summer in Sweden, free SAS airfare.

I couldn't understand my brother's and Clifford's fixation on breasts. As authentically Swedish as their fantasy girls may have been, to me they were forgeries of womanhood, wouldn't have surprised me if they were really transvestites. I seemed alone in my opinion because even the girls at school wanted straight blond hair and C-cup brassieres.

My mother doesn't think about being Swedish, though her hair's blond and her *äppelkaka med vaniljsås* has been prepared by five generations of Lind women. Unlike Papa, she's insistently American. She was born here and is crazy about American shock absorbers, parades, and kosher frankfurters. An aficionado of pomp, she's adamant about having a big boisterous Christmas and to this day knots a Marimekko scarf under her pert chin for church, Christmas and Easter being the only times she attends. She even refused to have me baptized, though when Jan was born she was too young and intimidated to tell the pastor no.

Papa in his herringbone slacks would shuffle into the Lutheran church behind his attractive wife. In singing Swedish carols he achieved deliverance. Mother may have been the professional singer, but I could see in Papa a pleasure that was a little orgiastic, vaguely disgusting. Christ is born, oh yeah. As a kid I had wanted to believe in Loki, god of mischief, and to keep Thor alive ever since my mother had first acquainted us, me atremble under the duvet and Him javelining thunderbolts overhead and into our muddy yards. My mother would throw her head back and laugh at the thunderclap, so I did too, and we peeked out the windows and smelled the god's fire and there were tears in Jan's eyes as he tried hard to be brave.

I looked up. There were no cartoon gods in the sky, no better place to go to, no angels with enormous wingspans. And we'd ruined the moon with those astronauts; now it doesn't belong to all of us.

I lit a joint outside the Gallaghers' and got stoned with a vengeance. My ugly new watch said 11:40.

McFee's Santa had an audience of me and the poodle walker up on Pine Street. Why wouldn't I wear gloves? my grandmother had asked that evening in the most beautiful English ever spoken. Not even a hat? What kind of Swedish girl goes out without a hat in the dead of winter?

I gave up trying to convince Grandmother I wasn't Swedish mostly because I felt less able to prove I was American. No one in Hell considered hippies American, and that was only half of it because then there was me and apple pie. ("You're as normal as blueberry pie," Fiona's mother had exhorted. What do they say in Paris? *Normal comme un croissant?* I'm French, then, twisted.)

Grandmother Anna-Maj worried about me, and though I saw no need for it, it made me feel so much gentleness for her I could hardly bear it and was glad when she went back to her friends in the Midwest after the holidays.

My Mexican sweater, though a highly coveted item of clothing among my friends, was impractical for winter in the northeastern United States. The wool stank when wet, and with its wide stitching it didn't provide much protection from wind or precipitation. My sweater fastened at the neck with a chain I'd made of paper clips and had a sewn-on belt. It was this sweater I had worn to deliver my *bûche de Noël*. But I was wearing the ski jacket home. It was a bouquet of her, the collar blooming with her perfume, the cuffs dainty takers of her pulse. I fought against my body's wanting to be sick with crying, and I recalled that as Fiona had packed me into it and zipped me up, she repeated what would become a mantra, "Paige, you've got to learn to let go." Of what? I wondered, though her saying it had terrified me. And after a while, I realized she wasn't talking to me, just offering some generic sleeping-pill–induced philosophy better meant for herself. Still it had ruined the thrall of being dressed like a dear child by Fiona Gallagher.

I turned, stiffening with the cold, to follow the spotlight as it passed in front of me then rolled away, zigzagging around corners of the neighborhood. I wondered if what Grandmother said about cold feet giving you the sniffles was true. Inside my shoes my toes no longer responded to my *Wiggle!* command.

Santa chortled. The spotlight flickered through the branches of another tree-named street. I blessed the rat McFee and made my way home.

"Where have you been?" my mother demanded, a mouth full of pie. She chewed furiously, swallowed hard, took a swipe at her lips with the damask napkin. This was trouble. She did not like to be caught in an undignified position—my mother even puts on lipstick to get the mail. How dare I not call. Who do I think I am, young lady, sashaying in so late when Grandmother had only recently arrived? Goggle-eyed at her pique and my nonchalance, Papa and Grandmother looked up at me from their midnight-snack plates of ham and pie.

What if they noticed the jacket? "Out walking." I was emboldened by the jacket. Not a single bad thing could happen to me while I wore it. And if it did, I didn't care.

I understood her anger. Daughters know their mothers' temperament better than anyone. In her eyes I was unpredictable, uncontrollable, and uncivil to boot. From my point of view, she was a shrew. But no one responded when I told them where I'd been. I thought they must have known the truth. Grandmother pretended not to hear any of this. She simply didn't care. She wanted more meat. Mother hushed her, said we've had dinner, now we're just having a late-night bite, Eustace don't pour the good brandy.

I headed upstairs.

Eating had nothing to do with hunger. If it did, I would be fatter than a hot-air balloon, that's how hungry I was. And not eating had everything to do with getting free of Eva's grip.

At the dining room table some taut discussion regarding what should be done about me ensued. *She should come down and eat with us. Why should she be given dessert when it obviously means nothing to her, she's getting a curfew, she's grounded starting right now.* I slowly made my way up the carpeted stairs, avoiding the two creaky spots so they'd think I was already in my room. It thrilled me to be talked about.

After lying flat on my back awhile, I heard Grandmother say she was going to bring me dessert, it's Christmas spirit, and that's the last word. Papa agreed in a baritone syllable. I slunk into my room.

All I wanted to do was rest here on my bed. But I knew my Grandmother would be coming up soon, tapping on my door, and it would provoke questions if she found me staring at the ceiling. I sat at my desk. I turned on my transistor radio, searched for a hit. I detested instrumental music; my being a singer's daughter, songs without words seemed a disfigurement, and how opera didn't give people headaches I couldn't understand.

Sometimes while scanning the stations I heard my mother's voice. When I was a kid it used to make me crazy with glee to hear her singing inside the little black box. I told my friends, "You know that Funland Amusement Park commercial? That's my mother singing it!"

Here's her voice now, along with two others, announcing our most popular local DJ in three whole notes. For 20 years the station has played the same tape of my mother's top notes every 15 minutes on that DJ show. But it's only recently, now that I have to avoid her for my life, that I've been able to distinguish her voice, second-soprano, from the other singers. The inability to pick out her voice used to give me a shudder, a fear as sickening as if I'm three years old and have lost my mother in the supermarket. But right in the middle of me still in Fiona's jacket came Eva trilling. Before I knew what I was doing, I hurled the transistor across the room. It broke open. I saw its guts.

Grandmother was the conciliator. I waited for her padding footsteps. Would she stumble on the radio parts, the batteries? I began to pick up the pieces. None of the music counted for me anymore. Not one song was ever written about my kind of love. So how do you learn what's permissible? Where do the lovers' great lines come from? What the hell are the rules? For all the help popular culture gave me, I could as well have had a passion for sheep. And they would be more of a comfort.

There were no rules, no codes of conduct. It was pure invention. And it nearly chewed me up and would have if it weren't for the ecstasy. The levitation. No one in the entire school was experiencing it. No one loved a woman, a Venus with purse, full hips, and Diner's Club card. No one loved an impossibility except me.

Many high school students kept a scrapbook, and so did I. Hannah's scrapbook contained concert ticket stubs, diary confessionals, photographs of boys cut out from last year's yearbook, flyers from the most recently attended moratorium. My collection, however, bore no direct connection with me. That was to befuddle my nosy mother.

My scrapbook contained newspaper clippings: FRANCE OPENS UNIVERSITY CATERING TO SENIOR CITIZENS and JOHNCOCK CAPTURES INDY 500; MECHANIC KILLED AND SAVAGE CRITICALLY INJURED; a photo of Boris Spassky in Reykjavik, an AP story on the woman claiming to be Anastasia, and front-page articles on hog men in the United Kingdom and skeletons preserved in alpine ice (no photos, unfortunately).

If my teachers had found out I was collecting such macabre, dissonant articles, surely I'd have been chosen to participate in one of those weekend encounter groups. Amelia was selected twice, and each time she emerged with a whole new set of friends who acted cliquey, as if they'd been long lost cousins.

I didn't want help. I just wanted to show everyone I was different, unique, interesting, noticeable.

But I slunk through the gates of mental health.

Mother wouldn't let me ruin her Christmas, I heard her say loud and clear through my open door, and she rose to light the angel chimes. The delicate *ting-ting* as the angels spun, driven by the heat of the candles, struck me. Oh, my God, it's Christmas week, and for a minute I wanted to retract the last few months and have an enjoyable Christmas, spice cookies, saying nice things about Jan's shy girlfriend, and allowing myself to be astonished by my mother's marvelous singing voice.

Breathing laboriously, Grandmother came up the stairs with a tray of cookies and a glass of hot lemonade for me. I heard the glass clinking on its saucer. I wish now I had kissed her long white braid.

You know what finally enrolled me in Fiona's mind? Homework. Our assignment: Write a poem in French.

Madame Foiegras gave me an A. Of her own volition she submitted it, with her translation, to the school literary magazine, which printed the poem in her English and my original French version. I swear it is what convinced Fiona to pay attention to me. Not that I was trying to impress her with any talent of mine. The truth? I was trying to blackmail her. To worry her into paying attention.

The Garage (*La Vie dans l'Enfer*)

The little girl I keep
in a motor-oily corner crouches
patiently among a week's worth
of feathered lettuce and brutal Del Monte tins.

But I won't feed her.
I'd rather watch
the body tremble,
sweat seeping from beneath her thin skin.

When I peek at her,
her gray knees lock and sweet
heart knocks, a raw
egg in a red hot pan.

And my own does the same
when I see her there, but I won't
go near, release her.
Won't she bite and torment me?

At night I am blinded
by her silent jaws
painfully stretching for food,
yaw yaw. In bed I am told

where my own bitter tears will fall
and the sound her body will make
when she dies out
and I drag her to the woods.

I conveniently forgot the school magazine on the Gallaghers'
coffee table. It was foolish, I know, precisely the kind of behavior you could expect from a junior high school student, but how
else could I prove to Fiona that I may have been normal, but I
was not ordinary?

It could have backfired. Fiona could have freaked out about
the poem and never let me baby-sit again. Gallagher was less of a
worry. I figured if a bunch of words in a magazine looked like poetry and not a spreadsheet, he'd walk right by it. I'm not criticizing
Gallagher. I'm the same way with the sports page.

Much to my chagrin, Fiona knew perfectly well I hadn't forgotten the magazine. Nevertheless, instead of teasing me about my silly deceit, she acted as I'd hoped she would, as I knew in my gut she would.

When I saw her a few excruciating days after my scheming drop-off, she was sitting on the edge of the bed waving the magazine at me. I had come to baby-sit.

"What am I going to do with you?" she said with a love look on her face shifting with a worried look, just like those Cracker Jack prizes where the clown's eyes are closed if you tilt the picture one way, eyes open when you tilt it back.

Fiona tied her tennis shoes, then walked over to me and put her hands on my shoulders as if to stop me from running away—just what I didn't want to do and wanted to do, with eyes in the back of my head to see if she pouted, because crying was out of the question. Getting Fiona to weep was like getting a cow to fly. Any psych major could tell you her heart was disconnected from her bag of tears.

"The French version is better," she proclaimed. Fiona was biting the inside of her cheek as she stared into me. That's how I knew I'd gotten her attention.

The little girl in that poem would haunt me for years. She entered the bathroom when the shower curtain was drawn and I was lathering up, she crawled out of dumpsters as I'd drive by, she'd try to take my hand when I walked home from school. She was my hallucination, my doppelgänger, and I thought I had it coming to me to scare myself.

There was one more crack-up, an attempt to overdose on aspirin and sleeping pills and gin. Well, that was my guess. I didn't think she'd slice her wrists, too much blood when there's a child in the house. Or maybe she simply quit, put down the oven mitt, closed her eyelids, slunk to the cold kitchen floor, and let the eddy of her misery swirl her off.

This time Gallagher called me. "Fiona's in the hospital. We won't need you this Thursday."

"OK."

"We'll let you know when we'll be back on schedule."

"Are they allowing visitors?" Who knew I'd had the nerve to ask?

"Family," Gallagher answered flatly.

That was one of the few times I loved myself, during that conversation, when I asked about seeing Fiona. I missed her, the sound of her coffee percolating, the refreshment of her perfume, the way she was sweet with me. The Plum Crazy Barracuda sat fading in her driveway.

Sad and completely excluded, I made Fiona a get-well card, carved the wood block myself, and stayed up past midnight to do it. Rays and rays of sunshine and a lone figure with arms outstretched. But by the time I'd decided what to say she had already returned home, so inside I quoted the part in "Chelsea Morning" about the sun pouring in and was too damn timid to even sign my name.

I delivered the card in person two weeks later. This time Fiona looked well. She was wearing a seafoam turtleneck and slim black pants with smart leather boots.

My card startled her, maybe it choked her up, maybe she was a bit ashamed of having been sick, but she quickly recovered, thanked me, placed the card on the glass shelf by the bar. There was something she wanted to show me.

Leading me by the hand—oh, her large, wonderful hand—into the dining room, as if afraid I'd scurry off, where a stack of sketch pads lay on the table, Fiona presented the drawings she had done in the hospital: a dead, bleeding raven, her right foot in a moccasin, and a self-portrait I swear I had seen in a daydream while she was away. In that portrait she stands in a white room in a white robe, her hair long and loose, her hands clutching her head as she faces a blue window, which is actually the sky. Then she showed me a wallet she had sewn in OT. We examined it, and I wanted to cry, I thought maybe they'd lobotomized Fiona, but then she burst open with laughs, and I wanted to cry more because she recognized the absurdity of her life. So maybe she would never make another leather wallet. It still made my heart feel droopy.

"I answered all the doctors' questions as honestly as I could," she explained to me after her laughter subsided. "I really wanted to get better, to be well."

"Did it work?" I whispered.

"We'll see," she said cheerfully.

Fiona told me her secrets! I could have done somersaults, but I was afraid my glasses would fall off. For one thing, there had never been any fetal position. The first time, Fiona had gone out in a blaze, having thrown the toaster at Gallagher, screaming, "I'm mad as Hell and I'm not going to take it," years before the movie *Network* was released. The more recent hospitalization was a placid event. Gallagher dialed her psychiatrist, Fiona got on the line, but could not speak, the hospital bed awaited her arrival.

I knew what it would take for her to get better. But I hadn't the impudence to tell her what was obvious.

Fiona was driving me home from baby-sitting, as usual, when she asked if I minded if we stopped in Hell so she could buy cigarettes. I was glad to spend time with her, said nonchalantly, "Fine with me," and she took the car down a steep, twisty, rain-slicked road. Coming out of the curve, where everyone else would still be braking and skidding, Fiona accelerated. She never lost control of the car, and she saw every disaster ahead of us, the squirrels by the roadside, the cars unyielding, the black ice, the child behind a hedge wanting to dart into the road.

After Fiona pulled cigarettes from the pizzeria's vending machine and we pulled back onto the road, I crumpled like a sigh in my seat. I hadn't been warned that was coming, though of course I knew I wanted Fiona's concern.

Resting my head against the door, I was thinking I had to quit the diner, let Eva have a fit. I couldn't bear the indignity of that uniform, even if it was just weekends.

Fiona pulled off to the side of the road. We were quiet for a moment, then she said, "You're very unhappy, aren't you?" For some reason Fiona's understanding made me feel sadder.

She brushed the hair off my forehead, and I turned to look at her out of one eye, a horse suspicious of a stranger. I noticed a peculiar but not unpleasant smell in the car as Fiona leaned toward me. Blood and molasses. I could see her coming, it was taking forever, like the slo-mo of a building collapse or the interminable seconds between when you trip and when you fall.

Hold me.

The spring rain began to let up, the roof quieted.

I smelled it again—blood, molasses. Was it the smell of her hair? Her breath? Was it menstrual stuff?

It was the mulch. Fiona had never taken the mulch out of the trunk, and in this humidity its perfume intensified.

And now Fiona's face was so close to mine I could see the individual hairs in her apostrophe eyebrows.

She kissed me. Gingerly. Her warm lips on my ear. The windshield wipers squealed. She put a hand behind my neck. She kissed me again. She kissed me skillfully, without knocking into my glasses. No one had been able to do that before. It was very considerate.

Fiona Gallagher kissed me. I thought I was going to pee in my pants. Suddenly I knew what it meant, a dog in heat. It was almost a whole-mouth kiss, but the corner is always sweeter anyway.

"I want to be your friend. Will that be all right?"

Fiona's kiss was a total-body experience, unlike the purely sexual kisses of John, the point of which was to remind me of that acre between my legs. But when Fiona kissed me, I felt my toenails sitting in their beds and a warm wash of blood attending to my legs, hip to ankle. My arms were limp, bones noodles, and in my brain, synapse telling synapse the great news.

I nodded yes, it would be all right if she became my friend. I knew it wasn't just friends, but what did you call it? All that came to my mind was that I'd be her dragon slayer, faithful and ever-present. A waterfall was ringing in my ears. Some people say they hear violins with a lover's kiss, but I always hear the crescendo of rebellion, street demonstrations, waves of blood crashing in my ears.

"Tell me, what is it Paige? You can talk to me about anything at all. Anything."

I was only 16. I felt as if I didn't know how to speak, how to assist the process of thought in the brain that transforms into words in the mouth. Fiona stroked my hair. She took my face in her hands. They were warm and sinewy and velvet. She looked into my eyes for something. I was hoping whatever it was was there.

The perfume of that evening was trapped in my hair, blood and molasses, and I'd been given everything I ever wanted while at the same time everything I ever wanted was teasing me, just out of reach. Desire hurt me in my body, there must be an emergency room protocol for treating longing.

HAVE YOU BEEN SERIOUSLY INJURED?

Not so much without speaking but in silence we continued on until we reached my house. Nothing changed. Even before her kisses I had always thought, *How could anyone not want to lay down their coat for someone kind like Fiona? How could you not want to see her every day you lived and died?*

She wouldn't say good night. I couldn't say it either. So we sat in the car, windows fogging us in, our heads against our headrests. How I wanted to know what she was thinking! Eventually, maybe five minutes later, Fiona inhaled deeply. I heard the air being sucked through her strong nose, and she placed her large, warm hand on top of mine.

Good night, I said quickly, before she could get rid of me. I threw my weight against the iron door of her car; being an average-size girl, I hadn't the proper leverage.

Once out of the car, I saw Annette Goldstein's bedroom curtains shift. They'd been parted, she'd been spying.

I walked on through the drizzle—it was effervescent on my skin—and I crossed my front lawn and didn't care that my father would scold me if he saw. It would have been a good thing to wear a path through the grass. We'd know we lived here, like giving a biography to footprints.

Fiona turned the car around and took it home.

When Jan and I were kids we used to play a game with Grandmother's grand piano, seeing who could make a note last the longest. It wasn't fair because I couldn't reach the pedals. Jan was good at it, every second of his massive D-note sounding like the deep ocean death of a whale. It made me want to cry when it was over. It was the same with Fiona's fading motor. You feel real small when it's gone.

I guess Fiona changed her mind.

Gallagher began driving me home after baby-sitting, no explanation. She'd walk in with the tennis racquets and, while dumping them in the coat closet, ask how Sean was and tell me Tom was waiting in the car, thank me, and march into the kitchen to make coffee. I can't say she was cold, not even indifferent. Something was missing, like she'd had amnesia about how she was supposed to be my friend.

Gallagher and I were spending more time talking to each other than Fiona and I were. A few times after baby-sitting, if they'd gotten home early enough, Gallagher would treat me to the movies, where he was careful not to spill one kernel of buttered popcorn, and I was careful not to let his Popeye forearm touch mine in our seats. And often on Saturdays Gallagher cruised down my street and found me heading to or from Hannah's. Fiona was stony in the passenger seat; Sean, a jumping bean in the back-seat; and Gallagher jovially invited me to join them for lunch at Vito's. That's when Fiona would come to smiling life and urge me to join them. If it was warm out she'd open her window and reach for my hands with both of her arms, give me a little squeeze, pull me toward the car. I thought that meant she wanted me to be her knight again.

At every opportunity Fiona would tell me I was so young. She'd use a word—*laconic, intrepid*—then turn to me and say, "You're so young, you probably don't even know what I'm talking about." She'd sing a golden oldie and shake her head because I had never heard it. She'd mention a car make, the Bel Air, the Nash, and smile wistfully because I had no idea what it looked like. Movie stars, dance steps, articles of clothing—I was of a foreign country and failed every test of recognition. Sock hop was all I knew, Eisenhower too. I understood perfectly why she was trying to insult me.

With my willpower I could avoid Fiona for a week, could make sure I saw her only from baby-sitting Thursday to baby-sitting Thursday. I didn't want to be a pest. I knew what it felt like to have a leech stick on to you because when I was in sixth grade a third grader leeched on to me, a little girl from down the block, Susannah Fahrenheit.

Every time I stepped out of the house, there was Susannah in her dirty knees and frilly jumpers. She didn't really bug me; she never whined, never asked me to buy her a troll or a Dixie Cup, and she wanted me to play cat's cradle with her only a few times, unlike some of the kids I baby-sat who insisted we play it over and over. The story on the block was that Mr. and Mrs. Fahrenheit punished Susannah by calling her "Retard!" and forcing her to sit in a steel tub filled with water in the utility room. Maybe that's why her skin was soft as rotten fruit.

Susannah smelled like milk and was just as vulnerable. I offered her Hershey bars and pineapple juice, but she accepted with apathy, was indifferent to anything I could offer except my company. I felt sorry for her. I didn't want Fiona to feel that way about me. A low profile was in order.

Then the Barracuda breathed down my neck as I was walking from school to Hannah's. I was going to ignore it, pretend I didn't see Fiona at the wheel, but she pulled into the oncoming traffic lane and kept pace with me until I looked at her.

"Come on in. I'll give you a lift." That was the point at which she should have called me an endearment. Honey. Sweetie. Cookie. But she didn't.

"That's all right. I'll walk."

"Paige, let me give you a ride."

I got in. Before putting the car in gear she looked at me long and hard, then zeroed in with a wet kiss on my face. I thought I'd had a pimple there, but if I did Fiona kissed right over it.

Fiona was in a talk-a-lot mood.

"You might want to consider doing some psychotherapy," she

said as we stopped behind a school bus. "It has done me a world of good, though I'm nowhere near done."

"There's nothing wrong with me." I meant that I was not disturbed by my obsession. I meant she shouldn't worry, I wasn't going to be a leech.

"You're sad. It might be good for you to talk to someone."

It was her I wanted to talk to.

"I can get you the name of someone I think you'd like."

For weeks after that Fiona kept needling me about seeing a psychiatrist. Good sign. The more urgent my getting a therapist was to Fiona, the more delighted I became. Clearly my seeing a psychiatrist would ease Fiona's conscience, which meant I wasn't simple for her, I wasn't just the baby-sitter. But maybe she wanted me to go to a therapist because she thought it was wrong for me to like her so much. But what if the doctor changed my mind about Fiona? Then what would I be left with?

With Fiona pushing so hard, I thought perhaps it was about time I got some special treatment from someone, so I agreed to see a shrink. Eva interfered.

Years ago, when my brother was still living at home, Mother, Papa, Jan, and I had gone to a family therapist. It had been my father's idea. No one ever said exactly why we were going, and I assumed it was because Jan and I were making too much noise in the house and not helping with chores or that Papa was having trouble with his forgetfulness and wanted to air his worries. Group therapy was the rage in those days, so of course Eva had to check it out.

At our first and only session, Papa did most of the talking, rambling about how his wife felt frustrated and furious because she wasn't getting any cooperation in the house, and he felt responsible for his forgetfulness, but his hands were tied. I think my parents must have talked to the therapist before we ever got there because next thing I knew, the guy was blaming 12-year-old me for everything, for being secretive and rude and unhelpful.

I was taken by complete surprise. I had thought I was normal and that my family liked me being the daughter. Jan was the only one who stood up for me. "It's not like that," he began, when the therapist interrupted him.

"Excuse me, Van...."

"It's Jan," my brother snarled.

"Jan, I understand you want to protect your sister," he said, cracking his hairy knuckles. "But that won't help us communicate better. Paige, do you have any thoughts about what I've said?"

"Are you talking about the chores?" I asked him. I could taste the venom in my saliva. It was green and nasty.

"What about the chores?"

"Why do I have to do all of them just because I'm a girl?"

"Why do I have to do all of them just because I'm a girl?" my mother mimicked.

Without reproaching my mother the therapist said, "But you are the girl, aren't you?"

I hated him, I hated my wimpy father, I hated my evil mother, and before I spat green stuff at their feet I ran from the office.

There I was, in downtown Flounder on a cold night feeling useless, ineffectual, a doll of myself rather than a living person. I heard the purposeful, far-off sound of the railroad. Where was it? I could lie across the tracks. The night clouds scudding overhead tried to spook me, but I didn't care. I could have run away, but then they'd just get hysterical and yell at me in the face. So, having forgotten my jacket inside, I shivered in the car seat until everyone finally came out. I saw Jan carrying my jacket over his shoulder. He got in the backseat with me and held my jacket out for me while I tried getting into it. He mussed my hair and blew down my back until I squirmed and nearly smiled.

No one spoke about what had happened except me. "I'm not going back," I said, refusing to giggle at Jan's tickling my ribs.

"Fine," Eva answered. "You don't have to be part of the family if you don't want to. See what that feels like. Just don't come to me for a ride to ice skating."

Fiona got me the referral from her psychiatrist, but I didn't call Dr. November right away. I kept her number in my change purse, where I also kept a butt from one of Fiona's Marlboros, a Mercury dime, a $10 bill, and a roach. I kept it like a charm. By the time I was ready to call I'd memorized the number and smoked the roach.

It was fairly easy talking to Papa about seeing a psychiatrist. I knew he'd be circumspect and not ask questions. Young woman stuff made him squirm, as did vehemence and crying. Papa said he would pay for me to see Dr. November, but I had to ask him three times because he didn't recall our having a private conversation, actually two conversations, about it.

My parents were driving me home from my consultation, and I actually was feeling pretty good because Dr. November said she thought I would get something out of therapy and because she was sort of glamorous, dark and lanky like a 1940s movie star, with a beehive hairstyle equally outdated. There was something eminently comforting about Dr. November. It wasn't a motherly thing; it was a tweedy, unpretentious thing. I was pestered by the thought that maybe I wanted to be in her office more than I wanted to solve any problems or admit whatever it was I was supposed to admit about Fiona Gallagher. But that would give me something to talk about during any nothing-to-talk-about sessions.

"So?" asked Eva in the car after my appointment.

"She said I should come back."

Eva went loco.

"You're not going back!" she screamed. She was so angry at me that I was afraid to look her in the face for fear she'd hit me. She was barking about dirty laundry and their vacation money and how I had my chance to do therapy but turned my back and now she was going to turn her back.

Of course I wanted to cry. So I told her to fuck herself.

"Eustace, stop the car." Papa gave her an anxious look, but Mother continued, "STOP RIGHT HERE!" and he obeyed her, pulling onto the shoulder, alongside a cemetery. "What did you say, young lady?"

I waited for Papa to jump in and make me apologize or try to cool Eva down. When he made no move to speak, I answered Eva, "You heard what I said." Eva ordered me out.

"Now, Eva," my father finally whispered.

"Get out of this car this instant!"

I shrugged my shoulders and got out.

If I slammed the door, she'd come after me. I wasn't afraid it would hurt; she never showed me her fist, and even if she grabbed me or yanked my hair, she couldn't hurt me. What I feared was that I'd puke if she touched me, afraid my skin would shrink tight if I even felt her breath on my face. I'd melt, shrivel up like a morel.

Papa drove slowly off. I saw him look for me in the rearview mirror.

Eva was screwed. She knew that having made me recklessly mad, there was nothing to stop me from confiding to Dr. November about her kicking me out of the car or about her boyfriend, the creep Jack Leever. Eva was afraid I would blame her for everything, afraid Dr. November would believe every word.

Too bad Eva didn't know how hard I tried to keep her out of my every conversation for fear she'd stink it up.

It was chilly for early spring and I was miles from home. It would take me almost two hours to walk it. With the Peugeot out of sight, I hitched a ride—straight to Fiona's.

To my five classmates, including the three Peters, who were accepted at Harvard, Yale, and Princeton, Miss Hitler sent congratulatory notes that included a certificate for a free pizza. The rest of us got nothing until the end of April, when the student office assistants entered every homeroom and handed out pencils in our school colors, embossed with the words GO, TIGERS!

Hannah recognized the unfairness of it and decided we should write a letter in response. At the critical moment, however, she backed out. The wise-guy note I sent Hitler was a retouched version of the letters she'd sent to the soon-to-be Ivy Leaguers.

Hitler's letter: *Congratulations! You're a superior junior-year student. The fruits of your hard work have ripened. During the next year, I hope you will feel free to stop by my office to discuss any college-related matters. Lindbergh High School is proud of you!*

My letter: *Gesundheit! You're an inferior infantile guidance counselor. The fruits of your idle hard work are rotting away. During the next year, I hope you will feel free to step into my locker to discuss any subversive matters. Paige Bergman is disappointed with you!*

I enclosed a photocopy of my SUNY acceptance letter. A big fat scholarship was also coming my way. Vocational school indeed! (The truth was, everyone who applied to the state university from Lindbergh got in.)

Some parents threw parties for their college-bound kids; in the Brook parents bought their kids sports cars. Peter got a Corvette Stingray, used, from the gas station owner in town. My parents were pretty low-key about it. "It's a good thing they're giving you a scholarship," Eva harrumphed.

Hannah's parents celebrated her admissions (every school she applied to accepted her) by taking her to Zorba's, a restaurant in the Brook with singing waiters. They invited me along. I managed a little *avgolemono*. Between the music and my hoping Fiona would walk in, I don't think I heard a word of conversation. In addition, the troubadour waiters had decided I was their mark and played song after song in my ear until I recognized a tune, the bouzouki version of "Over the Rainbow." By the time they disappeared, I was too embarrassed—and too mad at Hannah's parents for not shooing the waiters away—to eat another bite. I gave my untouched *rizogalo* to Hannah. "Mmm, I love rice pudding!" she said. I just shrugged and hoped her parents didn't want seconds on coffee, tempting the troubadours to return.

The next day I was suspended for insubordination (I'd say Hitler took it well, the suspension was only for one day). But after the incident she'd avert her eyes when she saw me in the hallway. I knew she felt guilty about playing favoritism, and I knew she couldn't tell if I had meant the letter to be mean or just creative juvenilia. Every time I saw her she looked like she was going to cry. I felt so bad and tried comforting her by giving my best smile, but I think she interpreted it as a curse.

All I had wanted to do was speak French. I had applied to the university because of Hannah, to spite Hitler, and because it was the only state school that offered a fully credited sophomore study-abroad program. But I wasn't sure I wanted to go upstate. It wasn't far enough away from Hell. I imagined bumming around the South of France for a year. Peter had said he'd go with me, but that was before I told him I didn't love him and before he'd gotten accepted at Harvard.

One way or another I was getting out of that town. Would Fiona miss me? I wanted her to.

Money was my immediate worry that junior year. The university's financial aid office determined that my parents would pay $1,500 for the first school year. A large scholarship and an on-campus job would cover the rest. Eva said I had to come up with a third of the money or she wouldn't pay a cent. For someone who wanted me out of the house, she was sure making things difficult.

Hannah's dad had lined up a summer job for her, as had most of my classmates' parents. Hannah would be taking inventory in her father's dress shop. It was air-conditioned. For part of the summer Peter and Peter would be working on the yacht Peter Mishmashkian's father dry-docked in Nantucket. Amelia, though her mother gave her $20 bills whenever she asked for money, got a job as an intern at a New York art gallery. During the week she'd be living with her mother's friend, the gallery owner, in an East Side town house. A postcard she would send me listed the contents of the lady's refrigerator: Danish cheese, caviar, cocktail olives, lime juice, Kodak film, an open can of cat food.

Since a number of high school students worked for their parents in town, summer in Hell had a bit of the fun house to it: Every shop contained a family tableau, a living portrait of the generations. At the delicatessen, the Gerhardts' son Francis poured coffee while his father sliced meat and his mother prepared sandwiches. The Zipper twins hauled manila folders up and down the courthouse stairs while Howard Zipper, Attorney-at-Law, explained torts and allowed them to sit in on criminal trials where defendants wore handcuffs. And every summer at least a dozen of us applied for a job with Dr. Cacciatoriani, the local vet, but he always gave the job to his eldest son, Steve, who'd rather have been taking life-drawing classes.

Everyone was innocent. They did not recognize the common morphology. The inheritance of noses, jowls, and a brooding brow made everyone sort of beautiful. Genetics, that was the true miracle.

Seeing my classmates with their parents made me feel a whole lot of tenderness for them. It's always like that, on Parents' Day in elementary school, visiting day at camp. Bullies and bombshells alike get cut down to normal size once you get a look at their parents. It works just as well for adopted kids.

Whenever we passed my classmates in the car, I cringed in my seat hoping I wasn't a family look-alike, hoping that if other kids saw me with my mother they'd think she was just a neighbor giving me a lift. It didn't matter to me that people found Eva attractive. John made me sick when he'd tell me how great she looked, especially for a mother. To me she stank, and my father's sleeping in the same bed with her made him just as disgusting.

No way was I going to see if there was work with Eva in the studio. Anyway, she had told me, "Most professionals won't want to hire you. What are your talents? Speaking high school French? You don't have any skills the studio guys could use. You're going to be in big trouble if you don't learn to type." I guessed that was true. Was my French going to get me a job hacking up bones at the Meat-O-Mat? Would it get me hired to trim mats at the historical society? And I failed the lie-detector test at the electronics store, though I told true answers to everything.

All I wanted to do that summer was learn how to drive, but I didn't dare ask because that would have evoked an unconditional *No!* from Eva.

"Wait tables again," Eva recommended. "You'll make a bundle in tips." She said she'd give me two weeks to secure summer work, then dropped me off at the dentist's.

Two weeks. I never think ahead like that. When Eva does, it ruins everything. Why does she have to tell me as soon as I come home from school that I have to set the table when we won't be eating for another three hours? It just makes me grumpy for the rest of the afternoon. And I just couldn't wait tables for another summer. Now that everyone was driving, sooner or later some kids from my school would come into the diner. If they recognized me, I'd be mortified in that hair net.

"More gas," I told my dentist.

"You seem upset," Fiona said. I heard a tinge of impatience in her voice. "Is there something you want to talk about?"

"I don't know." My tongue was dead in my mouth. It had been a struggle to speak even those three words.

"Is Dr. November working out for you?" We were on another cruise through Hell, the baby-sitting money folded into my book, Nancy Milford's *Zelda*.

Fiona was bugging me. She was restless, shifting in her seat. She wanted me to be satisfied with Dr. November so I wouldn't have to be her responsibility.

"Paige, you know you have to give it your best shot, be as honest as you can."

So what if I exaggerated about using heroin? So what if I refused to discuss Fiona Gallagher? She never talked about me to *her* psychiatrist! All I needed was Dr. November's concern, which had been what I wanted from Fiona. But Fiona never called me except to arrange baby-sitting. And she saw my room only once and did not linger, acting as if, as Papa would say, she had ants in her pants, though she said she liked my posters. It seemed that if I wasn't standing right in front of her, she forgot about me completely. What would I have to do? Jump in front of her oncoming vehicle my whole life?

Have you been sleeping OK? How long have you been disinterested in your schoolwork? Did you vomit much as an infant? Everything Dr. November asked made me buoyant. The tone of her voice alone, it was sumptuous, and I sank into it as if into deep sleep. How could I possibly tell her the truth? Everything was too embarrassing. That I hated my mother? How stereotypically adolescent. That I ripped my skin until it bled? How revolting. That my yearning for Fiona Gallagher was heliotropic, that I turned toward her the way the suntan ladies turn toward the sun? How blatantly mother-figure.

Unhappiness was the most embarrassing of all. With Dr. November I didn't pretend to be cheerful, but I certainly wouldn't let myself look down in the dumps. Instead, I perfected indifference, became cavalier, though I admitted saving children and animals from sinking in the sea was a cause to die drowning for.

All the time I was desperate to talk about Fiona. I didn't know how to begin. But in the day-bright hours, when the Barracuda menaced Hell, when I stood by myself in the street watching Fiona dance in her kitchen, I knew exactly what I wanted. I never heard of anyone wanting this from another person. I was ashamed. But that never stops desire, does it?

With Fiona I camouflaged the misery, though not well. Instead of answering her question about whether Dr. November was helping me, I changed the subject. Do you think I would admit my longing to her, say I wanted more than anything, more than the Publisher's Clearinghouse Sweepstakes or a Sorbonne scholarship, for Fiona simply to lie on top of me and kiss me all over my face? It was such a preposterous fantasy that half the time I didn't even recognize it as my own.

"I have to find a good summer job. I need to make $500 or else I can't go to college." Fiona tried to check her disappointment. I saw her expression go blank. She thought I was avoiding something, that I wasn't telling her the whole truth about why I was miserable. She wanted to hear something else from me. But what did I know?

Recovering from the letdown, the frustration, she asked, "Why aren't your parents paying for your education?"

"They think it's my responsibility."

"Well, at least you'll have your independence. I envy you for standing on your own feet." I thought that was weird since she did all this stuff on her own—have a baby, have an abortion, cook a turkey, drive at night, write a check, use birth control—that seemed daunting to me.

She put the car in drive. "I'll talk to Tom," she said after a moment. "He'll find you something."

$$\large(14)$$

A good fast driver is like the Lord unsleeping,
 he never kills and he is never killed;
 when he dies, someone else is always driving.
—Robert Lowell, "For Archie Smith: 1917-1935"

Fiona got me a job! Though I had to speak with Gallagher about the terms, Fiona had saved me from the humiliating part, having to ask for work. I could slap my thigh, if I were a thigh-slapping guy, from the pleasure I got every time Fiona understood me. The subservience of waitressing was over.

Tom would pay me $150 a week for four weeks. It was nepotism, make-work, obvious from the start. I would help with phones, paperwork, whatever was needed around the office, and at every possible opportunity I was to tutor his stock man in English. Gallagher would give me a lift to work in the morning, and on the way home he'd teach me how to drive. In the ship of his car, I learned how to get myself free.

Our first day out, a divine benevolence kept me from plunging us down the embankment and bumpering the Nova in the left lane. Gallagher seemed not to notice our peril. Or maybe he enjoyed my ineptitude, the spectacle of the largest car on the road weaving across three lanes. Maybe he was trying to get rid of me, a bedbug in his home. It seemed as if Gallagher wouldn't have worried had I *tried* to smash up the car. Why he didn't tense up was a mystery to me. Hannah, then in her Marxist phase, said it was because he thought his money could get him out of any scrapes—what was another new Cadillac to him? It was a Lincoln, I told her.

The backs of my T-shirts were absolutely drenched with sweat those driving-lesson days, which ought to be accorded the same recognition as birthdays or baptismal dates. They were the days that gave me the nightmares I've had my whole life.

It's driving itself, this shimmying Continental, yawing down the road despite my grasping the steering wheel steady at 10 o'clock and 2 o'clock. Sometimes I'm driving from the backseat where there are, of course, no brakes. Sometimes when there are brakes they don't respond, though I'm throwing my whole weight onto the pedal, pushing with my arms against the seat. Sometimes I'm driving so fast, and I know it'll kill me, but I won't slow down no matter how much I want to.

Those dreams are as harrowing as the ones where my teeth fall into my mouth and I spit them out like Chiclets. I thought Dr. November would be interested in those dreams, but she remained impassive until the day she finally said, "Are you familiar with the theory of castration anxiety?" Don't you wish Americans used the word *bosh*? The dreams are the body's memory of life in motion, a reminder of the horrendous trust we put into motor vehicles. If Dr. November means I fear things are out of control, why doesn't she just say so instead of bringing testicles into it?

An automobile is a loaded gun. I've seen wreckage on the highway, I've read A *Death in the Family*, I know you might never get home again.

There was something fishy about Gallagher Outdoor Furniture. First of all, I never had heard of an outdoor furniture store. Everyone in Hell went to Sears for picnic tables or got lawn chairs by saving enough Green Stamps. Second, I never saw more than two customers at a time in the showroom. Third, the only work Gallagher had to do was autodial the phone and shout business words into it: SKUs, High Point, occasionals, inventory, fiduciary. Once or twice a week he'd meet his father, who founded the business, for a three-hour lunch, then leave for the day, which meant I got to go home early too. Gallagher senior told dirty jokes with a fake Irish accent to the women on staff. His skin was earwax-yellow, and he smelled putrid, as if he carried dead mice in his pockets. I don't know how Gallagher's employees could accept his embraces. He must have given Christmas bonuses.

"In the old days we sold accessories. Gnomes and madonnas, sundials, birdbaths, you name it," Gallagher senior announced to no one in particular. "We did damn good business."

"It was a junkyard," Gallagher responded, chomping on a cigar and flipping through pink slips of phone messages, his back turned to his father. "All that stone crap surrounding the store scared people off. No, it wasn't a junkyard. It was a cemetery, Pop. Nothing sold." His father smiled, shrugged.

Gallagher spent most of the workday outside the office. I don't think he ever used his desk, an oak conference table so highly polished you could see yourself in it. There was nothing on the table (which is where I sat, alphabetizing invoices and reading *The Tin Drum*) except a telephone and two photographs: one of his son, one of his wife, which was taken before I had met Fiona. Everyone says Mrs. Gallagher looks like a movie star in that picture, and they mean it; they're not just trying to flatter the boss. That photo so proud on his desk was Gallagher's proof of ownership and I hated it, the Fiona who didn't give me a second thought. Whenever I sneaked a look at it, I remembered that she kissed me and I felt like a felon. *Criminel.*

There were no files, in/out trays, letter openers, pens, or paper-weights, no drawers or typewriter. Suited up, pomaded and smelling fresh, Gallagher sat behind his vast empty desk, smack in the middle of the length of it, and yelled, hollered, screamed, and pounded his directives to his employees while fingering his phone messages, deciding whom to call and whom to keep waiting. His telephone had been equipped with an intercom and all his employees' extensions were listed on the face of it, but he bellowed nevertheless. What a Humpty Dumpty. I waited for the phone to ring in his office, for his voice to soften when it was Fiona, for Fiona to ask him how I was doing. She never did ask. I didn't know whether that was a deliberate subterfuge or whether I was nothing once again, a blank in her brain.

It's not even debatable how much English I ended up teaching his stock man, but I had tried my best. It would have helped if he'd been a French speaker, but what had Gallagher known about languages? Portuguese sounded like French to him.

Gallagher surprised me by being an easy boss. He left me alone; he ignored me, in fact. He screamed obscenities at his employees when I was in the showroom, turned the air-conditioning up so high I had to wear my winter sweater to work, tossed me a roast beef hero with Russian though I didn't eat meat. Every day I spent with him should have brought me closer to Fiona, but it only magnified being apart.

If it wouldn't have been impolite, I'd have asked how Gallagher made so much money with this one silly store. I thought organized crime must have had a hand in his success. I don't know what set him off, but driving home after work one day, Gallagher went on this monologue about the business he'd built from his father's dinky store into an empire of patio and pool furniture. "Really?" "Wow!" and "That's great!" were my comments. It was still hard for me to drive and have a conversation at the same time.

Now I see Gallagher Outdoor Furniture franchises wherever I go. Gallagher gets richer. People will always need the beach umbrella, the rustproof chaise lounge, the hammock. Where's the real competition? I once heard Annette Goldstein tell Sean he'd inherit a lot of money one day, but how could she know? Sean could have lived a short life, Gallagher could've put his money in cyclamates. You never know.

After two weeks of great automobile luck steering the Lincoln home from work, I had just pulled out of the parking lot when Gallagher said, "OK, Celestine, turn onto the parkway." Papa used to say that parkway had more S's in it than Mississippi, though Jan pointed out that four isn't so many. There was no shoulder, only a ravine on the right and oncoming traffic on the left, no guardrail between us, just a strip of grass. Learner's permits were not allowed on the parkway. Gallagher was aware of that, but everything with him was life of Riley. He told me to head south.

I took on the parkway.

Passing a car in the right lane with scalpel certainty, I suddenly realized I was living at a higher temperature. I was unafraid of trouble, punishment, failure, and I was crazy about the adventure with my body. When I was that age, my body took good care of me, even at 85 miles per hour, though some say I was reckless.

"Good reflexes," Gallagher muttered. "That's how you take a corner." I understood driving thoroughly. Like horse and rider, car and driver were one. When I took my DMV driving test, I was calm almost to the point of indifference, and I passed with a perfect score, especially enjoying the U-turn.

Hannah was the worst driver in the world. She failed her driving test three times. When she passed on the fourth go, I asked her if the DMV wrote a restriction, "Must drive with flashers engaged," on her license. Hannah pouted for about five minutes. After that she always asked me for advice while she was behind the wheel: Should she slow down, was it OK to turn here, was there anyone in the left lane, when should she turn on her turn signal, could she fit into that parking space?

She couldn't even keep the car in her lane. She slammed on the brakes every time an oncoming vehicle approached. She'd talk aloud to cars merging into her lane, "Don't cut in front of me I'm not stopping just wait your turn." She'd honk when she went through an intersection on a green light. She scraped the car against the stanchion at the gas pump. She nearly hit a traffic cop. She knocked over rubber cones. She drove with the right tires in the shoulder. She tried to make her car very skinny by holding her breath whenever she had to squeeze through a space such as a toll or a drive-thru bank. And she never slowed down—she just stopped. I got out of her Pinto with a kink in my neck every time.

Nerve-racking as it was to be her passenger, I wasn't worried about being killed. My father would have said it was because I was just being a kid—a stupid kid, Eva would add—who, like all kids, thinks she's immortal. But it wasn't like that. No fairy had told me I was safe. And it certainly wasn't that I had underlying confidence in Hannah, the most uncoordinated person in the universe. It's just that I wasn't *afraid* of being killed, not that I thought it impossible.

Sooner or later it had to happen, and when it did, I was in the passenger seat.

Watching her make that mistake was chilling, far worse than the hollow boom of metal against metal or the shrieks of the Goodriches. To this day I wonder whether there had been enough time for me to stop her or whether instead I let her crash.

A good Samaritan hustled to my side of the car, yelling, "Are you hurt? Are you hurt?" while some lady in a hat started screaming when she saw the blood on the windshield.

It was only ketchup. My French fries had flown all over the car. Something from the backseat (I later learned it was a cigar box) beaned me in the head, and I conked out into charcoal darkness for a few seconds. But no one had been seriously injured. I wished otherwise. Stitches down my face. Plaster cast. Black eye. Fiona wouldn't be able to help noticing, and how brave I'd be. I'd have had an excuse for getting Fiona's attention and an excuse to be not-speaking-to mad at Hannah.

Poor Hannah. She'd had a moment of confusion, mistaking the gas pedal for the brake in the Pathmark parking lot. We had rammed a station wagon; a line of shopping carts ricocheted into the supermarket's brick wall. The Pinto's front end was relatively intact, except for the bumper and headlights. The passenger-side door of the station wagon would have to be replaced. Yet not a single egg broke in the collision (I checked the groceries to hide my face while the other driver ridiculed Hannah, which was more painful for Hannah than it would have been had the woman simply socked her).

"What the hell were you doing? Are you retarded? You could

have killed me you stupid hippie freak...." The good Samaritan led her away, calmed her, fobbed her off on the store manager who came out to survey the damage, and returned to us for Hannah's insurance information. Hannah was shaking and crying, so I drove the bashed-up Pinto home, at about ten miles an hour, and carried her mother's groceries into the kitchen.

I would have been afraid to tell my parents. I'd have to make up some lie about the accident, but Hannah's parents were bad drivers themselves. For them, dents and dings were part of the normal wear and tear of driving. They said if the car needed major work it was good for local employment. (Hell had two body shops, Flounder three.)

Drivers are ducklings, skill often an imprint, as imitative as Lorenz's water paddlers. Driving personality and ability develop in accordance with the type of driver to whom you've most frequently been exposed. Ages 14 to 16 are most impressionable, when you've become aware that cars are not simply appendages of parents and that your responsibility for them looms ahead. When your father (or, in my case, Gallagher) lets you start the ignition for the first time, you are heart-racingly afraid. You are petrified, the world is too much, brake clutch accelerator look behind you rearview mirror side-view mirror yellow light curve ahead don't forget to signal yield merge no shoulder no standing no parking illegal to pick up hitchhikers falling rocks bridge freezes first school zone yield to pedestrians stop no stopping.

My parents were unremarkable drivers. Neither had ever had an accident, nor did they have any bad habits such as speeding, running red lights, neglecting to signal turns, or tailgating. They usually got the parallel parking down on the second try but more often than not were too far from the curb. Because they were considered low risk by their insurance carrier, they had reasonable premiums, so they refused to teach me to drive in the Peugeot. I had to get my license first, and then they would think about teaching me to drive a stick. But how was I going to get my license without a car in which to practice?

Clearly they were resentful when Gallagher put me in the driver's seat, and Eva was even cooler when I opened my mail and showed her my license.

Eva taught me in three lessons. I learned quickly because she was so disparaging. Every time I pulled up at a stop sign, she'd act as if I'd given her whiplash. Every time I picked up speed, she'd grip the roof with her hands and tell me through clenched teeth that I was going too fast. And even though my shifting was smoother than Papa's, she ended the lesson by complaining, Now we're going to have to get a new clutch.

Even once I did learn standard shift, they rarely lent me the car. "You'll have to ask your mother," Papa dithered, and out of plain old nastiness Eva said, "You have to understand it's our insurance. You're not covered, and we can't afford any accidents." All Jan had to do was ask and the car was his, even if Mother had to rearrange her plans and have Annette Goldstein give her a lift somewhere. It didn't matter that Jan, always squealing around corners to impress people, had crashed into a trash can, backed into Dr. Goldstein's Mercedes, cracking a taillight, and stripped the gears, all within two months of gaining his license.

Why quarrel with them, why bring Jan into it? Fighting a losing argument was as embarrassing as mispronouncing a word in front of Fiona. Anyway, they were probably right. I *was* unpleasant to be around, as Eva said over and over, so why did I deserve to borrow their car?

I didn't. But I got around that.

For some unfathomable reason, perhaps just to be contrary,

Amelia refused to learn to drive. Nevertheless, once home from work her mother would always lend her the car—for me to drive. Her mother rarely used the car for anything beyond getting to and from the studio where she taught printmaking. She walked into town to do her grocery shopping, walked to the tennis courts, walked to the dentist. She cut her own hair and mostly stayed home tending her compost heap, cooking chicken soup with the whole chicken, head and claws sticking out of the pot, smoking her pipe, and reading her paper, periodicals, and mail.

Amelia's mother lent me the car regardless of whether Amelia needed a lift somewhere or preferred to stay home sketching naked men with her rapidograph, puffing on her hash pipe, and playing for the millionth time her Janis Ian and Iron Butterfly records. Her mother's only hesitation, and it was one she voiced each time, was that she thought teenagers were becoming too dependent on cars and that we should walk more. Since I had to walk the two miles to her house and back, Amelia's mother gave me the keys and toothless lecture, then retired to her easy chair.

I made sure Eva knew that someone who wasn't even my mother trusted me with her car and tried to make it available at my convenience. Big deal if I had to walk the two miles home. Sometimes I would run into Fiona, and she'd give me a lift.

I was the best girl driver in school and just about as crazy as the boys, though not as aggressive, never pretending to run someone down in the parking lot. I anticipated dangers—a child darting out of the hedges, a skid, a blind curve, a bicyclist spilling over—and could handle a Lincoln as well as Amelia's Toyota. I was the broncobuster of internal combustion. When I was behind the wheel, a car became my skin. It felt like all I had to do was think the car negotiating a curve or passing a vehicle on a one-lane blind-turn road and it was cleanly executed. I did drive fast, so fast that I once outran a traffic cop who'd summoned me to pull over. The pick-up drag races in the school parking lot? Never lost a single one, even in Amelia's mother's tinny V-4 Toyota. Speeding gave me a sense of excellence. And it enabled me to take my life into my own hands and challenge Fiona as an equal.

I had met her face-to-face on the road. She was making a left-hand turn onto the road I was about to turn right onto. I honked. She cut out in front of me. I ran after her in the Peugeot.

The road was a steep two-way climb with two sharp curves that made this particular part of it a perfect S. She was making headway in front of me in the Barracuda, I behind in the Peugeot, but not for long. I downshifted, pushed the pedal quick and hard, and veered sharply into the left lane of oncoming traffic. I could have passed Fiona cleanly, but I wanted to keep up the joyful daring. When I'd positioned myself side by side with the Barracuda, I looked directly at Fiona, saw her smile at me, shake her head as if to say I was incorrigible. She then slowed down, a maternal and graceful thing to do, so I could creep safely back into the right lane. But I remained like that, by Fiona's side for nearly ten seconds, parallel driving, ice dancing. When a telephone-repair van approached me head on, I sped up to it, then cut in front of Fiona and drove as if I were a motorcade leading her home. In her driveway she approached me with a sly smile and stood for a few seconds just looking at me, grinning. Suddenly she threw her arms around me and held tight. I'd almost lost my balance and could feel the rivets on her jacket impaling my neck. I was not too shy to hug her back, but I stood there, hands by my sides, in astonishment of my own happiness. Fiona did not let go until she'd rested her head on my shoulder for a second and her hair brushed across my eyelids. Then she caressed me further by placing her cheek against mine and hugging harder. Only the birth of babies gets me to smile that way now.

"You're playing Russian roulette," Dr. November lectured when I boasted my skill. I shrugged. So what? Maybe I did sometimes get mad as hell, but I was too good a driver to crack up. And I was ecstatic that she recognized my peril. But then it occurred to me that perhaps she was talking about my feelings for Fiona, which though unarticulated are written right there on the patient's forehead, if the psychiatrist is worth anything. I wasn't about to cease: Intuitively I sensed things would become glorious between us, we'd drive off and never come back. In the meantime, we would spend our days driving around in Hell.

I loved parallel parking, downright balletic with power steering. Cranking the Toyota's steering wheel into a parking space was a coup. I have to thank Gallagher for that. He taught me a systematic approach to parallel parking, and it took me only two trys to get the formula down. He'd said flatly, "That's it." That was a huge compliment. I was two inches from the curb.

My braking technique was velvet. This I learned from Fiona. I could take the most decrepit jalopy or a ton of overstuffed Lincoln into an adagio stop so smooth you wouldn't even notice you were no longer moving. I perfected this to spite Eva.

When I had told Gallagher I passed the driving test he'd said, "What did you expect?" I gave him a Chieftains album. He liked it, though I did it as a joke since all he knew about the Irish was the saga of the Kennedys in Hyannis. In fact, he drove Fiona crazy with the album, playing it over and over for four weeks straight.

Gallagher could be annoying. His constant finger tapping on the kitchen table. His mindless eating, devouring the whole bunch of grapes as if it were one serving just because you could pick them up in one hand, as if they were a single piece of fruit. His tailgating. His rudeness with waitresses. His loud voice. His bad taste (he once came home with a bedside lamp made out of a parking meter). His obsession with gadgetry. His inability to let a subject drop. Fiona was generally a patient woman, or maybe she was just preoccupied and didn't notice his eccentricities. But sometimes she cracked. Once she broke a plate of corned beef over his head because he was badgering her about his right to pick his toes at the kitchen table, a subject they had already put to bed. "I don't care where you play out your foot fetish," she'd said. "But it's really irritating to have to go over this again and again." Gallagher persisted. "Where better to perform my ablutions? Who wants toenail clippings in the bed?" Snip snip snip.

"Tom, if you don't stop, I'm going to smash this plate on your head." Gallagher could be maddening. She'd given him fair warning, but he persevered. I stayed with Sean while they went to the hospital for stitches.

I didn't want Fiona to love Gallagher, I'm ashamed to admit it, and I used to think that's what made them have big arguments. Clearly it had to be something other than his finger tapping and public pedicures.

"We have a name for that," says Dr. November. "It's called 'magical thinking.'" I think she's very smart, but my imagining that the Gallaghers had vocal disagreements because I wanted them to is not delusional. People have powers.

Arriving for baby-sitting, I often heard bedroom fights, Gallagher's voice getting high, Fiona cursing, someone hitting pillows and kicking walls. The violent one was not Gallagher. But he didn't have to be: He was 250 pounds of unmovable flesh.

During one fight Fiona put her foot through the oil portrait, which she told me had been painted shortly after their honeymoon. Another time she heaved the portable TV through the storm door. Gallagher told his tennis partner, Dr. Goldstein, about it, and Annette Goldstein blabbed it to the neighbors, which included Eva. Since it was pretty obvious to me that she was trapped in the wrong life, I didn't think it horrendous behavior at all, especially since Sean hadn't been home to see. It must have felt good, I even said to Fiona. It did, she smiled, adding it was a stupid thing to do, Tom was a good egg.

I sulked when she said that, feeling reprimanded. Fiona understood. She reached for my hand. "If you had been here, I wouldn't have gotten so angry," she said, lugging me to her for a hesitant hug. Everything sweet she said to me took me by surprise.

"We're unhappy together," she sighed one night in the car, and I didn't know if she was talking about me and her or Gallagher and her, and I sure didn't ask. Instead, I sat there hoping hoping hoping she would do something, lie on top of me like I was dreaming, say something magic.

Try as he might, Gallagher could never outstare her black eyes. It was probably a human impossibility. While I didn't doubt Gallagher deserved her anger, I couldn't figure out why they had married in the first place. And even more perplexing, why, after so many arguments, did she let him put his arms around her and kiss her on the nose?

Having completed my four boring weeks of work, the rest of July and August spread out before me and sparkled like an ocean. The summer was begging me to come out and play. But my good friends were gone. Summer disappears people.

Hannah's father had given her three weeks off in July. She would have preferred to work, but he wanted her to "get some great outdoors" and sent her on a bike tour along the Eastern Seaboard.

Amelia found the gallery a bore and was now off doing France-Spain-Germany-Italy, though somehow I got a card from her postmarked Athens. Her mother was a broken record telling us that when a woman has her own money she doesn't need a man. Amelia's parents had been divorced for 12 years, and her mother never had one single date after that. All she did was work, play tennis, and read newspapers. When I asked her how do you get all that money, she put her pipe in her mouth and walked away. The question I should have asked her is: What's wrong with needing a man? At the time I thought she just wasn't interested in sex.

A lot of kids spent the summer in Hell. We worked during the day and gathered like rats at night, skulking out of our parents' homes and, as unobtrusively as possible, walking the streets until we'd hear of a party or a house where the parents were not home.

In August they'd leave for their homes in Nantucket, but for June and July the three Peters (Peter Mishmashkian, Peter Gulderberger, Peter Cacciatoriani) were home taking science courses at a nearby community college. Peter and his older brother Steve were left with the house, the Mustang, the dog, and a freezer full of food while their parents yachted around Portugal. I went to the summer parties with them and talked Peter through a bad acid trip, ate too many burnt hash brownies, skinny-dipped in Peter's illuminated pool in the Brook, and had been ushered into one too many of their bedrooms, impressed that the walls were painted black, that they had resplendent stereo systems, that they'd grown hair under their arms, and that even the peewee now had rippling abdominal muscles.

The guys were nice enough. But the mere idea of having one

of my friends kiss me was unspeakably uninteresting, made me want to spit. Steve, Peter's brother, was handsome in that Jesus-hippie way, but I couldn't flirt—it was too hot that summer. And romance would have distracted me from Fiona.

What did I want from Fiona? Well, what were the choices? I did not want to be her daughter. I did not want to be her spouse. I did not want to be her sister. I did not want to be her friend.

I wanted...to live my life twisted up with hers. What's that called? What's it called when you like a person's smells as much as you like your own—the cozy smell of the scalp, onions and maple syrup on the breath, perspiration in a silk shirt? I wanted to be swaddled by that bucket seat, driving a long time to nowhere with her and not worrying about how soon saying good night would be. I wanted to know if she liked pie. I wanted to see whether she was still beautiful when the shower plastered her hair to her head. I wanted to compare her face with her mother's, to watch her try on shoes, to see how she applied makeup, to hear her voice when she speaks to her big sister on the phone.

I wanted to ask *someone* whether Fiona liked me. Just because she invited me to dinner didn't mean I was so special—surely Pansy had been invited numerous times, as had neighbors and unpleasant relatives. And some days, being in that Fiona fog, she'd seem to barely remember me. A conversation with her was as frustrating as those new fuel-injected engines, the disconcerting lag between the time you punch the pedal and the time the car bucks in response. Anyway, dialogue never was our strong point.

No matter. We understood the stuff inside each other, the stuff that makes reasonable people weep.

There was only one person whom I could ask, "Do you think she really likes me?" and it was Sean, second-grader Sean.

Sean clapped wildly and cooed when Fiona asked me to stay for dinner. I'd arrived early—it was Thursday, tennis night—having promised Sean I'd help him practice his two-wheeler on Chestnut Street.

Over stuffed peppers, definitely the nerdiest food ever put before a teenager, Gallagher asked, "Don't your parents mind that you're never home for dinner?" I thought he was trying to tell me I didn't belong at his dinner table. But on the chance that he was actually curious about my family situation, I responded, though I don't think I told Gallagher the truth. I was afraid to tell him I really didn't know how my parents felt about it. I thought he'd shoo me home, seeing as I hadn't had my parents' approval.

"Isn't your mother a good cook?" Gallagher persisted.

"Tom!" said Fiona, exasperated.

Actually, Eva was a great cook. Our spice cabinet held more intrigue than I'd ever seen in anyone else's kitchen. The neighbors had ketchup, molasses, food coloring, and Wesson Oil; Eva's redolent stock came from Hungary, Madagascar, Spain, Jamaica, Indonesia—coriander, marjoram, threads of saffron, lovage, vanilla beans, dry mustard, lemongrass, hearts of palm. When Jan and I were in grammar school, steak sandwiches with ketchup instead of the requisite bologna were packed in our lunch boxes. Swedish potato dishes, buttery desserts, and home-baked bread (though it was Papa who proofed the dough and Papa who forgot it burning in the oven) caused envy among housewives. But this is how I felt about eating at home: I hated it. Eva mocked me for refusing her lamb chops but wearing leather sandals. Papa sometimes seemed unsure of whose kid I was—a neighbor's? a friend of Jan's? a foreign exchange student?—drinking a tumbler of water at his table. Eva gave me all the chores except the one I wanted, shoveling the snow from the driveway; that was men's work. Whether it was clearing the table, scrubbing pots and pans, or loading the dishwasher, Eva would observe my every move, a prison guard with bayonet eyes. She did it when she made me vacuum and rake the yard too.

The few dinnertimes when I didn't despise my parents, it tore me up to look at them. Eating noodles one night, heads bowed over spaghetti bowls like penitents, they looked defenseless, vulnerable. I watch anyone eat, especially something tricky, noodles or lettuce leaves or a club sandwich, and see if I don't feel pity. That's why I never give someone bad news over dinner—it's malicious.

Eating in company is intimate behavior. Of necessity you're an exhibitionist, pleasuring yourself with mashed potatoes or something as sophisticated as an artichoke, your dining companions getting a glimpse of you every now and then gratifying yourself. The utmost trust is required: You can't afford to allow poison or a fork in the heart to interfere here. This is the most crucial service we perform—don't eat, you're dead.

Though I was pretty confident Eva wouldn't add a pinch of weed-killer in my tuna sandwich or stab me at the dinner table, I wasn't comfortable having her watch me feed myself. It felt as if she were doing it through a keyhole.

"They don't care what I do," was what I answered Gallagher, leaving it to him to judge Eva's culinary abilities. I certainly wasn't going to praise her. "Anyway, I don't eat much," I added so Fiona wouldn't urge more food on me and be offended when I refused, gagging on my own hunger.

Fiona was looking at me with a cocked head. It seemed she was trying to peer up my nose, but I had learned it was just a way of listening to me, not necessarily to my words.

At least twice a week the Gallaghers hosted me for dinner, which I didn't eat much of because what if I threw up or choked or skidded my carrots across the table? Always I offered to help clear the dishes but was told, a firm hand on my shoulder, "Sit."

It was Gallagher's birthday. We'd had scrod and spinach, stank up the house. Gallagher said he didn't understand fish, meat was what made a meal complete. Lobster would do too. Fiona paid no attention whatsoever. She served me a wad of her cucumber salad. By the way she looked at me as she approached with the serving spoon, I knew she wanted me to take a risk, to devour the food for once. I stabbed the slices of cucumber with my fork, building myself a two-inch bite that covered the tines of my fork and, with Fiona watching with amusement, opened wide and crunched. It was good. I smiled, she smiled, and then it was even better. Sean had been openmouthed at my feat. Gallagher was relieved he didn't have to be the clown for once. We were happy together, a tuning-fork contentment.

Fiona loaded the dishwasher and ran the garbage disposal while I read *Stuart Little* to Sean and answered his *why* questions. "Why is it raining?" "Why do my parents fight?" "Why can't you go to camp with me?" Gallagher peeled out of the driveway. He was playing in the men's doubles tournament.

Fiona came up to kiss Sean good night and utter mothery reassurances. Meanwhile I worked on translations in the faux-Breuer chair in the master bedroom. Like most newcomers to Hell, the Gallaghers had recently renovated their house—added fireplace, skylights, mullioned windows, walls broken through to expand the master bedroom. It was the master bedroom that became the sitting room, the living room for in-laws and cocktails. I'd felt comfortable in the bedroom, not only because Fiona hung a Kandinsky over the bed and the Miami Beach gold bamboo-patterned wallpaper didn't rise above the kitchen level, but also because I was familiar with the room, having sat there holding Fiona's hand until she fell asleep.

After she put Sean to bed and kissed his ears, she began to get herself ready for bed. I sat watching her every move. She ran a hand through her fluffy hair, and she was a French movie star. She threw her head back like a thoroughbred to swallow a pill. She grew distracted and distant from me when she answered the telephone. I was on tenterhooks, *sur des charbons ardents*. At any minute Fiona might explode, kick me out, good riddance kid, though she never was so rude (a single yawn could tell me all that bad news and wordlessly), or she might ask me to stay until the pills took effect.

Lying on the carpet, a hand supporting her head, she smoked a bedtime cigarette. Then she rose, did stuff in the bathroom that involved splashy water and the Water Pik hum. I waited with my Baudelaire and pen. It took forever.

Fiona returned in an ice-gray satin nightie. It must have shrunk in the wash. The only thing that could have made it look more ridiculous was bunny fur trim. I noticed for the first time that she had a little limp, barely noticeable. Perhaps she'd stepped on a thumbtack that morning. I had begun to scrutinize Fiona rather than avert my deep gaze out of politeness.

"How absurd do I look in this?" she said, reading my thoughts.

She was laughing as she whirled around 360 degrees pretending she had penguin feet.

As usual, Fiona warned me that the sleeping pill would make her "stupid" and I shouldn't pay attention to anything she said. I read into everything when I was a teenager, so was I not supposed to pay attention to that? She was telling me not to believe a word she said. She was telling me to pay close attention.

The sleeping pills walled her away from Gallagher. But I didn't want her to go to sleep. I wanted her to stay up all night with me.

Having taken her medicine she motioned me to the bedside. "Paige," she mumbled, "you're very special. Do you know that?"

That night, instead of our routine, Fiona mumbling her life story (which rarely went further than two or three sentences before decomposing into nonsense) or cautioning me about drugs or admitting how inadequate she felt, I was the one who spoke, who lullabyed her with a fairy tale, in French, *La Belle au Bois Dormant*. Fiona fell off to sleep with a faint smile instead of her serious, faraway face. She would continue to do so whenever I talked her to sleep, even if I spoke someone else's words, someone else's language.

Where was Gallagher all those Mother Goose nights? At Dirty Harry movies. On the tennis court. Working late.

Bonne nuit.

Eva was lying in wait when I walked through the front door. "Where have you been?"

"With friends."

"I hope they gave you dinner because the kitchen is closed."

"Fish."

I expected her to say something nasty, but all she did was smirk, put her hands on her hips, and swivel away. Over her shoulder she said with her usual sarcasm, "That Mrs. Gallagher must be some Julia Child to get you to eat, huh?"

She hadn't hassled me once that summer about coming home late. She'd known where I had been—I assumed Annette Goldstein told her—and she had made it evident a few days ago when, unable to contain her jealousy, she announced, "Your friend Mrs. Gallagher is a loose cannon, Paige."

I'd ignored her, but she followed me up the stairs.

"I hear she threw a television at her husband." I hadn't responded, not even with a shrug. "And then she dropped on the kitchen floor and had an epileptic fit."

A miniature giggle tickled my throat at that last bit of misinformation, but I hadn't let Eva hear it. She had to understand she had no effect on me whatsoever. I'd shut my bedroom door gingerly, not wanting her to think I was shutting it in her face, though I was. Eva had been looking for an excuse to come charging at me, give me a bloody nose.

It was chilly and damp the next morning, air smelled wonderful, smelled of camp—rain and cedar. It was flannel shirt and corduroy weather.

I squeaked open my dresser drawer and reached for my favorite shirt. Stewart plaid button-down, cotton flannel, with a pocket too. I shook it open and the sleeves fell off.

Horrified, I dropped the shirt on the floor. It had to be Eva. Who else would want to amputate the sleeves of my shirt?

My shirt could just as well have been moving with leeches, that's how awful it was. A dead brown rat in the silverware drawer wouldn't have been a worse shock. My eyes were fighting me, wanting to cry—but no more crying, I swore.

I hated her so much that I expected to short-circuit, have an aneurysm or something. Please, I begged, let being angry divide us in a way so extreme that I look like someone else, my hair reddens, and I plump up, appear nothing like Eva anymore.

Out of control with grief, with rage, I phoned everyone who was around that summer. And I wrote a letter about it to Hannah in mostly capital letters and French using all the curse words I knew.

I trembled through the day, finally deciding it wasn't too juvenile a story to tell Fiona. It was the first time I ever called Fiona to discuss something other than baby-sitting.

I phoned from the kitchen and didn't care whether Eva heard me. "What could she possibly have been thinking?" I asked Fiona with genuine perplexity. For a moment she grew so appalled she wanted to speak with my mother, but that didn't make me feel any better, and I was silent. Fiona listened to the telephone hush and then expressed sympathy, "Oh, Paige dear, I'm sorry." I looked for something to break; pencils were no good. I looked for glass to put my fist through. Now what was I going to do with my poor shirt? "Paige, you need a conflagration," said Fiona Mind Reader, and I mumbled OK while I looked up the word in the paperback dictionary next to Eva's cookbooks.

Gallagher started a fire in his outdoor grill. He and Fiona stood behind me American Gothically while I fed my shirt to the flames. I wasn't so sure this was the right thing to do. Maybe I should have preserved the remains, but Fiona was wise, I trusted her.

The fire was very sooty and stinky. I hoped my shirt understood I wasn't being mean, that the flannel molecules would find each other now. What an inferno, my shirt catching on fire and my hallucination of my hair a bonnet ablaze, and what if Fiona threw me in? What if it was a plot to get me out of her life? Farewell to Hansel.

I wanted Fiona to look at me, but she had retreated into the house.

Rage can make me feel bright, can make my heart an incinerator. If I didn't avoid Eva, I might consume her.

Gallagher and I were alone with the barbecue. He humored me and I was grateful, threw a bucket of water on the fire and suggested I join them for dinner at Vito's, which I did. He put his arm lightly around my waist and led me to the car. "Everything will be all right, Celestine," he said. "You'll see." I wondered how much he knew, how much I should read into his words of encouragement. It got my heart into an excitement.

After dinner I hung out in the Gallaghers' bedroom, Gallagher marching around in a satin bathrobe, then thumping down the stairs to work in his den, Fiona nuzzling Sean in his bed, me waiting for her—she told me to wait—in the fireside chair. I rubbed my oily nose on my sleeve and combed my hair with my hands so I'd look good when she came back. The room was redolent with Fiona the way a cabin is redolent of cedar. Out of the corner of my eye I saw a firefly, but it turned out to be Gallagher on the second line on the phone in his den. His voice could not be heard, which was unusual. Generally when he spoke on the phone he was so loud you'd think it was deliberate, that he wanted you to hear.

Fiona returned: Sean wanted me to say good night. When the four of us were finally scattered to corners in rooms in the Chestnut Street house, not a word was spoken among any of us, but between me and Fiona were the strains of difficult music, I guessed Schoenberg, on the radio. There was no language in the house at that hour other than what came to Gallagher through the phone. Sean was dreaming of monkey jungles. I can't say whether Fiona had sentences in her head, but in mine there was only the thrashing brain wave of *Verklarte Nacht*.

When it got late enough for my parents to be asleep, I returned home. Leaving Fiona was almost a physical insurmountability. The only reason I was able to tear myself away was because I thought my absence might make her miss me, might make her wake up to me. Someday she might grab me at the door, hold me back.

Once Eva had slashed my shirt, poor father had no idea how to begin to talk to me. So he didn't even try. He was in his pajamas at the fridge when I walked in, gave me a sheepish smile, as if I were to have pity on him.

Eva too was struggling. You can always tell she's in a dilemma because she holds her head higher and her neck looks like it's making a fist. Eva wanted me to adore her but at the same time was relieved when I wasn't around.

She was jealous. Not of me, of course, with my oily skin, patched-up jeans, and long hair I refused to braid or bun. She made that clear enough. She was jealous because while I showed my contempt for her, she also saw my devotion to Fiona Gallagher. A few days before she destroyed my shirt, I had heard her sobbing behind her bedroom door. She'd had the nerve to cry to my father because she couldn't control me anymore.

"You have to let your little girl grow up," had been Papa's lame advice. It had made my scalp shrink. I was not her little girl. She even said so, said I was no child of hers.

I slept late the next morning and stealthily snuck out of the house. There was no point in asking for the Peugeot anymore; Papa was too finicky about his car, and Eva's automatic answer to all my questions was no.

So I walked into Hell and hung around, acknowledging some kids I knew from school with a nod, reading magazines over an orange juice at Vera's Luncheonette, and trying to translate them in my head. Sundays are sluggish in Hell, or they're supposed to be, but people nowadays speed into town to get their Sunday papers and box of donuts before the next fool—a neighbor most likely—buys up the last dozen crullers or kaiser rolls.

Shortly after noon I headed for Fiona's. It was Fiona all the time now. No matter how much pot my friends and I smoked or how much fun we were having, I always kept ears alert for the Barracuda. Seemed like half the time Fiona would prowl through the parking lot where I was hanging out with friends, wave me over. Was that magical thinking? Fiona and I always had good timing, synchronicity; it was perhaps our best feature.

I'd jump into her car. We'd speed out of there, the cigarette lighter would pop, she'd light up, eyes never leaving the road. That was a sexy thing.

When I arrived at the Gallaghers' house, Fiona was walking across the lawn, car keys in hand. She hesitated, then invited me along. She was going to the nursery and to pick up a quart of juice, a roast, ice cream, and coffee at the supermarket. As would occur throughout the rest of that summer, Fiona hauled me around town on her errands, up to Debbie Court for an interlude, then home again. On days when her old sorrow pinched her in the face, driving helped her realign herself, to snap out of it, chin up, as Eva's always counseling Papa.

I hope everyone has a day like that early August Sunday afternoon. After we did her chores at the supermarket and were unsuccessful at the nursery, we drove through the suburbs and out into the country, flew past housewives waving their fists at us, past indifferent cows, up knolls in the Brook, and down dirt-road dales. In the 1970s no one but my father and Hannah wore a seat belt, so when that hedgehog crossed the road, Fiona flung her arm across my waist while managing to steer clear of a spiny-mammal death. It was the day I learned Fiona loved me.

Forget daisies, he-loves-me-he-loves-me-not. You could tell whether someone loved you if she shielded you, her front-seat passenger, with an arm. I liked that, the recklessness it took to be a passenger. You had to choose your driver carefully.

The convertible was exhilarating. Having confidence in Fiona as a driver was a way of loving her. I knew that the housewife who let two gallons of vanilla swirl go to glop in the shopping bags in the backseat, she was for me.

I looked over to her to thank her not for protecting me, but for the kindness. Out of her peripheral vision she saw me, and smiled. I never heard a woman sigh the way she did then.

There was no stopping Fiona from exulting in the heat. At the red light the atmosphere stung like exhaust. I was breathing exhaust, exhaust searing the top of my head, my eyes stinging with perspiration. Unlike Fiona, who enjoyed the heat on her skin and rarely sweated, the only enjoyment I got out of the oppressive weather was that it gave me something tangible to struggle against. Had it not been for the heat, I would have ejected out of my seat into the happiness of the heavens.

Eventually Fiona gave me the keys. My turn to squire her and the Barracuda around the neighborhood. It was my confirmation, my puberty rite, my doctorate. And after a while, when she saw I wasn't going to wreck the car, she would let me go to Hell alone.

I promenaded that mighty Barracuda through Hell, turning heads of classmates and mechanics, municipal workers, shop owners, and mothers who once had called me for reliable baby-sitting. That car was my stallion. It impressed the guys: furious engine power, Plum Crazy color, wood grain steering wheel, and air cleaner looking like the snout of a beast. It impressed me because it was Fiona's, and that sent me hurtling through paradise.

The night Fiona let me drive myself home from baby-sitting, I parked the convertible in our driveway and sat awhile under the summer sky. Fiona's scent was all over the place. She was probably snoring, not dreaming of me sitting in her bucket seat with adolescent longing and momentary knowledge of the constellations.

Had I not pulled out of the driveway and taken the Barracuda for a spin in the dark, I'd have been a disgrace to teenagers everywhere. I knew I might wreck it, the car speeding out from under me, a wild ride, a nightmare. But it was necessary to drive, absolutely imperative that night.

I rumbled up to the high school. Drag racing is combat; I was ready for it and drove into the back parking lot. A car pulled up on either side of me, bees to the honey of the Barracuda. Someone instructed us, "To the stop sign!" and he pointed to it. The intersection was about 300 feet ahead.

The Corvette revved up, the Mustang revved up, and at the last minute a LeSabre darted alongside the Mustang. I smirked at the ungainly Buick when suddenly the Mustang, the cheat, took off, and I ran after it.

The LeSabre made the mistake of flooring it, wasting time burning rubber. With a calibrated foot I pressed the pedal until it hit the floor. The Mustang veered too close to me, then oversteered himself quite out of the race. The Corvette should have beaten me, but Peter, who was down from Nantucket, hadn't the nerve, the car and his Ivy League future too precious.

Most drag racers jam on the brakes once through the stop sign at the intersection, they like to spin out, and that's the noise that usually brings the cops around. I didn't stop at the intersection, but instead swung left, Firestones screaming, pulling the car safely out of the curve with a touch of speed. I could hear the bystanders whistling and cheering me as I circled the lot, and I heard their puzzlement as I fled without so much as a wave "So long!"

Once out of earshot of the parking lot, I slowed down and it was waltzing all the way, weaving through town with a three-fourths–time purr, climbing uphill slow as an agricultural beast. For a moment I thought I must be feeling happy, the town so quaint and me hovering above like Santa in his sleigh. But it was not happiness. It was intoxication. I was a teenager with a sizzlingly hot car, and I was Goldilocks sitting in the just-right seat that was Fiona's.

I played a game with myself; I tried to make the Barracuda creep me home as quiet as crabs in the sea. I prayed Fiona would be waiting in the bushes, would *psst* me, and I'd lie down in the cool grass by her side, shoulder to shoulder, elbow to elbow, hip to hip.

In the morning I lingered over my grapefruit juice so I could be there when Eva noticed the Barracuda in the driveway. What entertainment it was! At first she wore a confused look, then it clanged into alarm at the thought that we had a visitor and she hadn't yet put on her lipstick. When she finally put it all together she was aghast, speechless. She saw the monster and felt kicked in the gut. I think the worst part for her was being confronted with how nice people could be to me, lending me their cars.

Fiona saw her psychiatrist, Dr. Strudel, three times a week. His Manhattan office on East 63rd Street was almost two hours from Hell because of all the overheating cars and standstill traffic. I wished it took longer. I wished Fiona would talk to me from morning way into the night. I wished we broke down and stayed by the side of the road forever.

"We've got to get home pretty soon or I won't last," she laughed. "Just wait until you have children." The mundane reality of the bladder deflated me. But I still wished what I wished.

If I were to show up at Chestnut Street before Fiona left for the city, she'd take me along. If I were to show up at her house and she'd already left, I'd have been stung and would be hating myself. But what did I expect? Fiona didn't owe me anything. I should be grateful for every attention she ever gave me.

Neither of us talked much during the drive—whose silence were we in, hers or mine, I don't know—but between us was the unspokenness of twins and her golden-oldie radio station. Often Eva's voice cut through on the station identification tapes. I never said anything about it, her singing into the car being a big enough interruption as it was.

I didn't care if we got lost, ran out of gas, had a blowout. In fact, I wanted a big applause of a wreck so we could have something permanent between us, so I'd be memorable, not a sidekick, apprentice, underling, junior. The garage attendant in Dr. Strudel's building was the only one in the world who understood my position. I saw it in the way he rolled his eyes up and down Fiona's body, then snickered at me at if to say, "Too bad you're too young to handle such a tomato." Fiona in her tennis dress was completely oblivious to him.

But no matter how disconsolate I was about being 17 in the world, there was always the approach to the city to look forward to. We whipped past bridges—cantilevered, steel arch, truss— pendulous wrecking balls, highway ramps, crash bags filled with sand, guardrails, and airplanes flying too low above us. It was an odyssey, the river running alongside us like a metaphor.

I'd heard the bromide a million times: New York City was the city of dreams. Papa likened visiting New York to the ride at the World's Fair where you got in a little boat and it pulled you along a track, past dioramas that were meant to make you feel you'd cir- cled the globe: Greenland, air-conditioning on full blast; ukelele music and free pineapple in Hawaii; elephants honking on a reel- to-reel tape in Africa. I could see why Papa thought New York was like that, a harlequin of characters, aromas and hollering. You could be at once seen and unseen in New York.

For me, heading toward New York was a spectacle, but I don't mean in a touristy way.

When I was in grade school, our class was taken to the World's Fair. For our essay I was thinking I could write about one kid puking outside the RCA Pavilion, more kids puking on the bus home. Too much pizza, chili dogs, Belgian waffles, Italian ices, and Cracker Jack. I had a headache of sadness for the real live Elsie the Cow, who lay in a manger listening to brats tell her they were going to make glue out of her. I told one kid "Shut up!" and his mother asked me, mean as mean could be, where is my mother, young lady! Before I could explain I was on a school trip and her son was a juvenile delinquent, he poked her in the rear with a souvenir American flagpole. I could write my World's Fair essay about that cretin.

But the moment I entered the exhibit from the Vatican, I knew what I wanted to write about.

We waited in the dark. The line was so long that most of the kids started whimpering, had to pee, or gave each other Indian burns and got into shoving fights. The two class mothers pulled the nuisances off the line and waited outside with them, which left the teacher and three or four of us kids holding hands in the shadows, shuffling along in church silence.

Ahead, the slight commotion—we must be getting nearer—of a clutch of nuns genuflecting, their black skirts rustling. My teacher scooped me up into her arms, and I thought there was danger.

But there was no danger. She just wanted me to see better. And there it was, eye-squinting bright behind bulletproof Plexiglass. I was in suspended animation until something inside cracked like a knuckle, and I was released, breathing again.

I knew, as my teacher carried me out into the light, that Michelangelo's *Pietà* was a prophecy. But because I was too young to arrange the words to explain it, I wrote my essay on Elsie. Now I was trying to explain it to Fiona because that's what entering New York was, the prophecy of passion. And ever since that Michelangelo I'd been looking for it everywhere, desperate for something deep to my bone to replace the tiresome child life in Hell, dullness fretted with predictable meals, predictable school, predictable kids.

The thruway was that long dark line at the World's Fair with its haunting possibility. The city was the emancipation, the way falling in love is, the way the *Pietà* is, the way a winsome red wine is. Fiona drove me there, drove me out of Hell and back. I'm sorry I couldn't hold on to those feelings, there was so much potential in them.

While she lay on the psychiatrist's couch telling Dr. Strudel what she could have told me if only she'd forget I was 17, I sat on a bench along Fifth Avenue reading Genet. (Of course I was trying to impress her!) When it rained, Fiona said it would be OK for me to sit in the waiting room, in which hung a framed reproduction of the Bosch triptych *Creation of Eve, Garden of Delights,* and *Hell.* Pretty obvious symbolism for a psychiatrist's office, I thought.

I preferred to wait outside. I didn't want to overhear anything, neither sobbing nor screaming nor my name unmentioned. Plus, I thought it best to give Fiona some time to herself after her session so I wouldn't be a nuisance and spoil the whole thing.

When the rain came I often wasted those 50 minutes browsing through the pet store on Lexington Avenue, tormenting myself by seeing if I could hold back what in anyone else would be tears.

Puppies and kitten made me want to wail. I guess I was afraid for them, motherless and at the mercy of my devious species.

Fiona met me under the awning of Dr. Strudel's building (I never saw tearstains on her face, just the faraway look that brightened when she saw me, as if, disconcertingly, I were a funny-meeting-you-here surprise), and we palled around for awhile. In a downpour once, Fiona took me to the movies, *Lawrence of Arabia*. We'd both gotten sopped even in the short distance from Dr. Strudel's lobby to the theater, and I shivered all the way through the film but was too embarrassed to say anything. Before the film started Fiona had tried toweling my hair with some tissues in her purse. When we left, I had snatches of white tissue in my hair. "Butterflies," said Fiona laughing. I was mortified. She gave me a butterfly kiss on my cheek, and that night I washed only around that spot.

At the cosmetics counter at Bloomingdale's she sampled a lipstick that made her look like a vampire. I hated it. She bought it. It was my first time at a cosmetics counter, and I thought the whole makeup thing a little absurd. Not only was it narcissistic, and not only did I resent that you weren't a woman if you didn't wear eye shadow, but also I found the look menacing—the hollow face, bloodied lips, darkness of disease under the eyes. Eva was as painted up as a warrior, but Fiona generally left it at mascara. I love the human face in the morning, vaguely sad and truthful. No wonder women wear foundation and men grow beards.

Without fail Fiona would emerge from psychotherapy absolutely ravenous. (One of the very few things she disclosed about her therapy was that Dr. Strudel often commented on her grumbling stomach. He'd thought it a good sign, that she was beginning to recognize how much she wanted him to satisfy her, father her, Electra complex her, etc. etc. Hogwash. This was her desire: to eat.)

Eva always lost the parking ticket, or rather was just too lazy to plow through her purse for it, but Fiona, as disconcerted as she usually was, didn't seem to have much clutter in her pocketbook. She handed over the stub and a $5 bill with an inquiring look. The garage attendant, deferential to the driver of such an impressive car, brought the Barracuda to us and gave Fiona a finger salute and to me raised his lip to show a fang, though everyone else assumed he was smiling.

We drove to the Burger Heaven a few blocks uptown. Fiona double-parked outside the restaurant, leaving the keys in the ignition in case the police came and I had to move it. I really didn't want the cops to come. Never in the life of the Barracuda had I thought I'd had full control of that beast. I had the image of me starting her up and being helpless as the car stampeded straight on down to Wall Street.

Apprehensively I watched Fiona hustle into the restaurant in that damn short tennis dress. She was ordering iced coffee, fries, medium-rare cheeseburger with mustard, ketchup, onions, and pickles. Every time she offered to buy me something, said she was concerned that I ate so little, but I, unlike Fiona, remained queasy throughout our years together in Hell. It was the delirium.

While she waited at the counter I observed her through the plate glass. She wasn't looking out the window for me. She'd forget to ask for extra napkins. The bloody juice from cheeseburger would spill down Fiona's face, and she'd laugh and she'd drive on, lunch in her lap in packets of foil while I'd hold the iced coffee to her lips, and she'd hold the dripping hamburger over the side of the car.

I treasured the New York jaunts, especially watching Fiona devour her meal with such hilarity. One time, however, things did not go so well.

After Fiona's appointment we window-shopped along Lexington

Avenue. A new store had opened up above the pet shop. It sold water beds, the latest craze. Fiona wanted to try one out.

She motioned me toward the entrance, and we walked sideways up a narrow staircase. It was a little creepy, and I wished I had gone in first in case the stairs collapsed.

The showroom wasn't quite finished. Carpenters were running circular saws and hammering away. It smelled good, fresh sawdust. I hope Heaven smells this way instead of powdery perfumey. The salesman glommed onto us before we had even caught our breath from climbing the stairs. I would have just let him go on and on, but Fiona cut him short, politely. "We're just looking." He blinked and backed off. Men never had to be told twice with Fiona.

So we tried out the water beds. There were two other customers, one couple about Fiona's age. They kept dumping their bodies on whatever bed we'd been testing. I was annoyed, but not to the point of wanting to leave.

It would have been nice to have had everyone else go away, to be able to jingle a bell and watch the customers, carpenters, and salesman file down the steep and narrow stairs. Then Fiona and I could take a water-bed nap in this exhausting city heat. Maybe that's all I wanted. To sleep beside Fiona.

We had been sitting on one of the queen beds. I hadn't yet had a chance to stretch out because the other couple was about to come over and make tidal waves. But seeing them talking to the salesman, I lay back in the quivering bed. I heard a few more people enter the store. This was fun, I thought as I floated on the bed, except what if you're nauseous?

All of a sudden Fiona grabbed my arm, pulled me up, and said, "We're leaving."

I didn't know what I'd said or done to set her off, but she was steaming. Maybe she recognized someone she wanted to avoid. Maybe she was panicking about some childhood memory. Maybe it was the absurdity of water beds. She disappeared down the stairs. Even if I found her, I knew I'd lost her.

I saw Fiona leaning against the pet shop window, smoking a cigarette, or about to once she found the matches in her purse. Even when I caught up to her she was so far away there was no point calling her name. We got the car from the garage attendant, hopped in, not a word spoken between us.

Fiona accelerated right past Burger Heaven and headed across town. I looked at her for an explanation as we entered the transverse through Central Park. Something was seriously wrong. I could tell because her nose got swollen and the skin above her lip bunched up, as pleated as a skirt.

She put her hand on the back of my neck and let out a heavy sigh. "Let's go sit by the river," she said. So she wasn't mad at me! I was enormously relieved. Fiona jammed the gas pedal and we flew along some street in the 50s.

A decrepit pier loomed ahead. It would never support the weight of the Barracuda, but I didn't care. Fiona sped through the yellow light, the car aimed due west, at the Palisades across the river. My hair snapped in the wind, the g-forces gently pressed me into my seat. I was alive. Furiously alive and free and 17.

I remember thinking that since the top was down we could swim away from the car instead of sinking trapped within.

Fiona swerved away from the pier at the last minute, spinning us in a 180-degree turn. She looked at me surreptitiously, perhaps to see if I was astonished or scared, but I thought the whole thing lovely. She shoved the gearshift into reverse and parked parallel to the river. Hands limp on the wheel at 12 o'clock, she slid down in her seat, her head resting against her seatback. Fiona cleared her throat, as she often did. Maybe it was too many cigarettes. I had thought she was simply preparing to justify herself.

I pulled my knotty hair into a ponytail. "Do you have a rubber band?" Fiona laughed at my calm. The view was great.

"I don't want you to kill yourself." The words came out of my head on their own. Prior to that moment I had maintained that Fiona had the right to do whatever she wanted with her life, to commit suicide if life were harrowing and she were plagued by voices, to throw TVs, stereos, pots, and pans at Gallagher. I would have respected any decision she would make.

Then I changed my mind.

"Did you think I was going to drive us into the river?" she asked with alarm. "Paige, you are very special to me."

I turned away. What that meant to Fiona was different from what it meant to me. To me, when someone is important to you, you call them on the phone to see how they're doing. You find out and memorize their birthday. You stop by their house to see if they want to hang out with you.

We let the conversation drop, both of us distracted by three clowns in satiny clothing moving near the pier. They had emerged from the river, as far as I could tell. Fiona and I, in our own miseries, stared vacantly at them, and Fiona pinned a strand of my hair behind my ear.

As they came nearer I saw they weren't circus clowns at all but three prostitutes in touchable clothing, one in a valentine-red satin miniskirt and fishnets, one in a sequined black satin bodysuit, one in jeans and a halter top that turned out not to be satin but stretchy rayon and didn't quite cover her belly.

"What are you looking at, bitch?" the valentine one called to Fiona. She had long nails and no good reason for a fight, and that was unnerving.

After all we'd just been through, now we were going to have our throats slit with a rusty knife. Fiona took a deep breath, put on her Ray-Bans, and drove slowly off. She was unruffled. I really didn't think she was a housewife at all. My cat burglar theory was gaining weight.

"That happens to me a lot," she said.

I was not surprised one bit, though I couldn't have explained why it was so. Fiona was everything a beautiful woman is: attractive, bewitching, beckoning, a Siren. Hookers would see her as competition, though I didn't think her allure was a sex thing, but what did I know about what's sexy? I didn't get Marilyn Monroe at all, and the first time I ever thought something was sexy, Eva laughed so much she practically choked on her gin rickey.

The gardener at Hannah's house had been nice to us ever since we were six, gave us Barbies one Christmas, so I always paid him friendly attention. One day—I was ten—the gardener was working at Hannah's, and we were running through the sprinkler in our clothes. It was the end of August, "a scorcher," grown-ups said. I knew we were too old to be playing in the sprinkler, but it felt too good to stop, and besides, Hannah's backyard was protected with greenery so nobody would see us and laugh us out of school.

The gardener had mowed the lawn and was working on the hedges. His green T-shirt was black with sweat. Just when we were getting cool, Hannah's mother called us from the kitchen window and let us in even though our clothes were sopping wet.

Her mother poured us lemonade, which tasted like soap, and, when she finally conceded I was not going to finish my glass, gave us a frosty tumbler to take to the gardener. Hannah held it out to him. I warned him it wasn't very good, he could dump it in the bushes, and he nodded repeatedly but held up a finger, asking us to wait. (I never knew he didn't speak English until Hannah's mother mentioned it years later. I'd always thought his quiet was gentleness.) Before he accepted the lemonade he first had to mop his face and the back of his neck with a handkerchief, then he took off his watch, and swabbed his wrist and palms.

I was startled by his nakedness, the pale white dial of skin on his wrist. A warm shiver surged up my spine, and I felt the alarm you feel when you come upon a garden snake. He passed Hannah the empty glass, smiling at us both, and we walked away, me imagining touching his wrist with my lips.

Months later at the table before dinner, Jan was trying to explain what made a girl sexy. Mother and Papa were bemused, both sitting with their chin in their hands, looking adoringly at Jan. We went around the table, defining "sexy." Papa, of course, said, "My wife." Eva said, "Sinatra, and a man lighting a woman's cigarette." I said, "The gardener's wrist," and explained how underneath his watch was that circle blinding like a brilliant reflection of light rather than the absence of it. Jan didn't have any idea what I was talking about, Papa had lost interest in the conversation or, more likely, lost track of what we'd been talking about, and Eva laughed so hard at my inexperience that Jan had to pound her on the back to stop her from suffocating.

Fiona is that kind of sexy, like the gardener's wrist, not the big-breast kind. Of all people, prostitutes are probably those most sensitive to sexy women, and that explained their animosity toward Fiona. But there was something else between them, some tacit recognition. Maybe it had to do with a woman like Fiona sleeping with a man like Gallagher. I once read about a prostitute who said it's common practice not to let clients kiss them on the mouth. That was how I imagined Fiona with Gallagher, having energetic sex, but with a paper bag on her head.

"Did I ever tell you I used to think about being a prostitute?" Fiona asked when we got on the highway. "Does that surprise you?"

It did not surprise me. There was an impenetrability about Fiona, the toughness, the distance, that had protected her so far. Whomever she told about this potential career choice surely comprehended that. What they did not understand was what her potential career choice said about men and about her dependence on them.

"Prostitution sounds just like many marriages," I said, plagiarizing someone.

"Hmm," she responded, and we didn't take the discussion further, but we did make long and slow eye contact. Fiona knew I knew.

The lights were out in Fiona's body, the rooms still and dusty. One of those rooms would accommodate her love for me, and her love would be irreverent and harsh in its devotion. Discover it, Fiona Gallagher. Flick the switch. I know it could save you.

With Dr. Strudel on vacation, we had no reason to go to New York. The city stank in August anyway.

We were just hanging around Fiona's house one day. I watched her make coffee and heave meat into the oven. To escape the heat in the kitchen, we went upstairs and lay on the bedroom carpet, the magic carpet, and listened to music, her new Stravinsky cassette, a Mozart piano concerto.

I began to grow one of my headaches. They weren't unbearably painful, but they were frequent, five days a week, and they made it impossible to smile or talk much. Eva was tired of me complaining. She'd tried everything—a cool cloth, two aspirin—and was convinced that since nothing worked my headaches were psychosomatic. My father tried massaging my temples with Tiger Balm, but that made it so much worse that I vomited from the pain. "You might have a brain tumor," Hannah said.

Fiona gave me two Excedrin and placed a quarter on my forehead, a method she'd learned from her father. "Why don't you take a nap?" she suggested. "Sean won't be back from camp until 3." She dimmed the lights and turned down the music. "It's OK," I whispered, wanting her to leave the Mozart on. "I like it."

The bed squeaked as Fiona sat on it, and for some reason I thought it hysterically funny, despite how painful it was to suppress my laughter. She leaned over the foot of the bed and mussed my hair with her fingers.

"What's so funny?" she said, smiling.

"Nothing." I looked at her eyes, their heavy lids, and my giggles were quelled. We stayed looking at each other long enough for it to be noticeable. It felt like a love scene in a movie. I turned back to my headache, and Fiona sat upright against the headboard.

She began writing letters and paying bills, folding paper, licking stamps. I was exactly where I wanted to be, tapping my fingers on Fiona's plush carpet, Fiona as nearby as a night nurse. By the time we got to the presto, my headache was only a shadow in my head. At last I was able to listen to classical music and feel the way I used to feel about it, that I needed it desperately. Somehow Fiona made it safe for me to feel that way.

"Do you mind if I turn the music up?" I asked.

Fiona leaned over the foot of the bed again and, smiling, picked the quarter off my forehead. "Whatever you like, dear Paige." And she again stared the unbreakable stare.

People want to know why I liked Fiona so much. What they should be asking is how come Fiona didn't come running to *me*? Adults have forgotten the feel of a teenager's love. For you a teenager will walk through glass doors, stay awake three days in a row, be an angel standing under your window in the rain. So what that we don't know how to order from the butcher or apply foundation or insert a diaphragm. Show us.

I would have to wear a dress. And I would have to eat. Fiona said so.

La Penombre was the four-star restaurant around the corner from Dr. Strudel's office. Tobacco-colored velvet window curtains prevented the riffraff from seeing through, and a grim guy in white gloves guarded the door as if it were an embassy.

I tried not to betray my inexperience by appearing too excited (too agitated is more accurate). After all, I'd been to a French restaurant before. Every year Madame Foiegras took our class to a French bistro in Greenwich Village, then to a movie at the Alliance Française. Taciturn waitresses in Breton costumes brought us onion soup and asparagus crepes and pretended not to understand our French. They probably didn't understand us the way they didn't understand President Charles de Gaulle, because they probably were as French as I was. La Penombre would be quite a different experience, frighteningly sophisticated, a culture where any blunders could be unforgiving.

"It's for the New Year," Fiona explained, though it was August. She'd already celebrated the end of 1968, 1969, and 1970 at the Goldsteins' annual bash, Sean sleeping over in his friend Fern Goldstein's room. I thought New Year's loud and arbitrary. I scorned it. But Fiona got this idea that she wanted to make up for never having wished me a happy New Year. In-laws, neighbors, and doctors thought there were demons in her head, but Fiona was actually a simpleton: She said she wanted to usher in good things for me.

"You don't have to take me out," I tried halfheartedly to dissuade her. "It's too expensive."

"Let me do this," she answered.

Every penny spent on me was Gallagher's money. That made it hard for me to treasure what I wanted to treasure. I felt guilty taking his money when I loved her, not him. I believed that if Fiona wasn't paying for me out of her own money, then it didn't count. It didn't matter to me that she had earned that money by being Mrs. Gallagher, Tom's wife, Sean's mother. She could have been a pipe fitter, a cancer researcher, a camel breeder, and it wouldn't have mattered; if Gallagher was paying her for her work, it was still Gallagher's money as far as I was concerned.

Fiona would not discuss the money. We were going to La Penombre and that was that; maybe she was even a little mad at me for being underappreciative. I hadn't immediately understood that money was a touchy subject for Fiona, that she felt dependent on Gallagher. I had viewed Fiona as sovereign, what my teachers would have called an "individualist." No one but Fiona herself would ever have seen her as inadequate, not self-reliant. Frankly, I thought she had to be brilliant to manage to live her life in Hell when to my mind she belonged in Berlin, smoking in the Tiergarten café, or walking the hills of Rome with a folio of Bernini's works tucked under her arm.

On the positive side, Gallagher's money neutralized things between us: I didn't feel indebted to Fiona for anything.

Wasn't my world of hope coming true? Fiona sitting opposite me on a velvet chair in a fancy restaurant? But I panicked: What if I had to throw up at the table? what if I choked on the soufflé? what if I spilled my ice water on her? what if I passed out from the wine? what if I said something stupid? what if I lost my French?

What was I so worried about? It wouldn't have been the first time we'd been at a restaurant together. We hit the Village Pizzeria at least once a week with Sean, though each time I declined her offer to buy me dinner and instead chomped on Sean's leftover crust. I didn't want Fiona to think I was freeloading, and, more importantly, my profound nausea made it physically impossible for me to eat anything substantial in front of her. What was I going to say? Fiona, you nauseate me?

Last time we were at the pizzeria she ordered eggplant for me anyway. "You can take it home," she reassured me. Once the waitress brought our food, the eggplant grew more and more ominous on my plate. Trying not to inhale the puky Parmesan cheese as I breathed, I cut up Sean's ravioli for him. Repeatedly he and I were amused by the way Fiona consumed a meatball hero. She took the hugest bites I'd ever seen, a whole meatball in her mouth at once. And I've seen big bites. My brother and his friends had had loads of eating contests: who could eat the most banana splits, who could eat a package of hot dogs in the least amount of time, who could stuff a dozen Oreos into his mouth at once. I guess they ate their eggs the way Fiona did, yolk down the hatch in one bite.

"You're going to be all right," Fiona told me, though I hadn't said a word about being afraid of La Penombre. I believed Fiona knew everything about what I felt and thought. That's why I resented the way she disrupted our silence, not by speaking but by being uncomfortable with it, forcing me to talk, to say something.

Honestly, I didn't know what to say. Anyway, who gave me the right to want to stay as close to Fiona Gallagher as her purse, to want to *be* her purse, held in her hand, minding precious items— her lipstick, money, matches, directions, Valium, lists?

I was going to be all right, Fiona had said so. Reviewing the litany of safety strategies, I told myself that for nausea I could press the cool, flat dinner knife against the artery in my neck. If the wine overcame me, I could sit in her arms like a baby. If the food slipped from my fork, she would spoon-feed me rather than huff and puff and snort in disgust as Eva would have. And even though I would be wearing a dress—the only dress I owned, a cotton Indian-print shift—because I was with Fiona I would feel protected, indifferent to whether boys could see up it.

It was just a few bites, couldn't I manage that?

No one would agree with us, but we thought we had perfect weather for the drive into New York. God shook hail out of the skies, scaring off most drivers. The road was ours, we had private passage, and I was eternal, the way I'd thought bomb shelters would make me feel, a baby in its cradle. I was precisely that with Fiona, all nerve endings and sweetly stupid, watching for cues and a smile.

Heading for midtown Manhattan, we drove straight through the hailstones, windshield wipers offering vision in fractions. Here it comes, not the city itself but the entering into it. Skyscrapers ahoy, I stuck my head out the window and sang full-throated the opening lines of "An die Freude" until I felt Fiona tug at my dress. I sat back down.

"Beethoven's Ninth?" Fiona asked.

"Beethoven's Ninth."

How had Fiona teased the classical repertoire out of me? I'd ignored classical music ever since my mother had implied I didn't understand it properly. I was just a kid in a concert hall then, probably could have had a career in music. But I quit it all after Eva's insult. "Don't be so stubborn," Eva had said when I refused piano lessons. "You're just hurting yourself." That's what they all say to kids, but it's not completely true; the parents suffer too. Good.

The hail had mussed my hair. Fiona's expression reminded me of a girl watching others play jump rope and wondering whether that might be fun to do. I think my singing in the hail spoke of the possibility of our own friendship. Fiona was wearing makeup, and this time it was for me.

Throughout the meal I spoke polite French to the waiter, and he was solicitous throughout. Everything had been going well until Fiona made the mistake of saying she had never seen him so docile.

My blood went in reverse when she told me that. I'd wanted this to be *our* memory, not some place she'd been with Gallagher or perhaps Greta. Noticing my disappointment Fiona impulsively, clumsily, reached for my hand. She was always being so damn nice; it confused me. I didn't know when to be mad and when to rejoice.

She would not look away or move until I made eye contact with her. A green vein was pulsing on the back of her hand. I looked up.

"Taste this," she said, raising my champagne cocktail to my lips. "Really taste it, don't just sip." She was still holding my hand.

Fiona ordered us *cotelettes de saumon au vin blanc, asperges Argenteuil, tarte aux pommes*. Her accent was definitely American but nothing to be embarrassed about. I got drunk on my champagne cocktail, which I didn't finish, and before dessert Fiona leaned across the table and kissed me on the forehead, right there in the hoity-toity La Penombre, her hand at the back of my head bracing me for the pressure of her smooch. It was a forehead kiss, the kiss you give to those who are sweet, children with fever, faithful old dogs, folks on the deathbed.

There was lots of jewelry noise and poufed-hair women and men in double-breasted suits with women or cigars, men with hair slicked back, men being a little mean to the waiters. The women, who sat so still and tall, didn't seem to notice us, but the men did because Fiona was so beautiful. I could see their brains calculating us then dismissing us—the two females must be cousins, maybe aunt and niece—returning to their fat cigars.

Bowing slightly, the maître d' offered me the flowers from our table, orchids, and I later preserved one of them. It had been a remarkable evening: the first time I had eaten in a restaurant that required reservations, the first time I had seen a dinner bill over $100. It was exciting and grown-up, and I couldn't tell anyone.

I didn't eat at all the next day. It's not that the food had been so good that nothing else interested me, though Madame Foiegras says that's why she loses weight whenever she returns to America from France. Rather, I thought that the longer I could hold on to that last meal, the longer I'd be in Fiona's company with only a bowl of orchids between us. But I was still mad at her for double-crossing me. She should have taken me to a restaurant she'd never been to with anyone else.

I dreamt of the jackknife dive that night. When you dive too deep, you aren't sure you'll make it to the surface before your breath gives out. But you make it, rub your stinging eyes, and explode, sometimes in tears, sometimes in silence, with gratitude, shame, unaccountable sorrow. You are completely aware that your life has been saved and you can thank only God, that is if you're a believer.

⑯

Etendue a ses pieds, calme et pleine de joie,
Delphine la couvait avec des yeux ardents,
Comme un animal fort quit surveille une proie,
Apres l'avoir d'abord marquee avec les dents.
—Charles Baudelaire, "Delphine et Hippolyte"

Lounging, serene and satisfied, at her feet,
Delphine looks her over with ardent eyes
Like a powerful beast surveying with pride
The prey bloodied by its bite.
—Paige Bergman, tr.

Fiona was Mario Andretti, Jackie Stewart in drag, the best driver many of us would ever know. Being poky like Hannah doesn't make you a safe driver, nor does speeding make you reckless. You've got to sit up straight in your seat. You've got to pay attention.

She saw me waiting for the ice cream truck at the shady corner of Larch and Chestnut. I'd heard her coming. She pulled over, rolled down the window. "Want to go for a ride?"

It was unusual to see the Barracuda's roof up in summer, unless it was raining, but it had been very hot out, too hot even for a heat-seeking missile like Fiona to play one set of tennis. Forgoing the Fudgsicle, I hopped in. The air conditioner made me feel very clean.

It was the muggiest August ever, and that steaming day would turn out to be one of the strangest days of my life.

Behind the wheel Fiona became as emotionally lethargic as a bus driver. Someone cut in front of her, and she let him. Someone pulled out of a driveway without looking, she stopped her vehicle, no honk. Fiona's always easy on the road, heat wave or not, though every once in a while she'll straighten her arms while holding the steering wheel and floor the Barracuda. Gallagher, on the other hand, sat on his horn with impunity, yelled "douche bag" at everyone who tried to pass. But you could tell he wasn't seriously angry because after cursing out the offending driver, Gallagher would hum, "Coming 'round the Mountain" or "The Girl From Ipanema." He was all pretense, trying on attitudes to see what got him Fiona's attention. Not an easy job.

"What were you doing hanging out on the street?" Fiona said, almost jovially. "Waiting for your fix?" Her humor was elemental, like knock-knock jokes, but when she teased me in the slightest I crumbled. I smiled back anyway.

Now that I was finally hearing the ice cream truck bells jingling behind us, they annoyed me. I plugged my ears.

"Ah, so I stole you away from your ice cream man?" she said. How did she know? I'd just made a gesture that implied the truck was annoyance, and she understood that, on the contrary, I'd been awaiting a Fudgsicle. She was always so damn right about me, it was kismet that we met, unexplained, destiny.

My mood was immediately ratcheted up a few notches when gravity pulled me back into my seat as Fiona thundered onto Route 22. We were headed for the Dairy Queen.

I waited in the car while she walked up to the window, her wallet sticking out of the small pocket in her tennis dress, and ordered me a cone. I'd told her to choose the flavor, anything but vanilla, and she said she knew that, her intuition again. Watching but not wanting to watch, I shook my head, amused at her lack of inhibition in that tennis getup.

Before long the Barracuda was surrounded by reptiles in motorcycle clothes just dying to get a look under the hood. They gave me the creeps, wearing leather vests and leather pants; snakes, dragons, and American eagles tattooed on their biceps; unctuous hair and skin and lips. I jumped when the fat one rapped on my window.

Just then Fiona came back smiling broadly, a coffee cone melting in each hand. Something she said to the boys made them all laugh, and they slithered off. I leaned over and opened her door for her.

Fiona drove us back to Hell with one hand, somehow averting ice cream disaster and a car crash. She didn't finish her cone and had actually taken some broad licks of it before flinging it out of the car into a field of wild grasses. We drove to the library in Bubbling Brook, where she paid for Sean's overdue library books, then back to Hell. Being seen with Fiona, even if it was only in the damn library, made me the happiest girl on Earth. It was the feeling of victory.

I finally thanked her for the ice cream. It had taken me a while because part of me thought she owed it to me anyway. "Paige," she responded, "do you know I feel safe with you?" Of course, I told her.

Once at her house, she suggested we sit in the den, where the air conditioner had been running three days straight. The room smelled of air conditioner. I was ill at ease, not knowing whether I should forget her taking me to La Penombre. Fiona seemed oblivious to my distress and said laconically:

"Sean is at day camp until 3." I already knew his schedule. "It can be dangerous to play tennis in this heat."

When I didn't acknowledge her, she said, "I want a drink."

Fiona was bored.

Fiona was a fire I could stare into, breakers in the Atlantic Ocean.

Languishing on one end of the sofa, me on the other, Fiona pronounced, "A vodka gimlet!" With great purpose in mind, she jumped off the couch and trod up the stairs.

I heard her cracking ice in the kitchen. She hollered to me in the den, offered me a cocktail.

No, I shook my head, too embarrassed to send my voice out loud up those stairs. A cocktail, how absurd! Not only had I never even heard of a vodka gimlet, but it was also so bourgeois. Her head appeared at the top of the stairs. "I didn't hear you. Did you say you wanted a drink?" I smiled, shook my head no. It seemed to take her a long time to mix that thing and come back.

"There was no vodka so I had to use gin," she said, offering me a sip. "Just a little taste?" I was scared of drinking, but said I'd taste it. She'd made it very weak, she promised, we could share it. If I got drunk and threw up, so be it, she wouldn't make fun of me, and I'd be able to face her again even if I slurred my speech. I said OK, I'd share it with her.

We lay foot to foot on the couch listening to Strauss waltzes, passing the drink back and forth. There was a lot of quiet between us as usual, but this time Fiona seemed edgy. How could I stay mad at her when she looked at me so intently?

"If you could commit any crime, what would it be?"

That stumped me. I was a pretty law-abiding kid, except for

smoking pot. What would I do? Charles Manson was in the news that year. My mind shut down even thinking about him, so I knew I couldn't commit any serious offense. I didn't consider making a skirt out of the American flag a crime. I didn't believe in shoplifting.

She was after something, but I had no idea what she wanted me to say.

"I'd race the Barracuda in the high school parking lot."

I guess that was a stupid answer because she made no comment. Maybe she was peeved because I didn't return the question to her.

"Do you know what crime I'd commit?" she volunteered. Before I could say, "No, what?" she had fixed me with that ardent stare of hers and said, "Rape."

Well, I didn't get it. I simply held her gaze.

"You don't know what I'm talking about, do you?"

I hated to seem naive, but I had to admit I didn't.

She was thinking of a way to rephrase her thoughts. Fiona was patient with me.

"If you could be anywhere, anywhere in the world, where would you like to be right now?"

This time I put more thought into my answer, hoping it would show Fiona I had big plans and should be taken seriously enough to meet her friends. "In an operating room performing brain surgery." Actually I surprised myself with such ambition. I would have thought I'd have answered something along the lines of teaching in French Polynesia. I guess I wanted to see blood in a respectable way.

She made no comment. "What about you?" I asked, having learned my lesson.

Fiona took a breath, gave me another one of those eye-to-eye looks. "I'd like to be in bed with you."

Was I cold or on fire, I didn't know. I listened to my memory again and again to make sure I heard her correctly and wasn't misinterpreting. But was I clean enough? I'd been sweating earlier. Was my hair greasy? Did I have dandruff? A pimple on my chin? My breath? Armpits?

Maybe she had a good idea. Wasn't that what I desired all along? To lie down. To be in her arms. To sleep together. I hadn't realized until then how tired I had been all these years. I was suddenly leaden, narcoleptic, needing to close my eyes and sink away....

It was daunting. Not because I was shocked—I wasn't—or thought I was too inexperienced to please a grown woman, but because after your dream comes true nothing's left, what do you have to live for? You invent the artificial heart, win Olympic gold, broker the deal of the century, and what is left for you? The high dive, Fiona would teach me, gives pleasure every time you plunge.

Fiona placed her hand on my shoulder to recover my attention. I flinched, I couldn't help it, it was automatic.

"Is that OK?" she asked me. I nodded. I didn't want her to worry she might have upset me, and I didn't want her to change her mind. "Why don't you think about what I've said? I'll call you tomorrow."

Maybe it was responsible of her to say that, but I was disappointed. What if she changed her mind tomorrow?

I let myself out the door, though I don't actually remember that part.

I'd probably had a total of four sips of the gimlet, yet I was smashed, reeling like a drunk in an alley. As I aimed myself homeward, one of the little girls I used to baby-sit for came chasing after me wanting to play. I thought I'd topple over her, but fortuitously she took my hand and walked me home. To her disappointment, I wouldn't let her in.

I flomped on my bed, and it began to spin, just like in the cliché. I grabbed on, steadied myself, then rose to throw water on my face. It's common wisdom.

Having fallen asleep in my clothes, I awoke at about 9 in the evening. My parents, not knowing I was upstairs, had eaten dinner without me. Eva was surprised and scornful when I sauntered into the kitchen to get something to eat—"Where did *you* come from?" I took some cheese, jam, and flatbread—and a donut I'd snuck under my T-shirt—up to my bedroom.

The next morning I tried to read my copy of Racine's *Phedre*, a prerequisite for next year's AP French, but I couldn't concentrate: I'd had the dream of a lifetime and was embarrassed by it. Maybe breakfast would sober me up.

I stirred a spoonful of instant lemonade into a tumbler. I saw my parents through the kitchen window. Mother was weeding. Father was sniffing flowers.

I thought I should stay by the phone even though it was a crystal-clear day. And the phone did ring, around noon. I picked it up in two rings, before Eva could run inside and get it.

It was Fiona. "Hello," she said, nice and friendly. My heart was hurting with all its beating.

We had silence. I couldn't hear her breathing. Maybe the phone went dead. It would be too stupid to say, "Hello? Are you still on the line?" But I had to say something; I would be just as idiotic to hang on to the receiver imagining Fiona on the other end when all it was was emptiness. The operator would come on and tell me to hang up. Meanwhile Fiona would be sipping something cool on her back porch. So I asked, "Did I have a weird dream last night or did we have a conversation?"

"No, you weren't dreaming…I'd like to talk to you about that," she cleared her throat, "I'll pick you up in five minutes, OK?" When she cleared her throat, oh, spontaneous dark wet action! I could have swung my arms and legs around her and kissed her like a baby brother.

Fiona showed up wearing a Mickey Mouse T-shirt and driving a preposterously ugly Karmann Ghia. I felt woozy, maybe I'd made a terrible mistake. The shop had loaned her the car while the Barracuda was in for a tune-up. Seeing her in that shirt and that car practically turned my feelings inside out—maybe I was all wrong about Fiona. I'd try to overlook the unsightly scene.

I got into the car, and we drove into the country. The air was much drier than the day before. Fiona pulled onto a dirt road, which cut through the field where she had tossed her ice cream yesterday. The grass was the color of wheat and as tall as the car. We couldn't be seen from the road. I could hear bees navigating through the dry grasses, wind rustling the stalks.

We sat quietly in the car for a while, feeling the sun plaster our faces. I thought she might want to take me out of the car and lay me on the ground for kissing, and was glad when that didn't occur because I was afraid of ticks.

After smoking a cigarette Fiona spoke up. She began by explaining why she had pulled me out of that water bed store so abruptly. She said she should have known better, it had been too much of a temptation. I would have welcomed her embrace. I said, "You should have!" and she tousled my hair and drove on. But I still wasn't sure what her temptation had been. To kiss me? Embrace me? Put her hand under my clothes?

On our way back to Hell, Fiona cruised past the house on Debbie Court where I'd spotted her car on Earth Day last year. She slowed as we approached the house, casing it without actually stopping. A Jaguar was parked under the carport. I knew I'd seen it somewhere before. Greta in the snowstorm.

Fiona floored it, and we crept out of there. This tin can was definitely not a Barracuda.

The way Fiona told it, her falling in love with Greta could have been a breath-mint commercial: eyes meeting and locking across a tennis court, a crescendo of white noise as the spine straightens with interest, a pickup game of tennis where they try to blow each other out of the water, great satisfying groping kisses in the cabana.

Deep, soul love? Nah, Fiona said. Single-minded lust. But she wasn't telling me the truth, and I knew it. "I was ambushed, out of my mind about Greta," she said. "I had to have her. It was an addiction, an obsession, and a compulsion. I had no self-control. Do you think I was immature?" How could I think passion was juvenile? To me it was the very mark of adulthood.

Here were these hypernormal suburban housewives, Fiona and Greta, slipping their tennis shirts off and kissing each other's neck while their husbands were bossing people around at work. Was I critical of that? No, I told Fiona. I was jealous.

"You have nothing to be jealous of," Fiona said stroking my hair. "Greta and I are over, done, *finis*." Why shouldn't I have believed her? Fiona was no liar, yet I wasn't convinced. She herself had no idea how much trouble she would have separating—*detaching* was her psychiatrist's word. Indeed, it was after Dr. Strudel told her she couldn't see Greta anymore that Fiona had her first crack-up. When she told me that, for some reason I felt duped.

Greta had had a nervous breakdown of her own, three actually. She was being treated regularly with electroconvulsive therapy, which shook her from the stupor in which she spent most of her time. Even her complexion improved after the shock treatments. I was fascinated and probably the only kid in the high school who knew of someone who'd been in shock therapy.

"Why doesn't she just get divorced?" I asked.

A laugh popped out of Fiona. "That's a good question," she said. I surmised that the answer had to do with Greta's children, alimony, child custody, her inertia, her reputation in the neighborhood. As if Greta had a reputation to uphold; she liked being the nutcase on the block. My type exactly.

> My swan, my drudge, my dear wooly rose,
>   even a notary would notarize our bed
>   as you knead me and I rise like bread.
>   —Anne Sexton, "Song for a Lady"

The vulgar word for it is *humping*.

Underneath my body in all its clothes—army fatigues, Sticky Fingers T-shirt—was Fiona Gallagher. Wasn't she beautiful? She was quicksand, and I was drawn into the plush of it. And when we moved together this embrace was the ocean with its undertow heartbeat. It was primal, elemental, as uncomplicated as rowing a boat. It felt unhuman, celestial, oceanic, tectonic. So this is sex.

How embarrassed we had been as children at the sight of animals mating. We didn't know what they were up to, but the configuration was grotesque, wasn't it? hee hee hee hee.

Now I had become an animal with animal rhythms.

Maybe I was ashamed. We were human beings, not dogs in the field! Yet this separate person—with a dental history I wasn't privy to, with memories of childhood illnesses I can't name, with aunts

I do not know, fevers that don't heat me—was willing to touch me, there, and blind me with pleasure. And I allowed her to.

"Are you an athlete?" Fiona was out of breath. "You have great coordination—and stamina," she laughed. (God, it was so easy for her to talk about sex. Does that happen automatically when you hit 20?)

I shook my head no. All high school girls had been required to run a quarter mile, do five chin-ups, and play field hockey, and I did a passable job as goalie, where shins were safer from being whacked by some nasty girl's stick. I took Fiona's inquiry to mean I was doing it right, and I did it every day until school began, weekends excluded, yet I thought of little else.

It was perfection, the expression of everything I hadn't the words for. But did that rolling around on the bedspread really count as sex? Or was it the sexualization of love? Did it mean Fiona wanted me?

Gallagher's car screeched into the driveway. We flew out of bed. I cracked open a book. False alarm. Gallagher ran straight to the fridge.

T.S. Eliot got it wrong. September, being the back-to-school month, was the cruelest. If I had to spend the whole day inside the stinking high school, when would I get to be alone with Fiona?

Luckily, school is a breeze for seniors. Having entered my final year with nearly enough credits to graduate, I had classes only three hours a day on Tuesdays, Thursdays, and Fridays. French. English. Social Studies. What this meant, I explained to Fiona, was that I'd be sprung by noon except on Mondays and Wednesdays, when I had Art and Gym and didn't get out until 3:30. Sean wouldn't finish his after-school activities, gymnastics and drama, until 4, and Gallagher, though unpredictable, did have a job.

"Looks like we caught a lucky break," she said indifferently. What could I expect? It had taken all my nerve to tell Fiona I would be available. I suppose I had wanted her to say "Fantastic!" and hug me to death. But if on one given day a married woman needs you to stroke her breasts, it doesn't mean you can count on being invited back tomorrow. At any moment Fiona could have shut the door on me and decided to have another Gallagher baby. She could have dashed back to Greta. She could have come to her senses and cut it off with a puny teenage girl. I never knew for sure whether I was in or I was out.

Perushka, the Goldsteins' housecleaner, worked for the Gallaghers two days a week. She was a recent immigrant, somewhere in age between me and Fiona. "You the baby-sitter" was the first thing she ever said to me, and she wasn't asking. I was The Baby-sitter. It was getting tiresome, the way it gets when everyone thinks you're 14 when your 17th birthday's come and gone.

I asked Perushka why her English was so good if she'd only been here a year or so. "Days of our lives," she answered. "As the world turns." I didn't know why she was being cryptic. Maybe she hadn't understood my question. I must have looked perplexed because she motioned to the television set on the kitchen counter. Some ridiculous soap opera music was coming out of it, and I realized she meant she learned English from watching television. She watched the soap operas while she ironed, even if there was nothing to iron. So we never had much conversation, at first.

When Perushka was in the house, Fiona and I withdrew. It was bad enough having to worry about Gallagher busting in on us in the middle of the day, which he did every so often when work bored him or he couldn't get the leftover pot roast in Fiona's fridge out of his mind. Then there were all the delivery people (dry cleaner, grocer, UPS) and servicemen (dishwasher, garbage disposal, boiler, a.c.). As a result we spent a lot of my after-school hours cruising in the Barracuda, looking for secluded spots.

Fiona was enslaved in the suburban seraglio, and what the hell did I know about getting her out of there? Of course I was aware I had very little to offer her, compared to Greta or Gallagher with the bags of money and tabs at tony restaurants and car registrations and deeds and taxes, but whatever it was I did have, she wanted. I had a heart cascading love, but she didn't need it. I offered my company, but she wasn't lonely. I offered some muscle, but the dropouts helped her with the groceries and carrying appliances into the house. What did she want from me?

Fiona Gallagher was counterfeit, rarely feeling like herself. But she recognized that with a 17-year-old French honors student everything was different. "You love me without all my bullshit, don't you?" Fiona asked me.

I'd surmised she was guileless with me because I didn't threaten her. But the day I told Fiona my French class would be going to South Carolina in January for the eclipse, I heard her hesitate, catch her breath. Rather than respond directly to the information I'd just given her, Fiona seemed to go off on a tangent—if I paid careful attention I would understand the connection. "Paige…I feel genuine around you…you're so full of feeling…you are my oxygen." She was rattled by my upcoming departure! Good.

In my family I got laughed at when *Lassie* made me cry or when I yelled at Jan at the top of my lungs for messing up my dolls' nylon hair. But now how queer for Fiona to think being emotional, excitable, is praiseworthy. "What are you so heated up about?" Eva would sneer when I enthused about something, watching a parade, going to a skating party, Grandmother arriving with cakes and fish. Fiona showed us both the best in me.

I wanted to languish in Fiona's perfume. I longed to learn her vocabulary. Fiona clutched her head, trying to stop herself from feeling out of her mind, from turning to zombie the way water in the tray turns to ice, and all along I knew I could help her. But there was no place to go to shake her out of it. She certainly wouldn't have wanted to hang out at the pizzeria or at one of my friends' hazy parties, and I didn't want to have nothing to contribute to her friends' tipsy, bawdy conversation.

So we drove. That's how I remember my senior year. Looking through a windshield.

Candy corn was appearing in the stores. Halloween approached. It's the most romantic time of the year, the going to bed of the seasons. I directed Fiona to a reservoir surrounded by pine trees, a popular hangout where banal yearbook pictures were taken (I had mine shot in the driver's seat of the Barracuda, top down, but the jerk forgot to put film in his camera. He had to come back and photograph me in a stupid hammock, me pretending to read Camus, because Fiona had taken the Barracuda the day of my photography session.) I became afraid that state troopers would shoot us in the head if they discovered us kissing in our bucket seats. Had I been arrested here for possession of a nickel bag with my goofy friends I wouldn't have cared, but this fever in my gut and this unavoidable smile were private.

"I'm afraid," I told Fiona.

"OK, we'll get out of here." I never had to explain with Fiona. She always understood.

Intimidating Fiona was difficult. And in this she was just like all new residents in Hell, who thought they had a right to do whatever they wanted. During our after–baby-sitting drives when

I was a junior, she'd prowl past the chain-link fence that said RESTRICTED AREA into the ravine where the Department of Public Works stored sand for the winter roads. The landscape was eerie, flat, but surrounded by steep hills, piles of sand shadowing us like craters on the moon. She would take my hand and pet it as if it were a cat's head, ask me my age yet again.

We had nowhere in Hell to go. Once, after the Gallaghers returned from a night out, Fiona drove me to the small recreation area near Flounder. We got out of the car and walked toward the radio tower. We followed its red light until our necks were crooked backward from looking up at it through metal ribs. It was deserted here at night, a good place to dump a dead body.

Fiona leaned against a tree and pulled me into her. The way she smelled completed my life, and I could have stayed like that, being received by her and breathing deeply in the night. She kissed my mouth. I wasn't sure what to do.

"Don't kiss me back," she whispered. "Just let me kiss you."

And so I learned kissing. Even though I'd been doing it wrong for so long, and she was correcting me, I wasn't ashamed. When her tongue came into me, searching like a blind kitten, I was suddenly aware of all veins and arteries, felt my heart and stomach and kidneys flush with my overheated blood.

A car honked us out of our looking into each others' eyes, and we scrambled toward the Barracuda, hoping it wasn't the police or a lynch mob.

For another year Fiona serenaded me with the car. We coursed through neighborhoods I'd never seen before, peered into windows, turned around in strangers' driveways. Her hand found mine in my lap, and she didn't let it go unless she had to shift. Holding her hand was my childhood. We have photographs and home movies of me and Jan and the neighborhood kids holding hands at birthday parties, holding hands while we raced across fields, holding hands on a diving board, each free hand holding a nose. It was the sweetest thing, holding hands, and maybe a little silly to be doing as a grown teenager.

I could tell Fiona was annoyed whenever she kissed me on the lam. She'd pull back, say banal sentences. I would have to wait. Could be years. I didn't care. She didn't have to kiss me. As long as I was the passenger in her car forever, she could wear a space suit for the rest of her life and I would be satisfied.

At the end of our wandering, day or night, when Fiona dropped me in front of my house I disintegrated, faded away until I became a teen ghost in Fiona's passenger seat. And saying good night, I might have broken up like static on a radio, except seeing Annette Goldstein spying out her bathroom window forged me back into a normal girl.

I would wait that whole senior year for Fiona. I had already waited a year for Gallagher to finish his dinner and split for the driving range. And I'd waited for Fiona to see me hanging out in town with my friends. I waited on Chestnut Street until her bedroom light flicked off. I waited for my phone to ring. I waited for the Barracuda to hunger the streets of Hell and scoop me up. I waited in the vinyl seat for her to touch me, to put her hand on my knee, behind my neck, my jawbone traced by her unpainted fingernail.

I was outrageously excited and had been for years. But I said nothing. Two years of nothing.

My silence began to unnerve Fiona. She was frustrated with me. "What is it you want, Paige?" she asked tenderly. But still I was mum, couldn't speak. Because I didn't know what what I wanted was called. And because I had no damn right to my desire. And because I believed she used my name just so she could remember with whom she was conversing.

If people called me a homosexual, it was fine. It's always fine when you love the girl you love. It's not fine when the only lesbians you've ever heard of are Gertrude Stein and your gym teacher. So it wasn't that I'd been afraid of being called a homo.

"We are two people in the wrong place at the wrong time," Fiona tried to warn me, tried to convince herself. But she was holding me in her arms on the couch as she said so, so of course I persisted.

"You're probably still a virgin," she winced. It wasn't a question, and I didn't answer.

Fiona was trying her best to get me to leave, but I wouldn't go.

I don't bother contradicting people who say Fiona was bad for me—people don't want their opinion changed. But if they want to know the truth, I tell them that what murdered me wasn't Fiona's being married or older or a woman in whose bed I would never sleep.

It was the bourgeois (one of my generation's favorite words) suburban world that was killing me, and killing her too.

It started with a tennis skirt, a gift-wrapped box from a fancy department store. The store wrapped it, not Fiona. I tried it on for her, and seeing her reaction—very pleased—I'd learned my first lesson in seduction: Wear skirts.

Fiona showed me the correct grip, the backhand, the service toss. The better I became, the more I became unrecognizable to myself. Who in the world was that girl flitting around a tennis court in a stretchy white tennis skirt! So I cursed and threw my racquet in the air at my flubs. Screw tennis etiquette. Let the housewives stare. Being unlike them was the only way of holding on to everything I knew about myself.

If I wanted to spend time with Fiona, I had to attend her world.

Go to restaurants and eat, play tennis, recognize the voice of Johnny Mathis, schmooze with her friends, stop wearing bell-bottoms and long hair loose.

While playing chameleon frightened me, I enjoyed the women who were Fiona's friends and tennis partners. Their candor, their humor, the books they put on the best-seller list, the tourist traps they'd been to, the words they knew, the diets they cheated on, the men they climbed upon. I didn't speak at all, but I was a good listener.

How large they were. I don't mean they were tubbies. Even Fiona, whose hipbones stood up like the Rockies, had this largeness. I could wear platform shoes and still I'd be a punk next to those women. They were indomitable, suburban housewives. Everything for them was a cruise, shock-absorbed, everything air-conditioned and ironed and vacuumed and on time, waiters bowed to them, cleaners knew how much starch they required, deli men knew to flatter them and sliced their ham paper-thin. I wanted such command and worldliness. It would make Fiona gather me up.

I tried to age as fast as I could, to become cosmopolitan so Fiona could take me seriously. I wanted savoir faire. Wasn't there a crash course, a fat farm for girls who need to bloom into women? But the only way for me to become more sophisticated was to learn it from Fiona.

At the supermarket she taught me how to test a cantaloupe for ripeness. I tasted my first cup of coffee in her kitchen. I learned that housewives with young children were having spontaneous sex with telephone repairmen. I saw her apply perfume at the temple, collarbone, wrist, and behind the knee. I stood in a million lines with Fiona, learned how to write a check and leave a tip, bought my first address book, shaved my legs, held on to so many of her to-do lists that I could have been made an honorary housewife myself.

Meanwhile, I was going to high school and handing in acceptable homework. Loving someone twice my age wasn't so difficult. Loving a married neighbor wasn't so difficult. Loving a woman wasn't so difficult. It was that horrible bamboo wallpaper in her kitchen, her white pumps, her hiring someone to mop up her family mess that twisted me.

The last straw came when I let her hairdresser, Mr. Frederick, cut off my waist-length hair. The goo he sprayed on made me smell elderly and utterly foreign to myself. I ran off, wouldn't let Fiona drive me home, couldn't spend that afternoon with her, had to be alone, in the attic—after I'd soaked my head in the sink. I was enveloped by panic, I was panic: I had been rinsed out of my body. I was gone. All because of Fiona having trouble with my age. For trying to make me look like one of her. Why couldn't she for once call me on the phone and say, "Come quickly, I miss you"?

The way I loved her bailed me out of my disappointments. And kicking the boxes stored in the attic helped, even when I realized I'd shattered my inheritance, Grandmother's china and Orrefors crystal.

On Friday I got out of school at 11:45 and went straight to Fiona's. Hannah wanted to come, but I told her no, Mrs. Gallagher was giving me a lift to the dentist. Liar.

It was Perushka's work day. We sat at the kitchen table, Fiona drinking a cup of coffee. I could tell it was very hot from the way her eyes watered when she sipped.

Fiona lectured me about drugs. I reveled in it to such a degree that I refused to forswear smack, even though I believed I'd never

ever go near the stuff. It was sadistic of me, but I enjoyed it.

She took my hand and pressed it against her heart, and we did the deep-into-my-eyes look. Fiona squirmed, then sat up back-bone straight. She spoke quietly. "I want to go to bed with you. Now." That's how she said it, not that she wanted to have sex with me. I preferred it that way, my knees blushed.

I had never seen Fiona naked, and I wasn't sure I was ready to. But I thought the chance may never come again, so I didn't try to squeak out of it. I wanted to know her nakedness, I wanted to be thoroughly familiar with her. The shoulder blades. The vein network head-to-toe. The smell at her hairline. The birthmark on her lower back. The pulse at her gut. The anxious heartbeat.

Our problem was that Perushka needed to clean the bedrooms upstairs.

"Come on. I have an idea," she said.

We got in her car. Fiona drove into Hell, circled the shopping center once, then pulled into the parking lot of the Easyrest Motor Court. Though the Easyrest had been here all my life, it had never occurred to me that anyone actually checked in.

Fiona turned off the ignition, clutched the keys. We sat in the car for a long time, five minutes.

Then Fiona got out and walked away, toward the back of the motel, away from the desk clerk who was ogling the car. Never before had I seen Fiona slam the door.

I waited. She'd get it together.

Minutes later she returned with a pack of cigarettes. She ripped out the foil, and started up the engine to heat the lighter. She breathed in the cigarette so deeply that hardly any smoke came out when she exhaled. Cigarette between her lips, she sped out of the parking lot and headed for home while all I could think of was falling myself out of the speeding car. I'd felt not only rejected but also hoodwinked. I knew in my gut that this is where Fiona had been with Greta.

To my surprise she drove straight home instead of dropping me off. As I walked down the driveway toward the street on my perplexed way home, Fiona lunged for my hand and jerked me along the path to the front door. Thank God. I thought she'd forgotten about me. I thought it had all come to an end.

Perushka had cleaned the master bedroom but was still upstairs doing Sean's room, then the second bathroom. Nevertheless, Fiona led me by the hand into the bedroom and locked the bedroom door.

Fiona lay down on her bed. I was flummoxed. Was she going to take a nap? Should I leave? Was I supposed to undress? Lie next to her? How did it all start?

"Come, lie on top of me," she whispered.

It was polite to keep shoes off the bed and the couch, so I had to sit on the floor and untie my sneakers.

What timelessness it was resting on her river-and-dale body, her heart beating into my breast.

"Relax," she smiled and combed my hair behind my ears with her fingers. I was preoccupied with the thought that I, 100 pounds of me, was crushing her. "Relax, I want to feel the weight of your body."

We talked and mumbled and outlined each other's lips with our fingers—everyone does it. "Could I be charged with statutory rape?" she fretted, so I kissed her, for the first time I kissed first. And the kiss took over me and sent my fingers down her body.

Fiona was transported. I could tell she had moved to another state of consciousness, her eyelids droopy and words turning to moans in her throat. She whipped off her shirt, buttons popped, wriggled out of her bra, and pulled me to her chest.

"Do you talk to Dr. November about us?" she asked breathily, the way lovers interrupt themselves to ask if the door is locked. "I think you should."

To have my face this close to a breast was…unusual. I was too inhibited to take it into my mouth. But how silky the skin, cool against my cheek.

"I'm going to the bathroom. Why don't you take off your clothes and get under the covers?" Good thing she was older and knew what to do.

I folded my clothes on the chair and jammed my underwear in my jeans pocket. Unclothed under Gallagher's sheets I felt more naked than I would have felt standing in the center of the room. And I didn't feel sexy anymore. I felt small, like a kid, Fiona's Sean. I could have slept the sleep of fairy tales.

Fiona came out of the bathroom just as I was nodding off. She peeled off her watch as she moved unlimping, eyes fixed on me, toward the bed.

I was horrified.

My whole life, from that defining moment on, I have experienced absolute fright at seeing a naked woman approach me with the intention of having sex. It doesn't matter how crazy I am about the woman, and it only happens the first time I'm with her, passes quickly. But I didn't know that then. Fiona's pubic hair patch was big as a baseball field, I could get lost in there. Her thighs, bolsters on a couch. And when I saw between her legs I didn't know whether to run like hell or put my hand there, do the work.

OK, I reluctantly admitted to Dr. November, my stomach seasick, this is the reliving of the birthing flash, which wouldn't be half as appalling if anyone but my own mother gave birth to me. I wonder if children of cesarean births experience this astonishment.

While I may have been astounded, I was up for it. I placed my glasses on Fiona's night table.

"Paige, I love that you wear glasses." That was good for her, but without my glasses I had to trust in God.

"Ugh. Why?!" Actually, I was less inhibited without my glasses.

"Because when you take them off, you enchant me."

You know what that sounds like when no one has ever said it to you before? If good news could kill, I'd have died of a heart attack right there on Gallagher's side of the bed.

Fiona's body was so different from mine, another sex completely. She was like a snake, cool to touch. The skin on her face was as thin as sausage casing or the sheath on a chickpea, merely a filmy covering that I imagined I might be able to slip off to kiss the muscle meat underneath. When she lay on her side facing me, her hip rose from her body the way the new Ford Mustang's fender rises above the rear wheel. I ran my hand over it, and doing so reminded me of when I was eight and the blanket became the topography for my toy cars.

I didn't know what she wanted or what would hurt. So I, impudent dog, sniffed her, breathed in the smell of her toes, creases behind the knees, navel, armpits, ears. It wasn't my idea. I saw it in a foreign film.

Fiona had put her hand between my legs and it felt good. Perhaps I ought to try the same, I thought.

Not yet. I was scared. I wanted to see it first.

She rolled onto her back. Her breasts flopped against her chest, and deep in that mound of strawberry pubic hair lay an odor that brought my grandmother's kitchen to mind. It was annoying, Grandmother's intrusive presence, but it wasn't until after weeks of repeatedly lying in bed with Fiona that I figured out what that smell reminded me of. I've been in women's bookstores in college towns, I've browsed through the novels and poetry that are supposed to be an erotic celebration of women. I can't bear to read another line that says a woman smells like fish or the sea between her legs. Who wants to be compared to pickled herring?

There was no brine between Fiona's legs. Fiona was the smell of warmth, of potato bread in winter in Grandmother's old-fashioned toaster. The bread didn't pop up, but rather you had to open the silver doors on either side of the heating device, and it lay there browned and steaming, hoping for marmalade. Fiona smelled of the promise of toast.

Fiona guided my hand, but when it came to touching me she was always shy. I would feel her thigh riding me between my legs, and a finger, sometimes a fingernail, making circles outside my jeans, but that was as far as she would take me.

We lay on our backs, side by side like spouses in a grave.

Fiona's hesitancy was fine with me, because it meant I always got to see the look on her face. I never forget the way a woman's face pleads and screws up when she's excruciatingly aroused. I own a mental gallery of their faces, I never forget. And that's good, because that's my collateral, against loneliness, worthlessness, and being brokenhearted. I remember what I've done to them, how I'd shipped them out of an ordinary day. I always keep the light on.

Each time we slipped into her cool bed and I climbed on top of her, all the clocks in the world fell in sync. It was the way everyone wants love to be.

And then there were the rest of the days and the rotten future where Fiona not only acted as if it had never happened between us, but also in Fiona's mind it *had* never happened between us. Maybe it was the moral impropriety, and maybe it was that she couldn't face what it would take in herself to be with me. I'm just talking about the truth. A psychoanalyst will tell her she had an "unintegrated personality," but that won't make me feel any better. I no longer snickered at the adolescent poetry my classmates wrote because I felt close to death, though I didn't ever spell it with a capital D the way they did. Death was in me, in my longing, and every time Fiona didn't suggest we go to bed when I'd stop by after school, I felt ulcerated by my own desire.

I was both surprised and not surprised to learn Gallagher and Fiona had come to "an understanding." Before the end of October, Gallagher had moved into an apartment he'd rented in the Brook, though he ate the dinner Fiona cooked most evenings, left his suits in the closet on Chestnut Street, and spent weekends sleeping on the couch in the den. He had a bubblehead girlfriend who as Sean's stepmother would be idiotically doting but would have no idea how to wipe pudding off a child's face. She was as different from Fiona as Fiona and Gallagher had been incongruous as a couple.

We are naive by necessity. Why else would I have believed Gallagher had been going to the driving range when he was going to get sex? I knew he hated the outdoors. It made him feel buggy, and he got rashes easily. But if I'd known Fiona was scot-free and still wasn't mine, I'd have been more miserable and sooner.

Though Fiona and Gallagher were not legally separated, Gallagher's departure made afternoons more relaxed. What I had gathered was that Gallagher had at least a tacit understanding about Greta but knew nothing about me (God, sometimes Fiona seemed to know nothing about me!), yet somehow he knew better than to arrive unannounced—at least we counted on that. When it rained Fiona would light a white candle, we'd get under fresh sheets, and I'd recite French Surrealist poetry to her. And when the leaves came loose from the maple tree by her bedroom window, she'd play her waltzes and violin concerti while she smoked in bed and I lay beside her wanting more. We were parted the gentle way, by Sean's imminent arrival from gymnastics or camp or a playmate's house. We'd dress, and Fiona would fix her hair and check the whiteness of her teeth, put out her cigarette, and receive Sean in her magnificent arms. Then Sean would pull me by the hand into the kitchen where I would reach something wonderful for him—a dish for ice cream, the Ring Dings still hidden from Gallagher, the kite on top of the fridge. Fiona prepared dinner, Sean amused me, and every time he touched me I felt it was with the part of him that came from Fiona.

By the time Eva's birthday party came around, Gallagher's oak valet no longer stood in the corner of the bedroom. He was pushing for divorce because he wanted to marry the ditz. Fiona too was eager for some kind of embarkation. She didn't know what it would entail, but she was good and ready.

My mother threw herself a party every year on the Saturday in November nearest her birthday. When I was a kid at her parties, I used to captivate myself by balancing the hors d'oeuvre tray in one hand while making the rounds of guests in the living room. Once I got into junior high, though, I didn't want to be Eva's slave anymore, taking this out of the oven, filling that serving bowl, collecting and washing used glasses, smiling at Annette Goldstein, who always found something about me to criticize (my skin, my hair, my clothes), running to the garage for ice, telling guests their ashes were about to fall on the couch and set the damn house on fire.

This was the last birthday party I'd ever have to attend. This time next year I'd be in college—or on the West Coast or under the Eiffel Tower, who knew?

The party clanged on as usual, the room filling with smoke, chatter, and an occasional shooting star of laughter. I had no idea it would become a vexation the way the plague was a vexation.

I'd just gotten my arms around the punch bowl—Eva hollered for it from the living room—when I was brought to attention, summoned, by a whiff of Fiona's presence. Someone else must be wearing her perfume, I thought, it is simply wishful thinking to sense her here. But it wasn't just the perfume. It was the fragrance of her skin, the lime in her hair, the claylike scent in her nostrils, and the smell of raw meat on her tongue.

Fiona was there. She'd been invited by Annette Goldstein, who was already, Gallagher gone a week, trying to set her up with an eligible man. Qualms in my guts told me Annette Goldstein knew about Fiona and me and was trying to pry us apart.

I set the bowl on the buffet table and grabbed the hors d'oeuvre tray, an excuse for getting close to Fiona. Why hadn't she told me she'd be coming to Eva's party? I despised my mother for having the privilege of setting eyes on Fiona and was delirious with anger, feeling like the family retard locked in the crawl space while upstairs the family's getting greasy eating ribs.

"Meatball?" I approached Fiona and offered an hors d'oeuvre. She took one of Mother's Swedish meatballs, slid the toothpick out of her mouth, placed it on my tray, but didn't give me any secret wink. She was too busy seducing Uncle Edbert. Fiona didn't flirt by batting eyelashes or showing cleavage, but by letting him smile the way he did, and letting him lean toward her the way she did was definitely an enticement.

I couldn't believe what was happening. Did I storm out of the house and fling the whole damn tray of meatballs into the street or did I simply detonate? I thought someone would come out to investigate the clatter, but apparently no one had heard. I sat on the curb hoping a big old Caddy would run over the silver tray the way they'd run over Trudy, the neighbor's cat. A few birds came to check out the mess, then a squirrel that scared the tweeters away.

I'd run off so many times and where had it gotten me? Was it going to make me any less furious? I clenched my fists and dragged my knuckles along the cement sidewalk. The hackles on my shoulder blades shuddered with the sensation of no pain. I watched the cherry blood make its way to the rough surface and bloom, bloom, bloom like a flower in a time-lapse photograph, then shook off the blood, leaving splatter in the street. I waited until the blood bloomed again, painted the street again. My fingers were sticking together with blood. With my bloody hand I waved good-bye to a few departing guests. No one looked askance. I was hoping Uncle Edbert would split, but it seemed only the nice people were leaving. I could hear Annette Goldstein's cackle from the street.

Finally I returned to the house to cleanse and bandage my knuckles. When Eva asked ("What the Hell happened to you?"), I told her I'd burned my hand taking the pigs-in-a-blanket out of the oven, but she'd walked off before I'd even finished the fib.

Fiona called me that night. I knew she'd apologize!

She was wondering whether I was free the weekend of November something. Sean would need dinner on Friday, but he'd stay at the Goldsteins' Saturday night. I just had to pick him up after breakfast.

I was stunned. All I could say was, "Sure."

When I found out where she was going, I should have gone berserk with drool and claw marks down my cheeks and running around Hell in my nightie. At the very least I should have refused to baby-sit. But I had a better idea.

I would have sex and lose my virginity—in her bed.

So while Fiona spent Friday night eating teriyaki in the sunken living room at Uncle Edbert's country house, I lay in a puddle of my blood, not even in the middle of her king-size bed but on her side, the right side. Steve Cacciatoriani, the veterinarian's son, my friend Peter's older brother, was the guy. The sex had been no fun at all, though I did like the smell of Steve, with his cumin-scented armpits and the black fur cascading down his back and across his shoulders. Steve helped me launder the sheets, then left when I asked him to.

I felt great. I could have smashed through walls.

Late Saturday afternoon, just after I waved Sean off in Annette Goldstein's Mercedes, a taxi pulled up to the house. It was very unusual to see a taxi in Hell. Mostly they were used in the Brook for shuttling commuters to and from the train when their fancy cars were in the shop. I was sure it was just going to turn around in the driveway and find its way home. I shut the door and went upstairs to my French.

I could hear the door opening downstairs. My heart starting banging. It was autumn, dark out by 5:30. From the bedroom window I saw the taxi drive off.

The screen door slapped shut. Gallagher, it was Gallagher coming to kill Fiona—I remember seeing a baseball bat in the closet downstairs. Who knew what he'd do to her if he saw me in the house? Smash my head in too? On tiptoe I scrammed into the bathroom and pulled the door until I could barely see out through the sliver opening with one eye.

The hall floor creaked. The bedroom door brushed against the carpet.

"Paige?" It was Fiona.

I stepped out of the bathroom and saw someone who looked like her standing at the bedroom door. Her face was scratched up, black-and-blue too. She was not leaning on the cane in her right hand. She made a motion to remove the eye patch, but then thought not to.

"What happened?!" I asked, heart still going from fright.

Gingerly, wincing nevertheless, she sat herself on the bed. "I'm fine," she reassured me with a wave of her hand. After a pause she said, "I must have been out of my mind to spend the weekend with your Uncle Edbert." Sense came to Fiona slowly.

"You think it was a mistake because he's my uncle?" I hoped she'd say yes, the folly of her ways, etc., etc.

"Not because he's your uncle. Because he's so *weird*!"

I was crushed, though I'd been the first to say he was a nimrod. But I guessed she was trying to tell me it was over with us the way it was over with her and Gallagher.

Uncle Edbert had a circular bed and a mirror on his ceiling, so I really didn't want to hear the details of her overnight, but Fiona was not faint of heart and expected everyone else to be as valiant. She told me that by Saturday before sunrise she had realized she couldn't spend another minute with my uncle. I think he drove her crazy the way Gallagher drove her crazy, scrambling on top of her every time she sat in a chair and pinching her rear every time she passed by him.

I wanted to never see my uncle again.

During Saturday breakfast she told Uncle Edbert it just wouldn't work, and he said he was sorry and would drive her home. I bet upon hearing Fiona break it off he rubbed down his oily beard with the flat of his two hands, and I bet he pleaded with her to first finish the goat-cheese omelette he'd made. She wouldn't have been able to. She'd have slugged down some coffee, and it would have been good.

Next thing she knows, the car's veering off the parkway at 60 miles an hour. Then boom! Hearing the noise, she said she wondered what had exploded. They'd hit a tree.

"Edbert had a seizure at the wheel," she said. "Some neurologic condition. Did you know about it?"

"He's dead?"

"He's going to be fine," she said with some disgust. She threw off the cane, started pacing with her new limp. "I'm incensed, outraged, livid that they let your uncle behind the wheel."

She was blaming me! How would I know if he had a disease? My family doesn't tell me a damn thing except "clean up." It was Fiona's own stupid fault.

What did I have to do to get her to pay attention to me? eat fruit pies, cheeseburgers, until I gained 500 pounds? wire myself to a vest of explosives? total the Barracuda, send it into the river, become seriously injured?

Then I remembered the bright sight of blood on her sheets and was calm again.

It was cold rain, it was soggy snow. I got soaked. (Hannah was the only kid in the whole school who'd wear a hat or carry an umbrella. The rest of us didn't so much battle the elements as let them embrace us. That's why we all loved *Singin' in the Rain*.) My denim jacket was sopping wet and heavy as armor. Perushka helped me extricate myself from it, "I'll put it in the oven."

"It's OK," I chuckled, holding the leaden thing over the kitchen sink like a carcass of holiday meat. Perushka yanked the jacket out of my hands and tossed it into the oven. She'd been baking a potato for her lunch. "Mrs. Gallagher's upstairs," she said in a none-too-friendly tone.

I started up the stairs to Fiona's bedroom, when Perushka came waddling out of the kitchen at her highest speed and grabbed my sleeve. Her face was too close to mine; I could smell her vinegar breath. "It's not right!" she said, staring hard at me. Then, with a little shake, she let me go.

Perushka didn't want to tell anyone about us. But all Annette Goldstein had to do, should she suspect us, was ask a few basic questions of Perushka: How often does Paige visit Mrs. Gallagher? What do they do in the house? Do they close the door?

I filled Fiona in about Perushka. At first she just shrugged it off, didn't panic. Then she got angry. "What goddamn business of hers is it anyway?" That was mild, but Fiona could really curse. I tried to remember her swearwords and string them together to better recall them, but I never could remember. Anyway, a good curse has to be spontaneous with ice-clean rage. I'd wanted to spew some good curses at Fiona for dating my uncle, but even though I rehearsed many conversations, I couldn't fake the outrage. It was absurd of me to think we could make a life together, wasn't it?

Fiona whipped back the covers.

Being in bed with Fiona in this black-turtleneck weather, the room stinking of wet wool, filled me with despair. And yet I was happy. How can I explain it to you? It was the quintessence of my heart: Fitting inside Fiona under clean sheets, the roof not leaking, the winter not whistling through, being whispered to—what more could I possibly want? The trouble was we were in Hell, and it was no place for us.

I kissed Fiona's ears and the baby-skin space behind them. What if we did ever sleep the night together and I woke up to find she wasn't pretty anymore?

People are fertile flower beds. They're rich and loamy. They produce a variety of pungent smells, and no one likes anyone's stench but their own. Oozes exude from their bodies. And you never know where something will sprout up, a wart, a pimple, a cyst, a mole. Then there's varicose veins and bunions and dandruff and calluses and horny toenails. There's hair loss and hair growth. There's all kinds of crud that can grow while you're not looking, moss between the toes, rash spreading like a shadow. Does true love mean you have to kiss the nevus? The hairy one?

Why don't we smell like lilacs?

Shut up, will you shut up! Everything here is shame and reproach—
Satan saying that the fire is worthless, that my anger is ridiculous
and silly. —Arthur Rimbaud, "A Season in Hell"

I had promised Fiona I'd look after Mr. Cat. Sean would be
staying with his father for the Christmas week, and Fiona, to distract herself from not having Sean for the holiday, was off to a
California spa.

What a joke. I didn't even restrain myself when she told me.
Though I should have been more sensitive to her sadness about
having to leave Sean, I burst out *ha ha ha ha*, my beautiful Fiona
among those tiresome women, out out damn flab is all they pray
for, and I can't imagine what they yak nonstop about, but the
masseuses want to gag them, and they think they're so smart with
their diet trick of smoking in the lounge instead of eating
dessert—it's Jell-O anyway, grapes, ladyfingers—but after midnight you can hear them digging through the Samsonite for stow-
away cookies.

I was on my way to pick up the house keys. Once I'd rounded

the corner I could see two cars in the driveway. The Plum Crazy paint job you couldn't miss, even without glasses I could see it. The other car I assumed to be Gallagher's dipstick girlfriend's gold Mercedes. I don't have to explain why Gallagher preferred to drive it instead of his car.

It wasn't Gallagher. He'd picked up Sean on Thursday. It was the Jaguar. Greta.

Fiona once told me it was her mouth. Greta's mouth, "perfection." Greta's lips, "haunting." Greta's smile, "endearing." I got the message: Greta was Kryptonite, and she enfeebled Fiona. Can't blame Fiona, love is love. I listened to the laurels only because she'd told me it was over between them, she'd told me that when Gallagher drove her home from the nuthouse she was bitterly forlorn: Dr. Strudel had instructed her to stay away from Greta if she wanted to get well. I'd never criticized her self-confessed compulsiveness, her driving by the house day and night, because what's wrong with passion?

Fiona could bring me the stupid keys herself. I walked right past her house.

She'd lied to me. She'd betrayed me. She'd abandoned me. She'd cheated me. For months she'd been driving me by Greta's house just on the chance she'd see Greta; it was not for the view. And now I knew, incontrovertibly, that I'd been right about her going to the Easyrest with Greta. And it was most likely Greta with whom she'd frequented La Penombre, and I was just a distraction for her.

I would go away, she'd notice, I'd disappear. If I'd had a credit card I'd have gotten on a plane out of there, flown over oceans, and so what if we were hijacked to Cuba?

I was in a trance and found I had walked myself all the way into Hell. First my uncle and now this. Just forget about Fiona, no more baby-sitting, she can drive herself to Dr. Strudel's, I'm not even walking by the house any more. I would go to fucking France, change my name, Celestine de Fenestration. Good thing there were no bridges in Hell. I had a mind to jump, to peel my skin off, get some blood on myself, some relief.

And then I saw my little garage girl darting across the street. She wanted me to run after her, follow her ragged spindly body past the Meat-O-Mat and into the woods. But she wasn't to be trusted, especially after I'd treated her so badly in the poem. So I let her take her ratty hair and evil thoughts up the tree she'd be sleeping in without my company. My poor girl, I could see with each encounter that she was becoming increasingly deranged.

It was damn cold out. Fuck the foggy glasses. Into the pizzeria, get warm. Patrons looked at me as I entered. I whipped off my glasses and got in line, leaning against the marble counter, though the idea of eating made me madder than I already was.

I heard my Peter friends. They were talking about the Marx Brothers. One night during that week I'd spent in Nantucket, Peter's father had projected *Duck Soup* on the beach house wall, and I'd thought it was totally unfunny though I hadn't said so. I didn't want to say hello, but it was too late to creep out. I ordered a slice and then had to count the loose change in my pocket to be sure I could cover it. Please burn the crust.

There was no refuge at the pizzeria. Peter's crush on me was as obvious as the smell of fish. The idea of kissing him was so uninteresting it gave me a headache. When another Peter tugged on my jacket, I turned and smiled and tried not to let my body touch Peter's as I slid into the red booth. Right in front of the guys Peter asked me if I was seeing someone—I seem to give him the cold shoulder. (Is that what Fiona had given me? Be glad you got the cold shoulder. You could have gotten a knife in the back, a kick in the head.)

I put my glasses on after wiping them with the most unab-sorbent napkin in the world. Peter offered me another from the dispenser, but he was getting pathetic. I would have felt miserable lying to him, especially with that tomato sauce on his cheek. As one of the confident Harvard-bound boys, Peter was smart but not so smart that he could imagine someone being averse to his embrace or to the notion of eating canned corn at his parents' dinner table. His little sister was a brat, and their intact house, glass figurines, and expertly dusted bowling trophies reeked of mildew.

I ripped the crust from the pizza and left the cheesy triangle for any takers. Gnawing on the crust, wanting it to pull out all the teeth in my head, I told Peter the goddamn truth. That I was in love with someone else. But I wouldn't say whom. We played a guessing game. It was cruel of me, but how else could I have told him it was someone older, someone married, someone a woman? Would he freak out?

He was stumped for a minute, then realized I was only kidding. The other two Peters weren't paying any attention to us, instead playing some game writing numbers on a paper napkin. Peter offered to buy me a soda. I politely refused with the lie that it was too cold out. I didn't want any connection with Peter, none at all. I let him think what he wanted, with a strange sense of relief I might add, and declined a ride home. I wanted this winter to bite into me like a shark.

I shoved my leftover pizza across to Peter on its wax paper. It's the only forgiveness I was capable of at that moment. I said bye.

I trekked home in a cold winter. Wind began whistling in trees, something I'd never heard in Hell before. The exhaust from a Torino curled home after the family within like the tail of a white stallion. I waved to it. And out of the corner of my eye I saw my little girl peeking out from behind the billboard. I could hear her kicking it over and over.

HAVE YOU BEEN SERIOUSLY INJURED?

I wondered if Fiona would call me that night, if she'd notice I hadn't shown up.

No word for two days. And she wasn't dead either—I'd heard the Barracuda, and it made me throw stones at the curb. On the third day she waved me in off the street on my way to school. I'd been weak. I'd taken the route past her house and now I was going in. Because she asked.

"You never came by for the keys." I smelled her percolating coffee. She knew neither that I was furious nor why. I began to hope she was schizophrenic. It would have been better than her being mean.

I'd never thought Fiona looked for me through her picture window, yet I had tramped on just the same, at least ten times a week. Even when she was expecting me after my classes got out, never once did I see Fiona look for me from her door, her bay window. What an idiot I'd been.

We sat at the kitchen table. Fiona wouldn't look away from me. She reached for my hand across the table. I didn't pull it away, but I didn't squeeze back either.

"What's up, Paige?" she said in that damn tender voice. "Are you angry at me?"

I couldn't speak.

"Come on, talk to me."

The coffeepot gurgled, and Fiona rose to tend to it.

Once she wasn't looking at me, I could speak. "So, did you have a good time with Greta?"

Without missing a goddamn beat she answered, "Being with Greta makes me appreciate you."

I was dumbstruck. What a great lie she'd told me! I'd remember it, see if I needed to use it on someone someday.

"I've got to go." Seeing it was no use with me, I was a boulder, she got the keys off the front-hall table and placed them in my open hand. I refused to engage her tender gaze.

Thank God the darkness was coming, three more weeks. South Carolina would fix everything. She couldn't get to me there. *L'eclipse, j'y vais.*

senza speme vivemo in disio
(having no hope we live in longing)
—Dante, *Inferno*

Facing the terrible face of the ocean, I crouched on the beach. I'd expected to have poignant last words with myself or to have my heart torn by the riddle of the surf. But it was all so ordinary.

I slipped out of my rubber sandals, pitched my sunglasses into the sand.

The water was take-your-breath-away cold. Even if it was way south of Hell, it was still January. Dive under, plunge in. It's less painful that way. But I did it the excruciating way, stones pinching the soles of my feet, sleepwalked against the water until it was up to my armpits. The neck was the decisive spot, where the thyroid stays. I couldn't torture the neck.

I turned around on tiptoes, fell back flat on my back. My weightlessness reminded me of the levitation my friends and I tried as children, the body rising, like layer cake, off the rec room floor. The magician swept his wand underneath. No strings.

On the beach, children were tense as ants, dashing to the water's edge, then spinning away to flood their sand castle moats with a pailful of seawater. My classmates were at the snack bar setting up to properly view the eclipse. I couldn't believe that I, dead man's float in the ocean, was spending this time thinking how grateful I was that Madame Foiegras didn't bring a bathing suit. You don't want your last sight of someone nice to be disfigured; you don't look into the casket of a motorcycle accident victim.

Raising my head a bit, I could see my beach sandals. How polite, how well-behaved they were, carefully aligned with one another. Had I arranged them so, my puppies, waiting for someone who would never come back? I lay back, shivered at the nape. Good-bye sandals. Tears spilled into the sea.

The tide rocked me, tugged me farther from the shore and the shouts there. A seagull circled and screamed at me. I could no longer smell the fried food or mustard from the refreshment stand. I couldn't distinguish between the cries of children and what I remembered of the cries of children.

I was weary. I was spent.

Keep your eyes open. Shut them and you're sunk.

I should paddle back. But such lassitude, breathing was an effort. And I needed to take a deep breath—now.

A wave dumped itself over me. I choked, I spluttered. Another wave. I heard gagging. And another. This time I wouldn't resist. Swallow it. The briny liquid up my nose, it was so familiar. Let's taste it again. Ah, now I remember. The days when I'd been dressed in a sunsuit, I'd been timid, afraid of the water. Eva tossed me in. Eva pulled me out. Eva, that's the name of my mother, isn't it?

The water was now inside me, I was flushed by ocean. My lungs were incapable, drenched in clay. My neck let go of my head, relaxed at last. Once before it had been like that, my body gently pitched in blood-warm sea, then under the green and into the explosive light. I was pickled, as I had been that time before when I'd spent all I'd known of my life rolling and head over heels with the vague sounds of emergency and aria around me but not yet graspable, on the other side of the wall.

Someone would probably save me.

But I would hate that—unless it be dolphin or dog, let that kind of savior nose me to the shore. Couldn't I sputter back to your world if I wanted to? Or have I already gone under? Hit me on the back. Turn me upside down. Put your lips upon mine. Lick me and whine.

⑳

No one is unique. No one is the only one. It hit me during graduation. There I was in the gymnasium, in a folding chair in the last row, Appleton to Byrne. In Sunday clothes, parents, proud siblings, and a few sleepy grandparents sat in the bleachers listening for the countdown, getting all heartbeated up as the alphabet got closer and closer to their family name. Doran Dziadzik Elmiger Evans Figueira Fonseca Fontana Gerhardt.

Surrounding me was the congregation of kids I'd known my whole life, the hundred of them thinking about The Future, flying an optimism they'll never have again. Even the kids who could barely contain themselves waiting to get drunk after the ceremony, even they were hopeful.

God knows what the parents were thinking. They were overcome with something, maybe the smell of adolescent sweat. Women dabbed their eyes, men examined their shoes. Not Eva. Sitting ramrod straight, she was disgusted by the hooting and clapping in the bleachers. My father was proud of me earlier in the day, but suddenly he was disoriented again, he was hindered from making eye contact. He didn't even know what row I was in.

And here I was, thinking about Fiona, about how I loved her

though she hurts me again and again because I'm too young and because she can't let me go.

The valedictorian was saying something about leadership. He'd practiced his speech too many times. Everyone managed to find the dough to rent the cap and gown, but I was the sole Lindbergh High School graduate who would not wear my mortarboard. You had to be kidding! I was 1% of the hatless. But one in a hundred could also be two in two hundred. So if 1% of the 300 seniors at Bubbling Brook High School weren't wearing mortarboards, that meant there were three of them. Peter could clarify my theory, since he was going to Harvard to study Probability. I'd never even heard of such a subject.

So, being the only one doesn't always mean being the only one. Maybe I was the only 18-year-old in the entire school who ran her fingers through the hair of a grown woman nearly twice her age. But somehow it didn't make me feel special anymore. Just forlorn and weary. I faked the smile in the class photograph and afterward crushed the diploma with my hands, dumped it in the gymnasium trash.

After returning the gown to Room 202, my sophomore-year French classroom, I hung around outside chatting with my friends. John Radnoti was back in town; I heard his bike rip across the parking lot. I turned away.

Whatever I was saying I was saying in an echo chamber. The words tumbled along and I heard them outside of me, as if I were underwater and someone were talking to me from above. Perhaps my little girl from the garage had stuffed my ears with newspaper. Oh, yeah, Dr. November suggested I try loving the girl by taking her back in, clean sheets on the bed and a shampoo daily. But the doctor also thought it was she I tried to drown in that eclipse. That was just ridiculous, I'd said. The girl's a phantom, and the doctor nodded as if I had been on to something.

My parents drove home without me. They'd gotten tired of waiting.

Another one of those June sunsets where you know you won't go on forever makes you more tender toward everyone. Maybe I'd show up at Amelia's party later, probably not though. As I was leaving the school property, I waved to Madame Foiegras. who was surrounded by chirping parents. She smiled back, cocked her head in a very French way. We both knew it meant she wanted me to wait for her, she'd ride me home, but when someone gives you mouth-to-mouth resuscitation you send them a Christmas card every year and keep a respectful distance.

I passed the Gallaghers' home on Chestnut Street. Everything was a dream because there was Gallagher's car parked alongside Fiona's, cars belonging to their guests parked along the street and up on their grass. Like any married couple, they were entertaining with a barbecue. I could smell the meat.

Noticing me on the street, Gallagher motioned with a grilling fork. Fiona turned to see what he was waving at. She looked trapped, like a woman facing the artist in a painting.

"Have some steak," Gallagher yelled. I was too tired to remind him I was a vegetarian, so I gave a lazy wave and continued walking down the street. I could feel Fiona tugging me back. She was at the end of my leash, a belligerent canine insisting on slow walking.

Gallagher still had the girlfriend with the Mercedes, but Fiona and he were limping through the tail end of their marriage as best they could. They both had a lot of tolerance, which would fade when Gallagher decided to fight to keep Sean. Fiona, a "female homosexual" with "a history of mental illness," wouldn't stand a chance in court.

Sean came running out from their backyard and threw himself against me, clamping himself to my leg. I whispered a secret to him (I had just graduated).

He would deliver the information in some mangled form to his parents. Fiona would feel guilty she hadn't done something special for me. Maybe she'd drop off a card. Maybe she'd bury the guilt.

For graduation my parents gave me a clock radio. Mother had had no time to wrap it. She presented it to me, "Here," and I sat with it on my lap as we passed around Grandmother's raspberry pie and I paid attention to the sound her dentures made as she chewed. The radio, $15.95 at the drugstore in Hell, was the exact same model as the one by Fiona's bedside. The first phone call I would receive in my college dormitory would be from my father. "You left your radio behind!"

According to Dr. November, there are no accidents.

The Barracuda was totaled. The mangled roof reached skyward like a drowning arm, its canvas skin in shreds. Every window had blown out, and the windshield was a massive cobweb of fractures. Fiona's door had flown open with such violence that it ruptured the left front tire. The front end accordioned, air filter popped right out and landed 20 feet away alongside the side-view mirror. Smoke emanated from the vehicle as if it were a carcass burnt in the oven. There was more damage, but I had to look away; it was like an animal in death throes.

The fire truck arrived first, followed by the police and ambulance. The tractor-trailer that rammed the Barracuda in the parking lot appeared untouched; the driver didn't even have a bump on the head.

I circled the lot in a daze, then came to, finding myself back in the restaurant, leaning against the cool window, which kept my nausea at bay. Through the window I saw the cops give the trucker a DWI test, then package him into a squad car. Someone handed him a cup of coffee through the window. Someone pointed in my direction. The ambulance light blinked and blinked its bloodshot eye.

I'd been checking out the vending machines when the truck had hit the parked Barracuda. Fiona had said she'd wait in the car, would I bring her a Baby Ruth. My body shook like a vibrating bed.

Then I saw Fiona, her face a horrible mess of incomprehension. I moved toward her.

Thank God she'd had to use the rest room. If that incident exhausted my share of luck in the world, I would consider myself fortunate.

Without the car Fiona had no transportation home, and I had no means of getting back to college. Over the years we'd kept timidly in touch. I sent letters and phoned a few times, she took me to a diner, showed me her apartment when I'd snuck back into Hell avoiding my parents. I think also she probably wanted to drive by her old house, which was now occupied by Gallagher and the girlfriend. Fiona always wanted to do me a favor, and giving me a ride back to school was a favor she'd done a few times.

Now her help nearly killed us. All my belongings had been seared beyond repair, my extra pair of eyeglasses smashed up, and my one piece of furniture, a night table, so hideously splintered that stakes of it had gone through the roof.

We were free.

We had dreamed this so often, being stranded together, no possessions, a life to start in an unidentifiable city. Fiona said it's what she needed now. There never had been a custody battle: Gallagher threatened to tell the court of her hospitalizations and her homosexuality as well as her now-penniless state. She'd had no choice but to leave her son. For years Fiona had dreamt of disappearing, moving to some unsuspecting place and taking up an anonymous life. I wasn't afraid of losing her. I knew she'd be in Cincinnati, she'd told me.

Ever since she'd left Gallagher, refusing alimony, I no longer heard her sing her favorite song, "Don't Fence Me In." Sometimes she'd mumble "Bridge Over Troubled Water," but that wasn't a song to sing if you couldn't carry a tune, and I made that clear by scrunching up my face when she sang it. But the song was popular that year, and Fiona would often sing along with the radio just to get me to laugh. What was under the laughter was the knowledge that the song had something to do with Greta. I've always disliked it, sentimental treacle. "Cecilia" better suited me: *You're breaking my heart, You're shaking my confidence daily…I got up to wash my face, When I come back to bed someone's taken my place…Oh Cecilia….*

Fiona Gallagher was released; you could see it on her face. Now there was a homunculus inside her eyes, bright and mischievous, instead of the woman in a veil, a trance. She still had that barely noticeable limp, childhood scoliosis or something.

While I was trembling and we were answering police questions, my legs buckled under me. The cop helped me over to a picnic table. Fiona and I gripped hands across the table and became hysterical, laughing as if we'd been plugged in. The cop kept trying to calm Fiona, calling her Ma'am, which only made me laugh harder. He gave up and walked away. "Call your insurance!" he yelled from a distance, shaking his head like we were loonies.

We didn't run away together. We didn't romp across the meadow and hire on at a dairy farm. Instead, we took a ride from the perplexed cop, who dropped us at a bus station, and 24 hours later we were unpacking nothing in my apartment in ice land.

I never thought it would happen or that it would occur with such suddenness, but in a snap I became a grown-up. I had offered Fiona water from my tap. I held the glass to the light to make sure it was clean. I rinsed it with hot water, filled it with cold. Such a hostess thing to do! What a grown-up I'd become. It felt taller, purposeful, if not more confident then at least less self-conscious. It also felt like being in a rush.

For a moment I wasn't sure I recognized the woman in the armchair. I was accustomed to seeing her in Gallagher's house or behind the wheel of the Barracuda. Now she was in another country where she'd have to maneuver without her accessories: I had no ashtray, no tennis racquet, no coffeepot. She didn't know her way around town, where the garbage was kept. Would she have a breakdown? Would I? Could I stand to look at her now that she was an alien? Would she become uglified as had Amelia and Hannah? It was Fiona Gallagher's mastery I had fallen in love with, her eminent capability, for driving, mothering, understanding, ushering along her life in Hell. Now what? What if I couldn't tolerate her vulnerable fear? I had to keep moving.

We took the bus into town. I was relieved to see Fiona completely at ease. I had seen her on public transportation only once before, yesterday, when we took the bus to my school. It could have gone either way. She could have been intimidated by the strangers and by not knowing her stop, or she could have reveled in it, like the prince being the pauper. She was the prince.

She was also suffering from motion sickness. Ironic for a speedster, huh?

We went to a foreign film, Lina Wertmuller, and during the opening credits Fiona whispered hot breath in my ear, "I'm going to always know you, wherever you are." She caressed my hand there in upstate New York. Maybe we'd get killed, shot in the back of the head by the projectionist's 12-gauge shotgun.

When I was still in high school, Fiona rolled over to me on her bed after we'd been kissing and said, "What do you think if I came with you to college? I could get a waitressing job." To my surprise

I was horrified by the suggestion. I think I wanted not so much my freedom but to start off with someone who'd be good to me from the very beginning. Me and Fiona, we weren't ruined exactly, but now I was already 21, I'd pretty much gotten over my good hopes, I'd counted her out. Anyway, now that she and Gallagher had split she was driving the hour to Hell every single night to put Sean to bed with kisses and the blanket pulled tight, then the hour back to her garden apartment in some other rotten town. She'd never move up to this cold college village.

After the film we brought back a pizza which we ate on my bedroom floor. I suspected the tomato sauce was actually ketchup. Fiona told me she had legally changed her name, to Fiona Pineapple, because she could no longer be an appurtenance to Gallagher and why not, she loved the tropics, and I said she was nuts.

And saying the truth and offering water, I was no longer shy of the beast. I could manage her. I could watch her leave in the morning, and I took off her clothes and took off my clothes, and in an undergraduate's apartment with a mattress on the floor, she opened up to me and I wept in her turbulent hair.

So we drove on toward death through the cooling twilight.
—F. Scott Fitzgerald, *The Great Gatsby*

Manhattan cocktails

Students do not get crushes on me. I have a face *comme un navet*, with just a wisp of a nose. ("Little Turnip," my family called me, "Little Turnip, come sit on my knee," and the aunts and uncles would splatter me with kisses and tie ribbons in my hair. That was in Nullepart; we had a country house there, Languedoc—you're nodding your head, you know France?—it had been in the family for six generations.) My hair, you see how it is thick on my head, a pot of curls. When the humidity is high it is as impenetrable as steel wool. If I am not vigilant with the tweezers, three bristly hairs sprout from my chin. My figure? I cannot complain, especially for a woman of my age. Brigitte Bardot I am not. But high school students cannot take their eyes off eccentricity and *c'est si bon*, a teacher wants their attention, not their love.

No, I have never married. My marital status is often cause for hilarity among students. Spinsterhood scares many of them, every *célibataire* a witch, a gobbler of children.

The students? Often there are no signs that a student is in trouble. Maybe someone with your training could detect problems, but we are not specialists. And even when the obvious signs are there, it is difficult for us to intervene. The administration has directed us to bring behavioral problems to the attention of the principal ("The Warden" in teen parlance). Detention and suspension rather than a visit with the school psychologist are his idea of therapeutic intervention. Not to malign your colleagues, but it is true that the psychologist at the time was an *ivrogne*, a sot.

Mademoiselle Paige Bergman was an outstanding student from the beginning. She was with me from Freshman Introductory French to Senior Year Advanced Placement. I will not tell you she was an assiduous student. But she did her work, and she did it with unfailing imagination, and that, you know, is critical for learning a language. With a little prodding she could have been a brilliant student; as it was, she had greater fluency than many of the students I've taught who did win straight A's.

Five years before Mademoiselle Bergman (in class we called her Celestine) came into my classroom, I'd had another student, equally remarkable, more of the scholar. Mademoiselle Bergman's certain guardedness reminded me of this student, Dominique. During Dominique's senior year at a rather competitive university, you would recognize the name, she jumped out of a dormitory window.

My intention is not to be ungrateful for your sympathy, but how can I convey to you my remorse? It clenches my heart whenever Dominique crosses my mind. I can't stop this recurrent vision from intruding before my eyes. (May I tell you? As a psychiatrist surely you will not think me mad.) She is dressed in one of her beloved peasant skirts. She is tottering on the ledge. Then, as surprising as a beautiful sun shower, she blooms from above, her naked legs and the parachute of her skirt and the horrible thud. My stomach turns, *j'ai un haut-le-coeur*, I retch. That is the way guilt lives with me: It is a mouthful of rotten meat. Ah, but you are not interested in my troubles.

Celestine will not take that path, that is my firm belief and my prayer. Maybe she hasn't quite got much *joie de vivre*, but she is a keen observer of life, so curious, incisive. Certainly you have seen it. One reads it in her essays. French, you see, was an instrument. French enabled her to express her pleasures, her terrors, whatever was on her mind. My experience has taught me that many young people find freedom in learning a second language. If anyone understands the adolescent's verbal reticence, it must certainly be someone in your position, *non*? What do you Americans say? You put your money on someone? I have faith in Celestine. But what do you think? You're the professional. Ought we to worry?

I would have liked Mademoiselle Bergman to feel she could have confided in me or one of my colleagues. Her home life? I knew nothing, *rien*, as it was with nearly all my students. She was a troubled young woman, *bien sûr*, but perhaps not any more troubled than her peers. You ask me what was my interest in her? Isn't that clear? She was trying to speak to me in my own language.

Permit me to send you one of her essays; you may find it interesting. Do you read French? *C'est dommage*, I will translate it. A napkin will do. Just write your address. I will remember your name.

You know, Anne—may I call you Anne?—I couldn't brush her hair. I couldn't invite her to sleep on my sofa. I couldn't fix her a nice omelette. I couldn't inquire, woman to woman, whether something was troubling her.

Entre nous, I have my fantasies too, as I'm afraid I've already told you. I have taken her hand. I have led Mademoiselle

Bergman up to my desk. I have conducted class while she sat in my lap, much like so many of those Egyptian statues we have in the Louvre, a seated king steadying his miniature wife on his stiff-skirted thighs.

You think that means I do not desire a man? *Mon Dieu*, how wrong you are.

The last time I saw Mademoiselle Bergman? Once they've left high school—and Hell—it is not uncommon for former students to get back in touch with me. Some of the returnees, I have to admit, I do not remember. We deliberate over photographs of their children, their home, their car. I offer tea and madeleines, homemade! It's my own private acid test. Beware the student who discourses on Proust—insufferable. And yet…I treasure the way their faces glow with recognition of my small cakes. The getting of knowledge, *tiens*! Surely you see it, the shadow of insight crosses your patients' faces, *non*?

Celestine, or perhaps I should now call her Paige Bergman though she signs her cards "Celestine," was among the returnees. When she first came back, however, it had been many years since she'd left Hell. Her visits were hasty and self-conscious. Undoubtedly she was still ashamed of her swimming accident. Do you know that never once in 20 years of postal correspondence has she referred to it? You are aware of the incident to which I refer? Ah, I see guilt lives with you too. I thought you people were supposed to be unattached, objective. Tell me, do you think that ever works?

During one of her later visits she offered the usual platitudes about how I gave her—how did she say it?—"a visceral understanding" of the language, how grateful she was that I introduced her to Camus. He was her lector on the subject of love (Camus, of all people!). I was appreciative of the accolades, but Mademoiselle Bergman was being insincere. A seasoned teacher develops a nose for deceit.

She stayed a bit longer. I offered tea. She smiled at the madeleines, said only one word, if *hmm* be a word. *La neige, la glace, le vent, la froideur*—the Montreal weather, she said there had been a time when she couldn't get north enough. Things change. Then she got around to telling me what her real purpose had been in coming to see me: She had received a notice of acceptance, and she was to undertake her graduate work at the Sorbonne. My felicitations were on the cautious side; her demeanor made it plain she felt no cause for celebration—she had decided not to return to school, *elle en avez marre de lycée*, she was fed up with book learning, she said.

When I found out she would be staying in New York awhile, I invited her back for dinner the following week.

I'd roasted a chicken, some potatoes. She brought wine, French, *bien sûr*. I made a valiant effort to call her Paige throughout the evening but was not successful. After all, I had known her for four years as Celestine. Four years may sound like a long time to get to know your students, but in fact I'd had no idea about Celestine's life in Hell. In fact, I wondered if she were adopted because she quite deliberately avoided the subject of her parents. Perhaps they were divorced? Or deceased?

We ate the bird with our fingers, leaving nothing but the bones for poor Marat. I heard, for the first time, her laughter.

I don't know what she has told you of her family. What she imparted to me that night, well, I sputtered a string of good French curses at the so-called adults in her life. Yet while I was swearing like a sailor I was aware of the calm in her face—it was an ocean. Celestine made it clear that she had found the happiness. It had to be love, *l'amour*.

Cocktail parties are for somnambulists, *non*? Meeting you has been a pleasure. Serendipity, *non?* I must write Celestine about our acquaintance. Now if you'll excuse me, my one-eyed Marat needs to be let in for the night.

A letter

Anne, I'm sorry it has taken me so long to correspond, but it required some time getting into my attic files. We have a family of bats up there, and I'm none too fond of the creatures. There must be some psychological symbolism in that, *non?* At long last my nephew has shooed them out of the garret.

Had Mademoiselle Bergman shown this to you? I don't think she would mind my sharing it with you: She read it in class, though I'm afraid it was over most students' heads:

Just a little lift your long skirt for me doctor and the darkness underneath I crouch and hold on tight to your pillars like a parachutist to his straps and breathe deep to my hips the way you smell the first smell in the jungle and breathe breathe to swallow and climb up darker and through the portal place leaving no trace of me behind a stone into loam invisibilized going with you wherever you curled up in the tire all asleep by the hum of your talking and heart machinery the way it was before all this the way it was.

I'm afraid I went on and on at the party, but I guess in your business you don't talk much. I trust you are well. *Salut!*

—Celestine Foiegras

A thought on the bus

Ms. Bergman told me she wanted to crawl under my skirt and stay forever. Why would I have thought she was lying?

—Anne November, MD

A telephone message

It is Celestine Foiegras. Hello? Yesterday I received a card from Mademoiselle Bergman postmarked Nullepart, of all places! I'm afraid I have put off until too late informing her of our meeting. She writes she and an old friend from Hell are going off for a year to travel the Silk Road. She has bought "*une voiture rapide*." That's *a fast car*. I thought you'd like to know. *Salut!*

All correspondence ends here.

Acknowledgments

I learned to drive in a 1969 Volvo 145S white wagon with a four-cylinder, inline OHV two-liter B20B dual carb engine, four-wheel disk brakes, three-point seat belts, and an engine mounting that would have caused the engine to drop under the car rather than be propelled into the passenger compartment in the event of a head-on collision. That was my salvation, as were my earliest passengers, my brother Joshua and sister Amy Willot.

Also, I was fortunate enough to have had teachers Ellen Ishkanian and Naomi Lazard, who helped me find the way to tell the truth. Stephanie von Hirschberg has offered me her considered editorial commentary over the years. Lynn Kanter and Maggie Stern Terris benevolently read drafts.

Josie Sandler and Lizzie Helen Coit helped to finance my life during the writing of this novel. Their kind friendship has been invaluable.

My agent Malaga Baldi persevered.

My editor Angela Brown said Yes!

And Isabelle, my darling, had a birthday. So I told her this story.

About the Author

Jane Summer is a writer, poet, and editor living in New York City. A graduate of Kirkland College, she is the former senior writer for *New Woman* magazine and has won numerous writing awards, including *The New York Times* Dining In/Dining Out Contest and the *Literal Latte* Poetry Contest. *The Silk Road* is her first novel.